The Witch's Forbidden Promise

a tale woven with fire, magic, and tangled hearts

Juliette Vale

Table of Contents

Chapter 1

The Sacred Oath Broken

Mist curled around Elara's ankles as she moved through the Shadowed Wood, the world suspended in the delicate hush before dawn. Fronds dripped with silver beads, chilled and perfect on her skin through the thin linen of her skirts. The air shimmered blue and green between the trunks. Each step pressed dew into the pleats of her dress, collecting wild-scented moisture that would later stain the hem with the memory of the forest. One pale hand slipped beneath the roots of an ancient oak, fingers brushing the loamy earth as she found what she'd come for—bloodroot, its bulbs smooth and crimson, veins running like whispered secrets through her palm. She tucked the bloodroot into her satchel, careful not to disturb the sleeping moss or the hair-fine threads of a spider's web strung between roots.

A crow called, hoarse and distant, as if warning her back from unseen perils. Yet the wood knew her the way a heartbeat knows longing, each bough and briar familiar beneath her touch, each stray wind braiding itself through her dark hair. She pressed on, wary of the shadows. The kingdom had taught her to move with silence: in the Shadowed Wood, witches like her survived only by dissolving into twilight, wearing the morning's hush like a cloak.

This forest was a promise and a prison. The trees themselves respected the border—where the pines thickened, no common man dared tread. Witch hunters with iron dogs and torchlight haunted the edges; their presence tasted of ash and rust, even this deep. All across the land, witches vanished with the dawn—names forgotten, homes razed, the oath etched on their gravestones by the hands of those who could never understand the cost. Here, sanctuary was nothing but a thin line between concealment and capture. And so the witches clung to ritual, venerated the ancient powers with offerings, and kept the oath that bound both their magic and their isolation. Any broken promise meant death not just of the body, but of the soul—a consuming undoing that left sounds dead and soil barren.

Elara's cabin emerged from the mist, moss swallowing one corner of the sodden roof, a crooked chimney fingering the sky. She entered, shutting the door behind her with a careful shoulder, and poured her spoils onto the sturdy wooden table worn smooth by years of silent work. Herbs—feathered fennel, dried foxglove, black lily—were chosen with meticulous hands. She set the bloodroot among them, grinding stems and root between stone pestle and bowl, the air filling with a scent at once sweet and sharp as a blade. The cabin glowed with pale light, illuminating jars of rainwater and a battered cauldron. As Elara measured crushed bloodroot into a vial, her lips formed the words of the sacred oath, syllables older than the kingdom itself:

"To the water, the stone, the wind, the flame—my will, my word, unbroken, untamed."

The vow tasted of salt and nettles on her tongue, a familiar bitterness that filled her hollow places with resolve. For all its suffocating rules, the oath was a living shield—woven from generations of hope and despair. It protected, but it cornered; it set the world at a distance, cold and sharp. Elara honored it, hated it, relied upon it like she relied on the sun.

She poured the potion into a small blue-glass bottle and was about to stop—then a hush fell over the wood so absolute it rang in her ears. Birds stilled. Even the restless spirits faded, the elemental voices that usually danced around her mind reduced to silence. A chill pressed in, a fist squeezing her ribs. Elara went to the door, opened it with slow, deliberate hands. The mist was dense, heavy with foreboding. Somewhere in the unseen, a flock erupted skyward, their wings thudding a panicked rhythm that echoed over the brambled canopy.

Her mind reeled, cataloguing threat: Witch hunters? A wandering beast? Or something older, born of broken oaths? The forest had its own language of warning. She felt its words now, prickling along her spine, sending dread twisting through her like roots strangling stone. The price of survival in this kingdom was perpetual vigilance—she owed caution not just to herself, but to every witch who still walked free, unseen.

She reached for her cloak, the fabric thick and green as spring leaves, its hood stitched with sigils she'd traced with fevered, careful hands. Her pulse skittered. She could almost taste iron in the air as the cold deepened, as if the fog itself carried a memory of centuries of blood and loss.

Something moved—a shadow on the edge of vision, too swift and deliberate to belong. She stepped from the threshold, boots sinking into the wet leaf mould, and drew the hood over her head, drawing herself into the smallest possible shape. Her heart hammered, a thrumming drumbeat in her chest, but she kept her breath steady, her hands steady, her magic ready if the world should demand it.

"Hold fast, Elara," she whispered, to whatever kindred power might listen, "You have not failed yet."

The mist thickened, swallowing her form. The cabin—a fragile thing, beloved and now distant—disappeared in her periphery as she advanced into the unknown, the old fear sharpening her senses and sharpening her resolve. She vanished into the pale, trembling dawn, leaving behind the only safety she'd ever claimed.

Elara pressed through a tangle of briar and blackthorn, their barbed limbs nipping at her wrists, catching her cloak and leaving the faintest sting along her forearm. Shadows clung thick in the undergrowth; the farther she moved from the velvet moss and birdcall of her beloved woods, the more the land soured beneath her feet. The air sharpened. Ozone mingled with iron—each breath tasted like pennies, bitter and cold—and damp rot crept in, heavy as a shroud. Beyond the twisted boundary, the Forbidden Tower's silhouette cleaved the horizon, stone spires jagged against the bruised dusk as if some ancient behemoth had clawed its way from earth to sky.

She hesitated, chest cinched tight. As a girl, she'd listened in rapture to Lysandra's grandmother spinning tales of this place: oak-paneled halls lined with candlelight, the voices of witches and nobles braided in incantation and promise, their oaths sealed with magic fervent enough to set the stones aglow. The first Witch Queen and Crowned Prince, standing hand-in-hand beneath the crescent window —pledging peace, binding their realms and hearts beneath the gaze of the elements. But when vows shattered, when ambition eclipsed loyalty, the same magic turned to poison in the blood. Betrayals lingered in the bones of the ruined halls, teaching fear. The tower bore the grief of broken oaths in

4

every crack and crevice, and mothers warned wayward children never to linger where the ancestors once wept.

Her heart thudded, thick with caution and doubt. Even the witch hunters feared the tower's curses—its reputation had grown monstrous with every story whispered by torchlight, every grave grown cold. She knew the stakes. The very idea of working magic here was heresy; to break sacred law within these walls risked setting old wounds ablaze again. Yet the compulsion that tugged her forward was fierce and unrelenting. Her independence warred against the rules that had governed her since girlhood—was she to let a man die out of obedience, or to risk everything for a single fleeting mercy?

She pressed her palm to the crumbling archway. The surface pulsed, cool and wet with the rain that had worked its sorrow into the stone. Glass crunched beneath her boots as she crossed the threshold. Inside, silence rang sharp. Shafts of dying light bled through shattered windows, illuminating the detritus of an age—the floor littered with jagged glass, splintered chains, a rusted knife. Her steps carried her through the once-sacred space until she saw a figure sprawled at the base of a toppled pillar.

He looked a painting wrenched sideways, limbs tangled in the velvet of a noble's cloak soaked nearly black with blood. His face, elegant and splattered with grime, twisted as he drew shallow, staccato breaths. She could not look away. Two arrows jutted from his side, their shafts bound with thread that shimmered a dull, unnatural violet. Dark magic festered at the wounds, sending veins of shadow up beneath his skin.

Elara's hand trembled as she knelt beside him. The world outside the tower faded, swallowed by the gloom and gravity of this forbidden place. If she worked the healing here, she could not undo it; she could not take comfort in the simple spells of the woods. This would be a knot she tied in fate, as dangerous as any witch-queen's pact. Guilt flared and flickered, a breath away from panic. She remembered the stories: how a single oath broken in this place had condemned an entire generation, how promise-bound magic could not distinguish false hope from true.

She pressed her palms to his chest. The cloak, still warm, throbbed faintly with his heartbeat. She inhaled, tasting the copper tang of his blood mingling with her own fear. She whispered the ancient words —words her mother had buried deep in her memory, marked forbidden—and the air quivered.

A current caught her, an inexorable pull that started somewhere behind her eyes and surged down her arms. Silver light sparked beneath her hands, threads slipping into Kaelen's wounds, unraveling the poison within. The world splintered: for a dizzying instant she glimpsed burning cities reflected in deep water, saw fire devouring royal banners, rain falling on split crowns, a dance of elements binding and unraveling. The tower's stone thrummed with her heartbeat and his.

Kaelen gasped, lips parting, lashes fluttering. His eyes flooded with awareness—startled, impossibly blue—and she caught a glimmer of recognition flicker there before lightning arced between them. The band of light around her fingers grew brighter, brighter still, until it was a ribbon spun from moonlight and dawn, binding flesh to flesh, soul to soul.

She tore her hands away, stumbling backward. The tower reeled around her—columns leaning as if burdened by memory, dust swirling in the wake of her unleashed spell. A mark pulsed at the hollow of her throat, searing hot, echoed by a glow at the place where Kaelen's wounded heart beat.

Thin wind shivered through the broken stones, keening low. Elara staggered to her feet, her chest seared by what she had become—and what she had just bound to her own, irrevocably. The howl of the wind pursued her as she slipped into the gathering night, nothing left of the old rules but the scars written in light upon her skin.

Elara plunged through the yew-choked darkness, each breath stabbing cold into her lungs. She did not dare look back—the ruined tower, the blood, the stranger still gasping in the dust—all left behind her as she stumbled deeper into the night. The hem of her skirt snared on sharp brambles and the night air burned raw against the flush of her cheeks. Only when her feet sank into carpet-soft moss within a ring of ghostly trees did she collapse, fingers digging through green dampness, their chill seeping into her skin. The silver bark above caught the moonlight and shimmered enough to paint her hair with icy fire. Heart drumming wild beneath her ribs, she pressed her palms over her face and let the cold night swallow her silent sob.

She did not know how long she crouched there, breaths fogging and vanishing before her lips, body curled in on itself. Her shoulders shook with the effort to hold herself together. Beneath her hands, the beat of her heart had changed, thudding a strange new rhythm that rattled through her chest in time with remembered voices.

Never offer them more than you can bear to lose, old Liraen had whispered, wrinkled hands cupping the child Elara's chin as the lesson pressed deep into her bones. *Mercy is a sweet poison, and witches do not suffer for strangers.* In the cabins of her youth, beside a hearth sputtering with blue witch-fire, Elara had listened to tales of oathbreakers who bled out in the moonlight, their bodies curled around the wounds of their own kindness. *To bind your life to a stranger is to tempt the hunt, to curse us all.*

Another voice echoed in memory, shriller, spun from the dark: *Remember the price, girl. Life binds. Life betrays.* The words tangled with Liraen's warning, wrapping barbed wire around her resolve. Elara drew her knees to her chest and rocked, her hair veiling her face in shadow. The old stories had been clear—mercy was the beginning of ruin.

Yet the image of Kaelen's blood-slicked skin, the helpless flutter of eyelids as life leeched from him, refused to fade. Her fingers ached still from the force she'd used to press his wound closed, from channeling the forbidden energy she had sworn never to touch. That energy now trembled inside her like a second pulse.

She lifted her chin at last. Starlight glazed the glade, a hush gauze wrapping the world in silver. She forced a ragged breath out, willed her voice past the lump clawing at her throat.

"Why did you have to be there?" she whispered, voice rough as gravel. "Why couldn't you have died before I found you?" The words fouled the stillness, but the glade only listened. "What have I done?" Her hand pressed into her chest, fingers curling around the fevered beat beneath her ribs. "Was it so wrong to save you?" Her voice unravelled, threadbare and thin.

In the silence, her mind conjured risks sharper than any blade. The witch hunters would notice the tremor in the world's magic, the ripple of power that spilled from oathbroken hands. They would search for the spark, and if she was careless, they would find her. She thought of Lysandra's smile, quickly turned fear at every rumor of a new hunt, of Rowan whispering names of those dragged from their beds before dawn. If she was known—no, when she was known—her mercy could end not with her own execution, but with a dozen chained beside her at dawn.

Still, the memory of Kaelen's lips parting in soundless agony gnawed at her, rooted deep as bloodroot at the foot of the oak. Compassion warred with duty—a lifetime of hiding, of keeping clear from fate's barbed traps. She had been proud of her independence, her devotion to custom. But something had shifted, like a new current beneath the familiar river. The world was not as bounded as she had believed, and her role in it not as clear.

"Liraen would curse me for this." She pressed the heel of her palm until pain flickered through. "But kindness... gods, must it always be a threat?" Her laughter came bitter and low, but no one answered except the small creatures rustling through nearby ferns.

The throbbing in her chest intensified, sudden and wild—a living cord pulled waxing-tight. Power snapped through her, shivering heat and jagged cold twining from her heart to her numb fingers. She gasped, half in fear, half in awe, and for a heartbeat her senses widened: she tasted distant smoke, felt the cool sigh of moss under her skin, heard her blood racing in time with another's, a presence just out of reach.

The bond would not be quieted. Whatever she had done, whatever ancient rules she had unmade in the tower, could not be taken back. Her solitude—even the comfort of counting only herself among the lost— had been claimed by something vaster, older, unfathomable.

She drew her knees in closer, chest rising and falling with each uncertain breath. Moonlight fell silver-bright across the grass, flickering and soft, catching in her tangled hair. Elara watched its shifting pattern, realization flickering in her gaze. The night pressed close, cool and open, and she understood with a shiver that she was not alone. She would never be alone again.

The night air clung to Elara's skin, cool and soaked in the scent of rain that never quite fell. Each step from the glade to her cabin felt stretched by the shadows, her boots nearly silent on the leaf-laden path. Breath ragged, she ducked beneath the twisted branches. Her palm pressed hard to her chest, as if her hand alone might contain the pulse of something wild blooming inside her. Moonlight, bruised by drifting clouds, led her to the crooked doorway—half open, leaking faint gold into the dark.

She crossed the threshold, and a sudden heat tore through her ribs. The world spun, her knees buckled, and she gripped the wall. Heat roared out from her heart, a living pyre that threatened to incinerate her from within. Her hood slipped back as she doubled over, sweat breaking from her brow even as the air remained chill. Light spilled from her—impossible, unnatural, golden as sunrise and bitter as blood root on the tongue. The cabin glowed and shadows shuddered along the warped beams.

She raised her eyes. The source of the glow was not solely her. On the narrow cot, Kaelen lay motionless, his skin slick with fevered sweat. The same golden radiance poured from the hollow of his throat and shoulders, pooling in the crumpled blanket tangled at his waist. Between them a thread shimmered, diaphanous as spun spider-silk, tugged taut from her heart to his. It quivered whenever she drew breath, thrummed in time with a second heartbeat not her own.

Was this what the old stories meant? Binding magic as tangible as the taste of copper on her tongue, as painful as the moment spellcraft turned on its caster. She inched closer, compelled by both terror and something deeper—a craving, a necessity that tasted of hunger after days of fasting.

The quiet of the room sharpened every sensation. The moss-packed walls absorbed the storm's threatened fury, leaving only the distant croak of night insects and the persistent, mingled sound of two breathing bodies. Elara knelt by the cot. She watched Kaelen's chest rise and fall in shallow rhythm. Her own lungs fluttered in unnatural harmony. When he gasped, pain flickered through her sternum—dull, insistent, muffled as though filtered through miles of fog. His hand jerked; her fingers tingled, nerves flaring as if scorched. She pressed her lips together, silent witness to their coupled suffering.

The kingdom had no mercy left for witches like her. Oathbreakers were the cursed, those whose names were never to be spoken in prayer or song. The promise she had shattered in the ruins would never forgive her—nor would the spirits of the wood if she failed now. Still, the warmth pulsing from the bond dared her to imagine more: that merged fates might not only doom, but deliver. That in breaking the law, she had written a new one—her own, forged from agony and hope in equal parts.

She hovered, afraid to touch him, but she could not leave the tether unacknowledged. Was this magic a chain, or was it a bridge? Would it betray their position to the hounds and iron-masked hunters patrolling in the dark, drawn to the scent of witch-fire and forbidden vows? What secrets slumbered beneath Kaelen's skin, resistant to her healing, demanding a price older than any spoken oath? And still, woven through her dread, the shivering possibility that somewhere within this bond lay the root of transformation, something that might remake the world's cruel boundaries.

If the kingdom's priests were right, destiny was a pitiless road laid out by ancient promises. Witches were not meant to love, only to serve, and every act of defiance left a scar on the soul. But when Elara lifted her hand, the golden link swirling between her fingertips, she found no condemnation in the light. Instead there was a question, unspoken and insistent: What will you make of this power you have stolen? Who will you become now that you are both bound and free?

Elara hovered above Kaelen, his face bruised and half-hidden by sweat-damp hair.

"Can you hear me at all?" Her voice trembled, almost blaming the magic for its effect. "I don't even know your secrets. Now they're sewn into my bones. I—" She hesitated, nerves exposed. "I never wanted this."

He did not answer, only twisted slightly, breath rasping.

"Rest, then. I promise... whatever comes," she breathed, voice shuddering with the weight of an unbreakable vow, "I'll keep you safe. At any cost."

She let the final word fall as a whisper. There was no audience save the hush of night, the gleam of the promise-thread, and the wild, uncertain hope curling in her gut. The air pressed close, as if waiting for something to break.

Her fingers hovered over the line of light. It pulsed—hot, cold, then gone, fading to absence. The cabin's gloom rushed back, velvet and thick, but the memory of connection lingered on her skin. Dread and wonder crashed together inside her, and Elara understood in that moment that she would never again be alone—not truly. Some shadow of her choice would echo into every dawn. Neither curse nor blessing; merely the shape of fate, newly woven from pain, longing, and a dangerous, perfect possibility.

Chapter 2

Bound by Magic

Elara's body shot upright with a gasp, the last coil of nightmare flung aside as reality crashed in—a reality not wholly her own. She pressed a trembling hand to her chest. Waking came with an unfamiliar heat—something that did not belong. The warmth spiraled from her heart to the tips of her fingers, searing through muscle and bone with an intensity that made her breath snag. This was not her pulse. No, deeper than sinew—there throbbed a hidden rhythm beneath her skin, fierce and frantic, a second heartbeat violently out of step yet tethered to her own.

Shadows lapped at the edges of Elara's small cabin, the faint blue hush of dawn flattening breathless candle flames to pinpricks. The air was thick with sour wax and the earthiness of damp pine. Time stuttered as Elara realized what she was sensing— the fevered echo in her veins fell into sync with a sound that should not reach across the room: another heartbeat. Kaelen's.

Her thoughts unraveled in jagged, blistering fragments. Her breath rasped from lungs that belonged to her, yet seemed suddenly porous—open to invasion. It's him, the truth blazed through the panic, hot and merciless. I have breached the oath. I have broken the circle. The price—Mother's warnings echoed—there is always a price.

Anxiety choked the air. She caught glimpses—alien, half-formed thoughts flaring like will-o'-wisps across her vision, emotions colliding with hers that seemed as startled, as lost, as hers. She wanted to scrape them out, to reclaim the boundaries of self she'd so jealously guarded all her life. The fear was bone-deep, coiling around her heart, tighter and tighter.

The faint creak of boards snagged at her attention. Kaelen stirred, his form a pale shadow splayed awkwardly on a makeshift pallet before the hearth. In the space between breaths, she sensed a trembling confusion—compact and intense, an echo that rebounded through her mind. Then, as he peeled himself upright, a pulse of dizzying energy shot through the room, jagged with both his pain and a pervasive guilt that sheathed her skin with cold sweat.

Elara swung her legs from the narrow bed, feet meeting the splintered floor. The air in her cabin shimmered, warping with the trembling flux of untamed magic. Candlelight recoiled. She curled her fingers, summoning the smallest whisper of wind—a litany drilled into her since childhood, for comfort, for control. The incantation faltered.

Sparks—amber and silver—spilled violently from her hands, crackling as they skittered across boards and sent a dry reed basket tumbling. The air filled with the scent of burning birch leaves and electric ozone. Her magic was wild, jagged at the edges, swept up in currents she could barely command.

Across the narrow room, Kaelen stilled. His eyes, storm-grey in the unsteady light, snapped to hers. In his gaze she saw her own terror reflected back—no, not reflected: mirrored, refracted, as if the essence of her panic flowed through a conduit binding them together.

Elara swallowed back a cry. There were rules, always rules—promises made under the blood moon, the first of which was clear: never, under pain of uprooting, shatter what binds the Circle. Never invoke the wild bond to save an outsider. Yet here she was, branded by her own defiance. The fire of the oathbroken licked up her arms, impossible to hide.

Her magic braided through the stuffy room with every breath. Kaelen flexed his fingers, lifting them toward a shaft of sunlight slanting through a cracked shutter. Something rippled in the air, as if the dust motes themselves were caught in a current. Elara felt a surging awareness—a brush of curiosity not wholly her own, woven through with shock and mounting fear.

What did he see, waking in a witch's cabin, lashed to her by some lawless ritual neither of them could recall in full? Did he sense her guilt, her dread, the way her own power now quaked and quailed? And what was she to make of the fragments she glimpsed: a blurred feeling of longing, knives of pain and determination, alien but now inseparable from herself?

She was losing herself, shard by inexorable shard.

The two of them stood on either side of the narrow space, a low fire barely chasing away the shadows at their feet. Elara shuddered and felt the tremor echoed in the pulse not quite her own. She met Kaelen's gaze—searching, wide, and stricken. For a beat, words were unnecessary, forbidden. A shivering current leapt between them, visible, real—silver and gold, elemental threads snaking through the air to arc from her heart to his.

A single heartbeat—hers? his?—drummed in her ears, thunderous and unmistakable.

Elara felt the weight of centuries pressing down. Witches hunted by royal decree, promises encoded in the marrow of the Circle, had held fast for generations; broken oaths led to ruin. The wild bond she'd invoked to keep Kaelen alive was as forbidden as naming true names—the ancient Covenant spelled doom for any who risked it. Now, with each burst of emotion bleeding between their minds, any witch, any hunter, could taste the signature of their trespass. If the bond was discovered, there would be nowhere left to hide, not even here, at the edge of the Shadowed Wood.

She could not let herself ache for what could never be hers—freedom, solitude, safety. Not anymore.

Elara and Kaelen stood motionless in the hush of dawn, locked in the delicate light, hearts hammering the same desperate rhythm. The remnants of her magic shimmered between them—terrible, beautiful, and irrevocably theirs.

Mist threaded through the trees as Elara stepped from her cramped cabin, her cloak pressed close to her skin, the air cool with the tang of damp earth and crushed fern. Each breath she drew tasted of moss and loam, a grounding antidote to the roiling thrum beneath her ribs. Her boots barely brushed the spongy leaf litter, careful not to disturb the hush that wrapped the forest in secrecy. The world beyond the Shadowed Wood was hostile, louder, full of shouts and the sharp clang of metal—but here, the only sounds belonged to crows and the shifting whisper of branches.

Near the village edge, wild honeysuckle twisted around a fallen stump, dew clinging to its golden blooms. Elara paused, her gaze flicking across the soft blur of distance. A shape stood nestled beneath a hawthorn tree, cloak drawn tight and flame-bright hair vivid despite the gray light. Lysandra's presence —always an anchor, always a warning—drew Elara onward, past memories of gentler mornings spent safe in laughter and not in fear.

The glade was haloed in morning mist, shadows pooling at its edges where the trees crowded too close. Lysandra waited, boots sunk in the knotted roots, hands wrapped around her own elbows. When Elara stepped into the clearing, Lysandra's brows knit together, and she offered no greeting beyond a look, the kind that said she'd been waiting too long and worrying too much.

"Elara." Lysandra's voice carried the rough warmth of birch bark, steadying and unyielding. It snagged against Elara's nerves, unspooling the words she'd tried to bury in silence since dawn.

Elara let her cloak slip from her shoulders and drew in a breath, her tongue catching behind clenched teeth. "It's done, Lys." The confession landed between them brittle as ice. "I broke the oath." Her hands trembled, fist tightening around empty air. "He was dying. I... I couldn't let him die, not when I could stop it. But now—there's something wrong. Not with him. With me. With both of us. I can feel him. Even now, I sense his pulse, the way you'd trace the echo of water underground. It's inside me, Lysandra."

Lysandra closed the space, voice low as she gripped Elara's hands, her palms crisp with callus, fingers sure and unyielding. Elara tried to fix her gaze on the sharp green of Lysandra's eyes, but shame and terror hollowed her out.

"Tell me everything." Lysandra's words left no room for retreat.

"When I healed him last night, something... turned. My veins burned as if filled with starlight, and a thread—some kind of tether—knotted between us.

His feelings surge into me, like water breaking a dam. I don't know how deep it runs, or if the bond will ever let go. I was careful. I did everything the way the old scrolls teach. But it broke the rules, Lysandra. Broke everything." Elara's voice rasped, barely louder than the wind stirring the grass.

She wanted to run, to vanish into the bark and root and be only magic, nothing fragile enough to suffer. Instead, she let Lysandra's touch root her in place, the familiar warmth seeping through her skin. Her fears, so jagged and raw in the privacy of the cabin, ebbed just enough to let memory stir—years of sunlit mischief, shared secrets in the hayloft, the knowledge that Lysandra had never once betrayed her trust.

Lysandra's thumb traced a steady circle atop Elara's knuckles. Her voice dropped soft, words cupping Elara's heart. "You must hide it. Don't speak of this to another witch, not even to the council if their runners come. There are those who would see you bled or exiled just for sympathy, let alone for breaking a sacred vow. You know how quickly word travels. Even I... even I can only shield you so far."

Elara stared at their joined hands, its dusk-brown and gold, as magic hummed faintly beneath her skin. Lysandra's grip was iron—not unkind, but unyielding, a tether strong enough to keep her from vanishing utterly. "How?" Elara croaked. "If a hunter with a spell mirror comes within ten paces, they'll sense something twisted in me. The bond leaks out—sparks, surges, every time I lose my hold."

"Mask it with binding runes. Paint them on your skin, hidden under your sleeves. Burn mugwort and ironweed every dawn. Bury his hair and blood beneath your hearthstone. I'll gather what I can." Lysandra's practical confidence threaded between her words, knitting Elara's panic into something almost manageable.

The mist thickened, threads winding around their ankles. Elara realized Lysandra was scanning the edges of the glade, posture alert, and there were new lines of fatigue etched at the corners of her mouth.

"They're getting closer," Lysandra whispered, lifting her chin toward the drooping canopy. "Patrols at the outer fields, lanterns along the road. Last night I saw a pair of strangers drinking at the inn—a hunter's badge glimpsed beneath a cloak. Someone's watching, waiting for a misstep. They're after something, or someone." Her voice frayed, barely audible. "You must not be caught."

"They won't catch me," Elara said, but her voice lacked conviction. The words were ritual more than promise.

"Promise me you'll be careful." Lysandra's fingers squeezed, a silent plea threaded between the lines.

Elara could not promise safety. Only loyalty.

They clasped forearms, warriors and sisters beneath the dripping hawthorn. Elara's breath mingled with the scent of crushed grass and Lysandra's skin, panic tempered by a fragile, aching trust. As their grips tightened and held, Elara let herself believe—if only for a heartbeat—that here in the glade with Lysandra, she might yet endure what the world would unleash.

Sunlight slanted through narrow glass panes, distilling afternoon gold into pools atop Elara's cluttered workbench. Kaelen sat surrounded by arcane paraphernalia: dried fern sprigs, coils of copper wire, vials cloudy with sediment. Air heavy with tang of molten wax and sharp green tinctures lingered on his tongue, but his attention was captivated by the artifact cradled in his palms—a silvered oval, small as a sparrow's egg, its surface whorled with symbols both alien and faintly familiar. He pressed his thumb against a spiral. Old warmth rose inside him, threading through his chest with each slow heartbeat.

The grooves beneath his fingertips tugged at something deep, unfurling ragged images behind his eyes. White marble. Gleaming floors stretching beneath vaulted arches. A corridor lined with ghostly light, shadows bending in patterns almost like those etched beneath his thumb. He caught the impression of a golden-haired woman half-turned, her gown trailing behind her as she vanished past an arched doorway. The scent of crushed juniper, the distant clang of bells—then nothing, just the abrupt hollow of absence, as if the memory had never belonged to him at all.

He looked up, drawing a shallow breath. Elara watched from across the worktable, a charcoal-smudged notebook open and quill poised, her presence as steady now as his own pulse.

"There's something about it," Kaelen murmured, voice hushed as if speaking too loudly might dispel the images entirely. He raised the relic to catch the filmy light, turning it until the markings gleamed pewter-blue.

Elara's gaze flicked between his face and the artifact. "Is it stirring anything else?" Her tone was gentle, but there was wary curiosity beneath the words—a tension that hovered whenever they neared the roots of things neither dared speak aloud.

He closed his eyes, forcing himself to focus. "Fragments. A marble hallway. A woman—her hair bright as autumn wheat—and the echo of bells from somewhere high above. I..." His words faltered. "I know I should remember her. But she's gone the moment I try to—"

He snapped his fingers, frustration pinching his brow. "Like chasing smoke."

Elara's hand hovered over the tabletop, wanting to touch, but not crossing the gulf.

"The relic—did it belong to you?" she asked.

"I don't know. All I know is it feels like..." He trailed off, rolling the cool metal between his palm and knuckles. "It feels like it's part of me. Waking something that's waited years to be found."

He struggled to assemble the fragments, as if recalling the layout of a half-remembered childhood home, the way the sun fell across particular stones, the hush beneath cathedral ceilings. Long ago, perhaps, his family had roamed such corridors. Nobles bound by oath and name, sworn to duties older than the kingdom itself. Relics like this would not be keepsakes, but keys—links to ancient bargains struck when the world trembled with elemental power.

His thumb ghosted across a line of runes. He tried to trace meaning from their curls: maybe a house sigil, maybe something more. The marks shimmered beneath his touch. Faint, silvery threads of magic arced from the metal, rippling under his skin. The sensation was at once foreign and achingly right, as though the artifact was answering a call written in his bones.

Elara leaned forward, chin propped upon her knuckles. "When you held it just now, there—did you see that?" She gestured at the outline of sparks dancing near his wrist. "It's responding to you."

He met her eyes, uncertain whether to feel hope or dread. "Do you think it's tied to my bloodline?"

Elara's smile was quick, brittle with nerves. "Magic doesn't lie. Old families hoard relics like secrets. If yours wielded power once, that mark wouldn't fade entirely."

He nodded, weighing her words. The rituals whispered about in the kingdom—sacred oaths ratified in blood and magic, inscribed upon objects meant to last centuries. Legends claimed some noble lines forged pacts with the elements themselves, gaining favor and curse alike in exchange for loyalty. Kaelen's own past glimmered just beyond reach. If the relic truly bound him to ancient promises, what did that mean for him now—amnesiac, hunted, and bound to a witch by unspoken threads?

What if remembering would only deepen the peril for both of them? He imagined himself restored—reclaiming legacy, unearthing forgotten titles—and weighed the jagged possibility: that the kingdom could demand a debt, or that this binding magic would twist his fate beyond his control. Was he meant to rise, or was he only uncovering a different form of captivity?

He found himself watching Elara as her slender fingers scrawled quick notes. Would knowing the truth mean a way to break the bond that kindled between them—or only seal it tighter? What if the artifact was never meant to be found, its secrets a warning rather than a promise?

"We need to know what this is," he said, voice hoarse. "If it holds answers for us—for the bond—I want to find them."

Elara's nod was solemn, her gaze steady with a shared sense of purpose. "We'll look through the scrolls and the old books. Someone—maybe Rowan—has seen these marks before. We'll do it together."

He exhaled, feeling a strange comfort in the word.

She stood and crossed the room, shelving the relic beside battered tomes etched with faded alchemical sigils. Kaelen closed the workshop window, warm air shivering between them. He watched the last glimmer of sunlight catch in her hair, and resolved in that silent hush to chase the echoes of memory, no matter where they might lead.

Twilight clung to the edges of the Shadowed Wood, transmuting familiar trees into sentinels with burnished shoulders and clawing branches. Elara skirted the moss-rimmed path, cloak pressed to her throat, boots sinking with every step in the sodden undergrowth. The scent of loam and distant woodsmoke was a balm she clung to—but tonight, even the whisper of wind through blackthorn seemed sharpened by threat. She knelt in a shallow hollow, fingers brushing the wire of her last snare, and found nothing but a slit hare's paw and a knot of trampled grass.

A hush, peeled thin by dread, hung over the forest. Her eyes caught movement. Boot prints: broad, deep, too uniform for a poacher, pressed into mud, leading toward her hidden sanctum. Her breath tangled in her chest. She ran her fingers along the tracks: she counted three sets, the treads marked with the stitched insignia of the king's hunters—still fresh, still oozing inky puddles. Snapped twigs formed blunted arrows. Thorns caught a fragment of fabric—rough-woven, smeared with crimson mud, the edge of a witch hunter's sleeve.

Sanctuary, broken. Her sanctuary.

In the kingdom, the old protections had fallen swiftly —new decrees inked by trembling quills, scrolls nailed to gateposts in every village. Magic: forbidden by threat of fire or worse, condemned by men who believed devotion meant rootlessness and fear. The king decreed that all channels of power—witches, charms, sacred oaths—must be eradicated. Every hearth, every shadowed glade, might conceal a traitor. The witch hunters were no longer just rumors in the alleys; they were law, weighted by iron and lanterns, stalking with hounds trained for the scent of salt and spell-oil. Lord Dalen's voice, cold as snowmelt, resounded through the valleys, and the kingdom's steel-shod boots answered with thunder.

Elara pressed trembling fingers to her lips. Fear, salt-raw, gnawed her belly, but her guilt was sharpest of all. She had broken the vow binding her to the coven, risked ancient wrath for the life of a stranger. And now, because of that oath broken by mercy and longing, the world pressed closer—as if some barrier had thinned, as if her act had beckoned ruin.

A branch snapped ahead. Elara spun, heart a wildbird in her ribs. Lysandra emerged, her cloak torn and breath heaving, eyes wide in the last violet spill of daylight.

"They're here," Lysandra panted. "Two hunters, a dog, and a scout fast as a fox. I barely slipped the dog—hid under the bracken. They're circling, Elara. Lanterns everywhere."

Elara reached for Lysandra's hand, gripping tight, felt the pulse skipping beneath her skin. "Up at the cabin, Kaelen—"

"I know. Go!"

The world narrowed to mud and leaf, breath and darkness. Elara hurtled over brambles, the cool of night sliding under her collar as adrenaline burned fear to purpose. Lantern light flashed between birches, slanting gold and white into the gloom. Every step forward, she weighed hours stolen from sleep by worry, lessons whispered over frost-laced cauldrons about secrecy and sacrifice. Life as a witch had always been a quiet rebellion—but never hunted, never like this.

Her soul ached for the deer path winding toward home, the comfort of the shadows, the old song of wind through needles—but all that innocence was splintered. They'd never forgive this trespass—nor would she, unless she steeled herself to survive.

She slowed at the edge of the clearing, senses peeled raw. The hairs on her nape prickled. Someone watched—a presence, silent but definite, cloaked in darkness. She saw nothing but the hint of a cloak— the glimmer of eyes, the muscle-bound patience of a man who lingered just past certainty. She turned away, unwilling to chase mysteries into deeper danger.

Inside the cabin, dusk bled through shuttered slats. Kaelen slammed the heavy oak crossbar into place over the door. A glimmer of sweat shone at his temple as Lysandra traced escape routes into the marsh with a charcoal stub, hands shaking but sure. Elara shut the fire with a hiss, plunging the room into ember-glow and shadow.

"Three sets of prints. Someone lost part of their sleeve to the brambles. They're close," Elara whispered.

Kaelen's jaw clenched, shadowed eyes meeting hers across a tangle of half-packed satchels and scattered books. "How much time?"

"None," Lysandra said. "Once the dogs find the marsh, we're cornered."

"Do you trust this map?"

"As much as I trust the mud not to swallow us," Lysandra answered.

Kaelen's voice grew low, urgent. "Why are they hunting you with this much fury?"

"Because here, mercy is treason. Magic even more so," Elara said, voice fraying. She had thought herself untouchable, hidden by roots and the wild grace of the wood, but now her stubborn pride felt threadbare. If she'd sacrificed herself alone, perhaps this would sting less—but Kaelen's fate hung in the balance with hers, bound by an unforgiven promise.

Lanterns swept the far edge of the trees, flames moving one, two, three—hunters methodical as hounds, driven by faith or fear, vigilant for the faintest shimmer of forbidden power. The king's decrees were more than parchment; they were chains, forged for the breaking of lives, stoked by a kingdom's terror of its own children. Those found with charms or healing were paraded through the square, marked and broken—Elara could not bear the memory of the last girl, wind-choked, shamed into silence.

She pressed her palm to the windowsill, breath shallow, heart drumming its warning. The woods, her only home since girlhood, now caged her in: roots holding secrets, not safe haven. A thousand silent promises rushed through her, braided with regret and reckless resolve. She saw torchlight ripple across the bark—bright, hungry, searching. There was no peace left in all the Shadowed Wood, only the certainty that tonight would demand everything she could give.

Chapter 3

Shadows Over the Capital

The grand halls of the Capital swelled with an uneasy tide of silk and perfume. Sunlight fractured on the marble floor, pooling around ornamented slippers. King Varric watched the clusters of courtiers and nobles shift and shrink—a living mosaic in jewel-toned masks and stiff collars, restless hands tightening on fans or goblets. Their voices, soft as rustling leaves, braided together: a forbidden name, the tremor of a violation, the dangerous scent of magic roused from docility. Beneath amber glass chandeliers, laughter had the brittleness of frost.

He could not help but notice how ritual disguised dread—each elaborate curtsy, each affected turn of phrase, all concealing eyes that darted toward the council chamber's tapestry-draped doors. Among them, rumors glimmered like hidden daggers: a witch who had broken her sacred oath, the possibility of something unleashed and uncontrollable, the ever-present fear that their own words might slip into the wrong ears. In this kingdom, order was gorgeous and suffocating; each tradition wrapped tighter when threatened, as if protocol alone could deny chaos entry. Varric felt it in the air, an undercurrent humming below the scent of waxed wood and dried lilac; the space between what was said and what was truly meant.

His advisors formed a blockade near the council doors—six graybeards in gold-threaded cloaks forming their own insular circle, voices pitched for secrecy yet swelling in volume. The king drifted closer, unobserved, as they argued over the broken oath's repercussions. For some, the breach seemed a harbinger—a signal that witches, long cowed by edict and sword, might rally and ignite rebellion. Others counseled caution, eager to tighten the leash of law even as their words stoked new fear: If mercy could shatter a sacred promise, what other boundaries might waver? Already, distant villages nursed old allegiances and new grievances. Already, gossip galloped faster than the king's swiftest hawks.

Varric's mind wandered as the debate thrummed on, the air around the council chambers heavy with winter and candle smoke. Had it always been this delicate, he wondered—this balance of power and terror, this measuring of each decree against the kingdom's unsteady heartbeat? He listened, silent and still, his face schooled to placidity, feeling the burden settle anew on his shoulders. A single witch's mercy could ignite hidden tinder. In a land where promises were not just words but woven into the very laws of magic, transgression did not only threaten the order of things—it could unravel the very tapestry they all stood upon.

A bell chimed, its peal rippling through archways. Advisors hushed and straightened. The king's arrival in the throne room was met by a shifting of silk, the whisper of feet, and rows of expectant faces that gleamed above their masks. Varric crossed the length of gilded tiles, mounting the wide dais to his solitary chair—a thing of hammered brass and velvet, more prison than throne today. Sunlight traced the outlines of his signet ring as he folded his hands, giving nothing away.

In the hush that followed, voices rose again, now sharper. Advisors and councilors spilled their arguments at his feet: Witchcraft threatened the sanctity of their laws; mercy could not excuse revolution; lenience would imperil the throne. Varric's gaze wandered from face to face, searching for sincerity in the careful postures, the veiled glances. He let their words wash over him like cold river water, searching for the current beneath. At the edge of his senses, excitement flickered: some relished the uncertainty as if court intrigue itself was a kind of game, yet none dared step outside the lines. He felt the tension coil, a living thing, and kept his own counsel buried deep. Every response, every measured breath, would echo for days. He could not afford to waver.

A hush thickened as the hall's double doors boomed open. Lord Dalen moved through, silvered armor catching the light, his steps striking up sparks from the marble. The commander's presence carried the bite of frost—no merry games here, only sharp lines and harder truths. He halted at the foot of the dais, addressing the assembled with deliberate coldness. In a voice like drawn steel, he declared that order must be maintained, and that he would show no mercy to witches who dared defy the old laws. His gaze found those who whispered against him and pinned them in place, a silent warning writ in the set of his jaw.

As Dalen's words fell, the crowd's mood shifted from nervous anticipation to something tremulous. Varric watched the way glances darted like finches, how lips pressed together in pale masks of acquiescence. The councilors and nobles who had moments before spoken with such confidence now weighed their next words with caution. It struck Varric how easily fear could shape a gathering of the kingdom's brightest into something hunched and silent.

He steadied himself, feeling the weight of legacy and kingdom pressing closer with every heartbeat. Maintaining order meant never allowing the court to glimpse uncertainty—yet he tasted it on his own tongue. What would it mean for his reign, for his people, if fear became the only law? Would a show of iron bind them closer, or would it fracture what little trust remained?

No answer awaited. Lord Dalen's threat hung in the air, cold and measurable. Without a word, Varric dismissed the court. Silk swished. Masks hid fleeting expressions. The assembly retreated, taking their secrets and worries with them, leaving behind a silence fraught with everything unsaid.

Lord Dalen moved down the spiral staircase, boots striking the stone with rhythmic precision, each step measured, every descent deliberate. Beneath the Capital City, there was only the hush of trailing cloaks and the distant pulse of torchlight flickering against lichen-crusted mortar. One by one, his most loyal allies slipped into the shadow-lit chamber behind him, faces revealed only in fractured gold and ochre as they took their places at the heavy, oaken council table. Smoke curled from a guttering cresset, threading the chamber with the scent of burning pitch—damp, bitter, promising reprieve from the choking world above.

He let silence settle, surveying his assembled council. The maps he carried, stiff and stained with years of blood and wax, unspooled across the wood. A hand to the edge, fingers gloved and cool, he pinned the corners: swathes of the kingdom daubed in ink, veins of territory shaded with crimson where witches were rumored to gather, places where power was suspected to meet secrecy. Cold satisfaction rippled beneath Dalen's ribs as the others leaned in, breath quiet and taut with expectation.

"Every shadow they think theirs is known to us now," he said, voice low and clipped, drawing a line across the map that cut through a clutch of villages bordering the Broken Marshes. "Every oathbreaker draws eyes to themselves—and every eye leads back to Elara." He traced the sigil he had marked for her, a rune shaped like an open hand, and shut his own fist above it.

He valued the hush that followed—no one dared interrupt, not at this table. In these depths, beneath the city's bustle and the king's decorous paralysis, Dalen shaped his power out of darkness and anxiety. Above, fear threaded the gilded halls with ever-tightening knots; below, he pulled the strings. The ruling class understood little of the danger that beat beneath their jewel-hung revels. Most of them, born to privilege, could not remember the massacre at Moure Castle ten years before—could not scent the same sharp iron in the air that Dalen could, proof that witchcraft left scars that never healed. The city had lived with the dread of witches for lifetimes—an old song now given new teeth.

He looked upon each of his councilors, let his calm settle over them, then cut through the hush: "We let unrest breed in the dark. Make them clutch their throats at the thought of another oath shattered. Let them see rebellion smoldering in every gathering spark. Spread it in the taverns, in the marketplaces. Speak her name as you would a fever—Elara, who would tear down the walls between us and the curse." He lifted a single finger, summoning his trusted advisor—a broad man, face half in shadow, quick to bow his assent.

"You will see to the tales," Dalen commanded, "twist truth as needed. A witch who breaks bonds is no distant legend. Paint her as poison—no one, not hunter nor child, escapes untouched."

The advisor murmured compliance, voice as thin and quick as a knife's edge. Dalen relished practical men —men who did not trouble themselves with doubts or scruples. In every word, Dalen felt the kingdom tightening, confusion giving way to fervor.

He dispatched the next set of orders to the military captains. They approached the table as a wind snapped through a high vent, carrying the scent of petrichor and lamp oil. Dalen addressed them with the same restrained gravity: "Patrols double before dusk. Pick your squads by loyalty. No travel along the outer roads without sanction. Curfews enforced—no torches lit after midnight. Any rumor of magic, any whisper, you come to me first. The populace must feel that safety lies only within law—and law lies through us."

His words, sharp as flint, struck anticipatory fire in the room. The captains exchanged nods and recorded details with rigid efficiency.

While they conferred, Dalen's thoughts drifted. He had always known the kingdom's peace was brittle, a surface glossed to mask rot beneath. To govern was to wield fear—fear, when asleep, was dangerous; roused, it became a weapon. Witchcraft, that persistent myth, gave form to anxiety and permission to wield control, an old logic returned with the breaking of the sacred oath. The king might prevaricate, lulled by the trappings of diplomacy, but Dalen saw clarity in these moments—how history, every fire and purge, showed the only way to prevent chaos was to master rumor and wield the sword. He would prove that order was not a hollow or sentimental thing; it was steel, cold and inexorable.

Dalen turned to the last: his chief of spies, silent beneath the flickering torchlight. Leaning close, Dalen let his voice fall to a breath within shadow. "Infiltrate every suspected circle. No gathering is too small. I want names—Elara, and anyone feeding her rebellion. And Kaelen. Learn what binds him to her, and what secrets he carries."

The spies waited, faces unreadable, before slipping into the darkness along the chamber's edge.

At last, he allowed the room to exhale. "Traitors will find no refuge. You have all you need. Act swiftly. Retribution will be sure—and relentless." He let the torchlight catch the ice in his eyes, and as his allies bowed low, the promise of his intent burned steadier than any flame.

King Varric's footfalls hushed into the thick carpet as he withdrew into his private chamber—a sanctum above the sprawling, thunder-wreathed city. Candlelight breathed against the tapestries, gilding dragons spun in thread-of-gold and catching on the folds of his heavy mantle. The council's arguments still echoed within him, sharper, somehow, here in the layered silence. He settled into the embrace of a high-backed chair, gestured to his advisor for hush. The storm's rhythm—rain brushing colorless pearls down stained-glass—was their only music as he searched for words finer than command and weightier than fear.

He let out a shallow sigh. "What am I to do, Edrin? The hall is a tinderbox. Dalen is striking matches open-handed before a sea of oil. Yet if I do nothing— if I falter, even for a breath—every look, every whisper turns to suspicion. Today, for the first time, I felt it. The court's patience has teeth." His voice rarely fell so low, the syllables as fragile as melting wax.

His advisor, loyal Edrin, watched him from the modest shadow beyond the desk—lips pressed together, hands folded over a sheaf of sealed parchment. The older man's face betrayed nothing but patience.

"Harshness may break the spell, Sire, but hesitation may breed a hydra. Your line endures because it chooses neither extreme. A measured hand—wait, watch—let Dalen show his mettle. If the witches truly mean uprising, they'll reveal themselves soon enough."

"And if we force their hand?" Varric's fingers drummed restlessly on his knee, wishing they still held reins, not responsibilities. "If Dalen's steel shatters what little quiet remains—do you truly believe they would rise with such fervor? That the people would join them?"

"Rebellion's spark is never predictable," Edrin replied gently. "But fear—too heavily wielded—shapes its own monsters."

A silent contemplation stretched between them, broken only by rain pocking the panes and thunder shuddering somewhere above the turreted city. The scents of roasted chestnut and cold beeswax mingled with a thread of damp stone. Light fractured through colored glass, etching restless patterns over the battered ledger atop Varric's desk, and over his hands, dusted with gold and trembling only slightly.

What if the old stories, the ones whispered beneath festival garlands and around winter flames, held more truth than the council dared admit? Magic was never truly banished, not while promises bound the world together and blood remembered its own. Dalen's certainty in swords and flames ignored the old balances—the pacts signed beneath moonlight and within ruined shrines. The sacred oath, broken by a single witch with mercy enough to defy centuries: what did it mean, truly, for a kingdom stitched with ancient bargains? Was Dalen naive to think terror alone would hold the peace, or was Varric himself the fool for dreaming that fear could ever bind together hearts, not just wrists?

If he sanctioned purges now—with rumors swirling like storm-crows at dawn—could he stop the tide once loosed? Would the nobles, veiled and calculating behind sapphire masks, see his measured caution as wisdom, or as bloodless weakness? Perhaps some already plotted, speaking in riddles over goblets, drawing lines in dust where none yet dared cross. Perhaps even Edrin, silent and grave, glimpsed the precipice and wondered if his king would choose law or empathy if forced to gamble the realm's heart for the sake of quiet.

He rose, restless, and paced slowly across mosaic tiles softened by centuries' touch. Through the narrow window, lantern-lights quivered across city streets—fragments of constellations pitched against sticky dusk. From above, the Capital seemed gentle, almost enchanted, the violence of its secrets pressed beneath a breathless hush.

Suppose witches were more than outlaws and myths. Suppose mercy could birth not only curses but hope —no, that was too dangerous a thought. His advisors would warn him that such softness was a poison. Yet he could not shake the image: the risk, the trembling hands of a woman breaking an oath to heal, not harm. What else might such forbidden power heal, if given leave?

He halted before the fire, gazing into orange glow. "Wait, then?" he murmured. "We wait, and watch for the hollows in Dalen's story to open and swallow us?"

Edrin offered a subtle shrug, lips quirked into a thin, knowing line. "Patience often reveals more than action, Sire. A ruler's shadow falls far, and your silence will be measured word by word."

Varric inclined his chin in resigned understanding. He reached for paper, quill, and a slender dish of powder. In a careful cipher known to only a handful, he wrote—one letter, then three, then seven. Short, precise, bristling with implication. To each noble house, different assurances or reproofs; none would know the others' instructions, only that the king's eye watched from within the secret heart of the palace.

Stewards were summoned in velvet shoes, their faces pale in the flicker. Instructions were given with no theater: deliver these under night's cloak, speak of them to no one. Doors muffled sound as servants departed, each bearing a thread of the king's will out into the uncertain dark.

In the sudden quiet, Varric stood before the wide window once more. Fat beads of rain slid across the stained glass, distorting the spires and cobbled alleys beyond into rivered gold. Lantern-light shimmered along the ridges of his reflection, hollowing his eyes. Alone, he pressed a hand against the cold pane, chest tight with things left unsaid as the chamber door closed softly behind Edrin. Darkness settled at his back, patient and unbroken.

Marek's boots struck the flagstones in stern rhythm, footsteps muted by thick shadows clinging to the high, arched corridor. The cloying scent of lamp oil mingled with the damp musk that seeped from the mortar—bare, chill, and purposeful, as if the very walls of the fortified residence conspired to listen. Torches sputtered along the passage, throwing brief shivers of gold across his armor, painting battered steel with anxious, trembling light. He paused before a narrow door marked only by an iron ring handle, the office within as austere as rumor suggested.

Lord Dalen stood behind a desk bereft of ornament, his gloved hands clasped like a silent challenge. Marek kept his chin lifted, heart tethered tightly as Dalen's gaze ran him through: measuring, weighing, finding wanting or useful, it was impossible to tell.

"You'll guard Kaelen. Nothing escapes your notice— especially not lies," Dalen said, voice cutting through the smoky gloom. "Report every move, every slip. If he so much as flinches out of turn, you'll know before he does."

"Understood." Marek forced nothing into his tone but stony agreement, as required. Dalen's instructions bit like frost against exposed skin.

"Don't trust him. Trust no one. Dismissed."

He left with the scent of Dalen's leather and cold certainty following him into the corridor. As he walked, a distant bell sounded from the Capital's spires—too faint for any casual ear, but haunting for those who understood. The city, he thought, was a living web of vigilance and concealed knives, and tonight its threads were wound too taut. Sometimes he wondered if there'd ever been a day in his life without suspicion.

He stopped at another door, plain yet sturdy as the rest, and rapped sharply. The muffled shuffle within was the only answer. He entered without ceremony, keen gaze catching small details in a single sweep: cot, battered trunk, coarse blanket folded with soldier's discipline, a single lamp with a near-empty oil reservoir. Kaelen sat upon the cot, eyes wary and posture careful.

"I'm Marek. I'll be seeing to your security." His words fell flat in the cramped air. Arms crossed, jaw set, he did not move from the threshold.

Kaelen inclined his head. "I suppose you're to keep me from wandering into trouble."

"I'm to keep you from causing it." Marek's voice remained taut as drawn wire. His eyes flickered from the man's hands, empty and unthreatening, to the shallow lines of fatigue etched around his eyes. Every line and gesture was catalogued, added to a growing file of potential weaknesses.

"You'll find little excitement here. I keep to myself."

"I'll be the judge of that."

They regarded each other over the glow of the lamp, two wary predators feeling out the boundaries of newly forged territory.

Marek shifted, leaning a shoulder to the wall. He noted the way Kaelen's fingers curled and unclenched compulsively, how his gaze never lingered on Marek but never quite avoided him either. Silence gathered, thick as wet linen, broken only by the wind hissing at failed shutters. Marek found himself cataloguing, assessing, the way a player would study an unknown opponent's first move—a game begun and as yet unnamed.

"You've seen action?" Kaelen asked, testing the edges with the smallest of invitations.

"More than I care to recount," Marek said, not offering more. "The city's not safe for wanderers."

"I'm no wanderer."

"That's what concerns me." A practiced indifference shielded Marek's true thought: that it was not what lay before him he feared, but what slept behind Kaelen's even voice.

The conversation lapsed, uneasy truce settling over the cramped room. Marek let himself out, silent as a shade, leaving Kaelen to press his own worries into the thin mattress.

He returned to Dalen's office as dusk thickened, light bleeding purple through the high windows. The room smoldered with the residue of command—no sentimental trappings, only the discipline of order. Marek laid a folded report on the desk, details precise: Kaelen's movements minimal, his demeanor subdued, his watchfulness not yet open defiance.

Dalen's eyes moved across the page, his jaw grinding as he weighed the invisible dangers sketched there. "Keep close," he instructed. "If he so much as dreams out loud, I need to know." Marek nodded, swallowing any retort behind the familiar burn of loyalty and doubt.

Night took hold as Marek resumed his post outside Kaelen's door. The corridor was stripped of warmth, shadows spilling in silent pools at his feet. A draft crept beneath the stones, bringing the coppery tang of distant lamplight and the crisp promise of rain. He stood sentinel, senses stretching into the silence, listening for what might shift or whisper in the darkness.

He weighed the day's encounters, suspicion rasping against his mind. Dalen demanded vigilance—yet Marek wondered at the man inside, Kaelen's silence as calculated as his own. Was Kaelen truly a threat, or was he simply lost, caught in the kingdom's web as tightly as the rest? If allegiance demanded unfeeling scrutiny, what of the faint pull he felt, curiosity or something darker, each time he met Kaelen's gaze?

Duty chained Marek to the door, but his mind ran crooked paths through the fog of unknowns. Perhaps he would glimpse the truth before it cost him all. Or perhaps, like so many others in this city of secrets, he was already ensnared and simply waiting for the trap to spring.

Chapter 4

Whispers of the Past

Kaelen jolted awake, clutching at the tangled blanket, breath catching with the shock of some unseen drop. The world swam, blurred lines of shadow flickering at the edges of his vision before resolving into the frail blue of morning spreading across the hidden camp. His chest heaved; cool mist seeped into his bones, bracing him deeper than the restless night had ever soothed. The fire had died but not forgotten—ash and ember whispered their own secrets beneath the curling scraps of smoke. Clinging to consciousness, he pressed his hand to his head, the ache at his temples raw, images flickering behind his eyes: tongues of fire roaring wild and hungry; silhouettes, half-men and half-monsters, tearing through velvet darkness; a scream stretching across time, almost familiar.

He pushed up on trembling arms and stumbled free of the blanket, needing air, space, anything except the trap of memory he could not yet claim. His boots pressed damp earth—crushed fern and autumn leaves exhaling a metallic tang as he left the circle of sleeping bodies, moving through the hush. The Shadowed Wood loomed at the very edge of vision, branches twisted skyward, knit tight with lichen and secrets, dew sparkling on each blade as the light thickened.

Kaelen walked until he found a fallen log, mossy and ancient, sunk low beneath ancient sycamores. He ran his fingers across its rough back. A strange charge bristled—felt, not seen, in the way the air pressed closer and the sound around him muted. He closed his eyes, edging closer to the precipice of recollection. Mist coiled around his ankles, clinging and cool, and in its swirling forms he glimpsed fragments: a woman's silhouette reaching for him through the blaze, her voice distant but certain, calling a name he couldn't claim for his own—his or another's, he didn't know. He strained after the memory, mouth dry, heart pounding a broken tempo.

If these visions were omens, he wondered, what did they offer? Chains or answers? Noble houses fell for secrets less damning than what hid in his mind. The flash of a scarlet pennant—crimson against golden light—danced behind his eyes, sharp as a dagger's glint. He remembered swords, yes—cold against sweat-slicked palms, the scent of steel and blood clinging to the air—but the memory slipped every time, dissolving in the ebb of panic and a longing that bordered on grief.

He let himself imagine, for a heart's beat, that the golden tower looming above the flames had been his once—sanctuary, or prison, or both. If he reached for that lineage, would it embrace him as heir or enemy? He ached to remember, and feared what truth would dawn when memory returned, whether it would light the way to freedom or only deeper shadow. Beneath all of it, dread gathered, heavier than sorrow: what if the answer was only ruin, for himself and for the witch whose mercy had bound their destinies?

Cold now, Kaelen drifted back toward the semblance of safety—embers still cradled in the ring of stones, dawn painting the camp in silver brushstrokes. Elara was already kneeling by the ashes, head bowed, her hands sweeping slowly through the soot as though trying to read the future in scorched remains.

He moved closer, unsure. "I saw fire. Shadows. Someone... a woman, calling my name through the blaze." His voice faltered, barely above the hush of morning. "And swords. Not soldiers, something more —chaos, I think. Her voice felt so close, but I—" He searched her features, hoping for reassurance, for any anchor against the tide that tried to drag him under.

Elara's lashes lifted, sharp as a blade. He felt the prickle of her scrutiny, but her silence pressed heavier than any words.

"I keep seeing it," Kaelen continued, his hands tracing the memory in the empty air, "a crest—deep crimson. Like blood, but shining in the flame. And above it, a tower. Gold, or something brighter than sunlight. Every time I try to focus, it slips away. Like whatever I lost is protecting itself from me." His palm shook before he curled it tight.

He let the weight of not knowing crash through him: was he a survivor or traitor; son to a doomed house, or the reason that house had fallen? Would these memories brand him foe to the witches, or would they bind him to their cause by some fated legacy? He wanted to believe that the truth would save him. But the more he pressed, the more he feared it would destroy everything Elara had risked for him— and more.

His words trailed into silence. The ache curled deeper, squeezing air from his lungs. The wood, the damp earth, the sweetness of sap running in old trees—all of it sharpened round his aching uncertainty; not danger, yet, but the promise of it.

He pulled away, knuckles ghost-pale. The chill of the earth bit through his trousers as he settled at the base of a sycamore, knees hugged to his chest. His shoulders shook—small tremors, barely visible in the dimness—against a sorrow he refused to voice, and all the broken pieces of memory flickered and faded with the mist.

Elara slipped into the green hush beyond the camp, each step carrying her beneath twisted arms of ancient oaks. Bark shimmered where dawn pressed golden fingers into carvings no human hand had formed, shifting with breath and breeze—runes trailing like scars across the trunks. Dew beaded on low ferns and the loamy air curled in her lungs, charged with the promise of sap and life and the sharpened sting of memory. Sunbeams pierced the mist in narrow columns, turning suspended motes to ghost-lights. Elara moved between the trees, trailing her fingertips along ridged bark, the runes prickling her skin with old magic. She had loved this wood once—before exile, before blood and bonds and all that she could not take back.

Every pace away from the camp felt borrowed, a respite from eyes she could not bear, especially Lysandra's, steady and wounded and so watchful in the mornings. The oaks whispered overhead, voices rising in a language older than words. Elara pressed both hands to a tree's flank, as if she might draw courage from the solid heart inside, but only the cold seeped in. Her eyes followed drifting breaths of sunlight through the mist, and she tried to quiet her mind—tried and failed.

You know what happens when you lose control. Lysandra's voice, low with warning, echoing from the memory of night fires and scared laughter. Power is not promise, Elara. Promise is sacrifice. There was love in that caution, once—a reaching hand, a candle flame in a storm. Elara's mother tangled into the memory, sharp-eyed and sad-mouthed, pressing the ritual knife into Elara's palm all those years ago. Swear it, if you are to have this gift. Swear yourself to what is right.

But what was right? The memory of spattered blood-covenant was a living ache in her palm, a mark deeper than the scar. She had broken the oath by binding herself to Kaelen—broken it to spare a stranger's dying breath and now carried that act like hot iron in her chest. The guilt clawed at her, a thousand small regrets rasping beneath her skin. Even now, surrounded by ancient things, she could taste the bitterness of having chosen mercy over duty, both too much and never enough.

A ring of mushrooms glowed violet at her feet, their caps slick with morning damp. Elara folded herself to the ground, knees pressed into moss, spine curling forward as if to guard the fragile flame in her core. She brushed her fingers over the clustered fungi, and from her throat spun an invocation—syllables old as moonrise, voice barely more than a hush. Her palm hovered, trembling, willing light to answer.

Blue sparks flickered and threaded above her skin, writhing like newborn snakes. Flame, then darkness; light, then nothing. Elara's mouth tasted of brine, her jaw tight with shame that prickled hotter than the cold. If she could not shape even a wisp of gentle magic, what good was mercy? She remembered when weaving a spark had been effortless. The night she'd healed Kaelen, power had flooded her—a torrent, wild and sweet and reckless. But now it guttered. Every time her mind circled the broken promise, her hands shook, and magic slipped away from her like rain from stone.

She tried again, lines from her mother's lessons lapping her memory like an incoming tide. Focus your will. Fear is the enemy of balance. But what had oaths and warnings done except make her a stranger to herself? The blue light sizzled out, painfully weak, leaving only a fading afterimage behind her eyelids.

Her breath quickened as frustration cracked through her control. She slammed her palm into the yielding earth. Energy leapt—too much, wild, a ripple distorting the moss and flaring through the roots, all fury and no shape. The power rushed up her arm, more tempest than gift, and then faltered, vanishing into mud and silence.

In the fevered hush, her reflection appeared in a shallow puddle between roots. Her face shimmered, warped, eyes bruised by doubt. Dirt streaked her cheek, hair wild as brambles. For a moment she wished desperately to become something else: powerful, unafraid, whole.

"You're pushing too hard," Lysandra would say, gentle but unyielding. "You cannot hate yourself into strength, Elara."

Easy for Lysandra, whose magic moved like water— never choking, never stuttering. Elara pressed her forehead to her knees, squeezing her eyes shut against the wet burn behind them. Shame pressed into her, and she felt the vast, cold space that separation from her kin made. Did any witch, outcast or loyal, truly belong anywhere? Was exile the price of every mistake, or only hers? She longed to ask her mother, but that door had shut with her first broken promise.

How did one find her way back after crossing the line between kindness and danger? The wild magic meant to save had stained her with its cost, left her neither martyr nor villain, just uncertain—aching for the solace of those who might forgive her, hating her cowardice for still craving it.

A breeze swept through the oak ring, stirring the leaves overhead in a slow dance of trembling light.

Sun gilded the canopy above, dazzling her vision. Elara slumped onto a tangled root, arms curling tight around herself. Her gaze followed the fragile pattern of sunlight weaving through green, holding the tears at bay. In the hush, with the taste of earth and regret lingering on her tongue, she let her hope wither quietly, hidden, even from herself.

Kaelen waited at the edge of the campsite, a thin sliver of dusk pressing through the trees and bleeding lavender across the scattered leaves. The fire had collapsed into a ruin of blackened wood and faintly glowing cinders, the air tainted by the memory of smoke. His every muscle held stillness like a blade at rest, but his jaw ached from how tightly he pressed his teeth together. He heard Elara before he saw her, footfalls brushing the leafy undergrowth, a faint shift of fabric as she stepped back into their makeshift world. He watched her figure emerge from between the oaks: shoulders squared, chin high, though moonlight caught the smudge at her knuckles where magic had recently burned wild. He did not know what he searched for in her step—a sign of guilt, remorse, or anything to make sense of the pit at the base of his spine.

She came close enough for the silvery gleam of her braid to catch the last color of the sky. Kaelen straightened, gathering his questions like armor, trying to block out the echo of her hand pressed over his heart and the forbidden promise that still hummed beneath his skin.

"Why did you do it?" His voice landed between them, sharper than intended, a stone he could no longer carry. "You broke the oath. You risked everything— for me. Why?"

Elara's lips parted, but her reply snapped with brittle defense. "I had no choice. You would have died. What was I supposed to do—let you bleed out under a hedge and walk away?" Her eyes flickered—left, right, never meeting his—before she knelt by the fire, hands trembling as if she might scrape the last warmth from the moss.

Kaelen narrowed his gaze, pressing harder, as suspicion bloomed beneath his ribs—a weed he could not pull free. Her words threatened the fragile trust he hinged everything on; she, with her ancient oaths and forbidden rituals, had upended the world he thought he remembered. He needed to know if he understood anything at all, even if it left their alliance shattered.

"If you *had* a choice, then what, Elara? Did you save me to fulfill some secret bargain? Or is this—" he gestured to the invisible tether between them "—some kind of punishment you've cast on us both?"

Her mouth formed a grim line. "If you don't trust me, say it. Don't dance around the words." She sounded both tired and furious, a contradiction stirring the air. "Why should you be the only one with secrets? If you remember so little, how am I supposed to know you're not a hunter's spy or a lord's lost son?"

He let the accusation settle alongside the crackling hush of evening. With every exchange, the world shrunk further, the trees crowding in and the dying fire revealing more shadows than light. He could not stop imagining the moment her magic had tangled with his soul—a moment filled with heat and terror, the feeling of being laid open and woven anew. The uncertainty of it now festered. Was she protector, captor, or something that blurred the boundaries so fully that neither of them was free?

"You're hiding something about the bond," Kaelen insisted, his voice hardening, arms folding over his chest as if to press his secrets deeper. "You know more than you admit. There's power in ritual—even I can see it, even if my memories crawl just out of reach."

Elara's shoulders tensed as if bracing against a sudden frost. Her next words shot out, brittle and metallic. "What about *your* secrets? You flinch at every memory. You shut me out. Maybe the real danger is what's inside your own head."

He felt the echo of her accusation like a bruise. The argument pressed in—two shapes circling the same fire, neither willing to surrender their guard. He thought of the way her hands glowed with blue sparks in the mist, the unwilling awe he felt as her voice threaded through him the night she saved his life. And he thought of what it cost—a price neither of them could name, a chain that might tighten with every step toward dawn.

The silence that crackled between them was heavier than the words they'd hurled, and Kaelen turned from her, staring down into the glowing embers. The air shifted, spiced with the smell of burnt sage and earth, and the failing light threw jagged shapes across their camp. He couldn't unravel her motives any more than he could parse his own. Doubt corroded the edges of memory and longing alike.

He remembered nothing truly solid before her—only flashes, fragments of steel on stone, the stain of crimson cloth, the haunting chorus of a song sung for the dying. Now, with each passing moment, the shape of the bond between them grew more monstrous by definition and more precious by consequence. He needed answers but feared them. He needed trust but could not find the bridge to reach her.

Eventually he heard Elara's retreat, her steps crunching through the fallen leaves as she slipped to the perimeter of the camp, where the last golden streaks dissolved into violet dusk. He drew his knees up to his chest and wrapped his arms around them, fighting the tremor in his hands. The camp breathed in uneasy silence. The fire cast light and shadows in equal measure, pooling between their divided forms as night bled quietly, inexorably, into every empty space.

Mist crept among the gnarled trunks, drawing silver from the dusk as Rowan emerged at the fringe of the firelit hollow. Her boots pressed noiseless into the leaf-strewn earth, shroud of fog swirling around her ankles. She pulled back her cloak, chin tilting upward —refusing the shiver skittering beneath her skin. Beyond the ring of light, watchful branches loomed, every root and knothole marked by memory and threat. Rowan crossed into the warmth as if she belonged, though the camp's edges bristled with suspicion. She moved with the confidence of someone who had outlived ambushes and oaths, pausing only when eyes fell upon her.

It struck Rowan, as she halted before the battered sycamore, how raw the small camp felt. The embers glowed anemic in their stone cradle. Elara crouched near the banked fire, hair falling loose about her face, gaze unreadable; Lysandra sat beside her, arms folded, wary as a cat watching shadows. The strangers—a gaunt, haunted man Rowan did not yet trust, and another whose armor bore scuffs of long road—watched with open unease. Rowan took in the frayed silence, fingers ghosting over the hilt of the blade concealed beneath her cloak.

For weeks, rumors had trickled through the border woods. Witch hunters massed in the Capital—iron-masked and merciless, their dogged pursuit scattering the covens that clung to ancient magics in shivering pockets. Young blood spilled on cobblestones; promises broken in hurried whispers at midnight. Some witches, desperate, turned to forbidden bargains. Others vanished. Rowan had slipped through three blockades, bearing sigils no army could decipher, to find the hearts of the dying rebellion. Now, standing by this humble fire, resistance felt both close enough to taste and as fragile as frost between her fingers.

Rowan's eyes swept the camp—the wary faces, scars old and new, hopes knife-edge thin. She let her words fall sharp and bright. "You risk your freedom for a stranger, Elara? There are whispers King Varric's men are not far behind my own trail. Is your mercy worth the pyres they love to build?" Her voice cut through the tension, meant to shake complacency and draw truth. She watched Elara stiffen, Lysandra's jaw tighten. It was not cruelty but necessity to prod wounds—their unity, if it existed, must be tempered like steel.

Caution flickered through Rowan's thoughts, mingling with old scars. To trust too quickly was to invite betrayal; to question everything was to survive another dawn. Yet beneath that calculation a longing pulsed—a hunger to find kin who would not splinter when the storm came. Rowan tamped it down. She remembered the night the last promise was struck— clay tokens shattered, magic unraveling under Lord Dalen's decree. She remembered the faces of sisters lost, the lies told to keep the old ways alive, the taste of blood and old wine mingled on a tongue that refused to forget.

Elara stood slowly, the movement deliberate, green eyes narrowed in appraisal. "Rowan. I'd hoped you outran the hounds," she said, voice even and tight as a drawn bow. Her gaze darted to Kaelen, then back, weighing intent and the subtle threat Rowan brought trailing behind her. "This is Kaelen. He's… not what the Kingdom thinks. He's lost, hunted. I acted as I had to. Would you have let him die?"

Rowan's inspection shifted to the stranger by the tree. He radiated both fragility and the stubbornness of battered stone, watching her through the strands of dusk as though measuring the risk she posed. It was a dance—every question double-edged, every answer carrying the scent of concealed magic or betrayal.

"Lost and hunted is every witch north of the river," Rowan answered. "Being hunted does not make one an ally." She let the unspoken challenge hang, eyes flickering back to Elara, cool but not indifferent.

Elara held her ground, resolve flickering beneath the exhaustion. "None of us are allies by birthright, Rowan. Alliances are forged by choosing—who we spare, who we keep close."

Rowan met her gaze, weighing the tremor behind those words. She understood, too well, the arithmetic of alliances—old vows counted against the risk of discovery, every promise a potential chain. A misjudged bond could shatter them all. She was the keeper of broken pacts, the one who remembered how each hope failed. But she was also tired—of running, of suspicion, of the ache that grew each time another coven vanished to the pyres.

Rowan drew herself up, voice ringing low but steady. "If you believe this bond is worth the cost, let it be so. But do not pretend the cost ends here, or that the fire beyond the trees is not real." The challenge in her words was lined with invitation—there was room in her defense for the desperate and the brave, but she would not bind her fate lightly.

Kaelen's gaze lingered on her, a flint glinting behind uncertain eyes. Elara's lips pressed thin as she waited. Rowan watched the flickers of hope, doubt, and exhaustion sparking between the small circle, unseen threads binding them.

A pause stretched, tense and liquid. Rowan folded her cloak and settled onto the far side of the fire. Lysandra's watchful stare flicked to Elara, then Rowan, then inclined her chin—a nod small as a secret oath. The others eased by degrees, resigned or accepting, as sparks kindled and smoke curled upward.

As the night deepened, Rowan could almost taste the future shimmering on the horizon—promise and peril dancing in the woodsmoke, new battle lines sketched in light and shadow.

Chapter 5

Allies in the Hearthstone

Elara's boots caught on root and moss as she led Kaelen through the snarled arms of night-cooled branches. The damp velvet of her cloak swept silent trails across dew-beaded ferns. Above, bruised twilight pressed through the canopy in blade-thin bars, spilling silver across their hands and cheeks. Her pulse stuttered as she reached the edge of the clearing. She almost halted—magic beat here, electric and unspent, as if the wood itself inhaled and would not exhale.

At the glen's heart stood a woman whose shadow seemed to slip out ahead of her. Seraphine's hair shone black as rain-slick slate, threaded with strands of pale light. Her voice, low and urgent, wrapped each breath in syllables unlike any Elara had ever heard. The air shivered where her hand moved, weaving silver filaments into spirals that hung, suspended, refusing the pull of gravity. They squirmed like living veins. Elara caught a scent— sharp, sweet, cold as stone split by spring thaw.

She dared not move, nor speak. Unseen insects hummed on the edge of hearing, their song thickened by magic. Kaelen's breath rattled shallow beside her; she felt it tremble against the back of her neck, a strangled warmth anchoring her to the world. The silver strands wound tighter, then snapped into silence. After a final whispered incantation,

Seraphine straightened and cast a hard glance their way, eyes glinting green as storm-lit moss. The fading afterglow of her magic coiled and flickered, reluctant to leave.

Seraphine showed her hand. Etched across the palm burned a sigil—curving lines and jagged points, restless as quicksilver, shifting beneath translucent skin. It twisted, never resolving into one symbol, one meaning. The sight of it raised the short hairs on Elara's arm. She forced herself not to shrink behind Kaelen, whose foot moved back until it crushed a fern. Seraphine's mouth twitched upward, not in warmth—more the reluctant calculation of a fox faced with an unexpected hound.

"What do you seek here?" Seraphine's tone did not welcome, but it did not spell death.

Elara steadied her tongue. Words cost dearly, especially in these woods. "We mean no threat." She drew herself taller, pressing the memory of her mother's lessons against her spine. "I'm Elara. This is Kaelen. We... seek guidance." Her jaw clenched. She tried to glance past the persistent shimmer of that sigil. "Or perhaps, something more valuable— trust."

"Guidance is in short supply," Seraphine replied, the last traces of ritual lingering on her lips. "Trust, rarer still."

Kaelen shifted, boots scraping wet earth. "We were chased," he said, voice sanded rough by lack and fear. "Witch hunters. They... they have our faces. Wanted, now. We need to cross the marshes— safely." He pressed the words out as if revealing bruises.

Seraphine's head cocked. "You would turn to me, outcast among outcasts?" Her hand flexed; the sigil brightened, fading again before Elara could catch its shape. "You must truly be desperate."

Elara's mouth dried. She hesitated. The old stories haunted gatherings by firelight, warnings to shun certain magic—especially what bent the elements against the natural order. The kingdom's oaths bound all witches; to break them risked more than death. Devouring flames, iron cages, water crawling into lungs: they punished not just the forbidden spell, but all kin of the one who dared. Even gathering here, with Kaelen at her side and guilt lodged behind her ribs, felt like tempting fate.

Seraphine, spoken of only in veiled rumor, lingered on the tips of frightened tongues. Some said she could bend moon-shadow to blade, or set a man's secrets writhing out from his own mouth. Others whispered she was half-fey or had liquor of the old world in her veins, unclean as frost rot. Seeking her favor risked more than exposure—it risked a curse deeper than any hunter's steel.

Elara gripped the pendant at her throat. She no longer trusted even her own voice, since the breaking of her oath. She had sworn not to meddle with blood magic, not to save strangers with powers meant only for her people. Yet Kaelen's life had spilled into her hands—helpless, golden, impossible to deny. That act now bloomed between them, a strange flower with roots burrowing deeper each day. She saw the sense of that risk flicker in Seraphine's eyes.

"We're not here to bind you," Elara said softly, hating the tremor in her words. She wanted to believe in the possibility of alliance, yet fear twined close—fear that each new promise was a thread dragging her deeper into unraveling. "Just to ask for your company—a pact, perhaps, of mutual benefit. We know the dangers. We won't betray you."

"And I will not be yoked," Seraphine warned. "The terms must be mine. I demand secrecy about my origin, and no choice involving me can be made without my agreement. That is my price."

Kaelen nodded, wary and eager at once.

"That's fair," Elara answered.

Seraphine stepped nearer, breeze combing the stray strands from her face. "Then I will walk beside you— no further promise, but for tonight I am your shadow." Her words fell as cold and beautiful as the moon's own spell.

They turned, Elara leading, Kaelen close enough for their shoulders to brush, Seraphine's silence fluttering just behind. With every step into the deepening forest, Elara felt the future draw taut— hope braided to suspicion, desire to consequence. The night closed around them: three shapes, bound only by the peril of new trust, wading into unseen dangers.

The creak of the Hearthstone Inn's battered door sounded too loud in Kaelen's ears, echoing the restless pulse in his chest. Elara entered first, violet-cloaked, hair tumbling in defiant waves; Seraphine followed, her silhouette half-cast in shadow, the remnants of night's ritual clinging to her like cool mist. Kaelen lingered a heartbeat at the threshold, drawing in the scents—charred wood, spiced cider, and an undercurrent of incense—before stepping into the hush that fell as they crossed the threshold.

A fire roared in the wide hearth, flames licking old stone and bathing the room in amber light. Elara moved confidently, her stride drawing cautious gazes from the coven of witches who gathered in alcoves, their faces momentarily illuminated—sharp-jawed, scarred, weary, beautiful, always watchful. Two herbalists lifted their mugs in half-salute, eyes sharp above travel-stained gloves, fingers tracing idle circles on battered tabletops. Kaelen's every sense felt tuned to alertness, the memory of flight making his limbs heavy beneath his travel-worn coat, but he kept near Seraphine, hand hovering protectively at her back.

He recognized the rituals beneath the surface: a split-second meeting of gazes, a tilt of a chin, hushed words exchanged beneath cloaks. It reminded him of the coded signals used by nobles in the Capital, but here, trust had to be wrested from bitter soil, not inherited with a name. He watched as a silver-haired woman folded a map with trembling hands, the edge weighted by a scrap of tattered parchment—wanted posters heavy with lines and accusations. Kaelen's gaze drifted to a cluster near the taproom's far corner, where tension crackled in whispers between witches and outcasts over news of a burning. He caught the clipped words, low and urgent, spoken by a woman with bandages wrapped from wrist to elbow.

"They torched it. Ash and nothing left. No warnings, just the brand of the hunter on the lintel."

Nothing in his training among noble guards had prepared him for the desperation in that voice—a grief that ran deeper than anger. He listened, letting the chill settle in his bones. Beside him, Seraphine drifted, ethereal and half-withdrawn, her attention stolen by a hooded figure who appeared from the woodsmoke murk. Pearlescent eyes glinted from beneath the cowl.

"We walk the moonlit safe paths tonight. The willow bows. The wind listens," murmured the stranger, voice almost lost beneath the snap of the fire. Wordless, Seraphine acknowledged with a fractional nod, exchanging no names.

Kaelen's mouth felt dry, his thoughts snagging on the layers of secrecy, the artful weaving of language and body that kept trust just out of reach. He had maneuvered through courts where a raised eyebrow could seal an alliance or doom a petitioner, but among witches, the stakes hummed under his skin— more vital, more perilous. Betrayal here meant ashes, not scandal; loyalty came at the price of exile, even death. His own memories pressed at him: the night his father claimed loyalty would matter more than blood, a blade poised for his final lesson. Now Kaelen's loyalty was something else entirely—a silent oath to the woman who had touched death to save him, and the thread that drew him into these hidden worlds.

He trailed after Elara, weaving through chairs and tables carved with hidden sigils, worn smooth by years of subterfuge. A hand, gentle and callused, caught Elara's arm. Lysandra, a flicker of warmth passing between them. Kaelen could not hear their conversation fully over the murmur of the room, but he saw Lysandra's lips shape words—"allies," "city," "careful, always." The embrace was brief, then Lysandra melted back into the current of the inn, her presence lingering like a shield.

Turning, Kaelen caught Elara's searching glance; she didn't speak, only jerked her chin toward a table pressed against the paneling near the window, and he matched her stride. Seraphine remained alert and tense, jaw set, eyes darting from shadowed corners to firelight. Kaelen's awareness sharpened. Every posture at every table held a degree of calculation, each smile measured. He wondered how many here had fled burning villages, how many balanced vengeance in their hearts. It was impossible to tell which faces read as friend, which as spy—yet, impossibly, a fragile web of cooperation quivered.

He seated himself so he could keep watch over the room, the coolness of the table seeping through his sleeve. Elara nodded subtly to a group of cloaked newcomers gathered at a nearby bench—an acknowledgment, not a challenge, elbows tucked in, hands visible. The smallest gestures defined inclusion or exclusion here. Kaelen caught the flicker in the newcomers' eyes and saw the stiffness in their jaws ease a fraction.

He leaned toward Seraphine, voice low and meant for her alone. "We're not threats here. If there's a place to breathe, even for a little while, it's among those with something to lose."

Seraphine's fingers drummed against her thigh, and Kaelen held her gaze just long enough to offer reassurance—not in words, but in the steadiness of his presence. He remembered what it meant to be the outsider, to wear doubt like a second skin. Once, he might have dismissed these unspoken rituals as paranoia; now, he recognized them as armor.

He watched others—an exchange of tokens, a knot of thread, a candle slipped from pocket to palm. Signs of belonging, hard-won and fiercely guarded. The lines between ally and informant were blurred, but in this flickering space, guarded hope lived alongside suspicion. Kaelen's wounds ached, reminding him how close he remained to the liminal edge between safety and peril. Each wary alliance was a bulwark, every act of trust a rebellion.

When the three of them settled at their chosen table, the hush of the inn seemed to flutter—a growing comfort beneath the tension. Kaelen let himself imagine, for one fragile moment, that this was how a home might feel: voices low, fire warm, eyes meeting in wary understanding. Elara's gaze swept the room, alert and present, and Kaelen felt the weight of community gathering at their backs, a fragile boundary against the darkness waiting outside.

The backroom door creaked shut, stifling the sounds of distant laughter and the rumble of boots from the inn's clattering main hall. Shadows pressed in, broken only by a gritty band of gold bleeding from the single oil lamp set atop a crate. Kaelen slid across the splintered bench, elbows brushing against a sheaf of stained maps. The grain of the table was scored and warped by age—scraps of ink and wax curves, layers of writing etched and rewritten, smudged and folded from a dozen hasty flights.

Elara's hand lingered on the door handle an instant too long, her posture taut and regal—noble, even here. Marek, broad and wary, unfurled a tattered ledger across the table, its pages uneven and blotted, marking the roads and hidden paths twisting through the Broken Marshes. Lysandra reached for a charred bit of charcoal, tracing the spidery lines where the narrow causeways vanished into brambled bogs, checkpoints notched at intervals marked with a hunter's sigil. Two outcasts huddled close, faces inked with unease, hair braided in talismans meant to ward off curses and storms.

Kaelen's gaze roved over the maps. The world shrank to symbols: a pitfall marked beside a half-collapsed mill, a river bend haunted by the previous week's skirmish. He heard the scratch of Marek's thumb as it skimmed his ledger, naming distant villages—places already burned, smoked ruin in their wake.

"They're moving patrols farther into the marshes now," Marek said, voice low, fingers drum-beating a grim rhythm beside a jagged X. "Here, here, and another sighting at Dunwell Crossing." His finger hesitated, pinched hard between two pages. "No sign yet of Dalen himself."

Lysandra stilled, the charcoal in her fingers rolling, restless. "The checkpoint near South Bridge has doubled since the last moon. They questioned Myra's lot two nights ago about supplies—they barely slipped away." The smudged map bloomed under her touch, escape paths fanning out in uncertain webs.

"They'll keep tightening the noose," Elara murmured, sweeping a strand of hair behind her ear. "We need another way—signals, maybe." She glanced at Kaelen, something like stubborn hope resting in her eyes.

The flicker of the lamplight set shadows fluttering along Kaelen's jaw. He straightened. "If we're to survive the next sweep, we need more than routes and hiding holes. Some kind of warning—runic or not —so no one's caught alone."

A chill spilled along the room's seams. Seraphine, arrayed in her cloaked silence, lifted her head from the darkness near the wall. Her voice seemed to slip from the shadows, thin as mist: "Elemental wards could ring the inn, woven subtle. Smoke or water, something the hunters might overlook." Her eyes caught the lamplight—metal-bright, watchful. "But use too much, and they'll scent it in the stones."

The hush between them grew taut, shaped by uncertainty and need. Kaelen watched the others weigh the risk—one outcast biting her lip, the other's fingers clenching a threadbare talisman.

"What good's another ward if they barge in anyway?" Marek demanded, the words blunt, gruff. "We can't magic our way out of every pincer."

"No, but we can make them hesitate," Seraphine replied, unmoving.

A voice, rough with doubt, echoed from the end of the table. "You trust too quickly." The second outcast, unnamed, shook his head. "Promises are one thing—surviving's another. I say dawn's safest, before the fog clears. We scatter at first bell."

"We don't have agreement on the time," Lysandra interjected sharply. "No point all slipping out if there's an ambush waiting. Some should wait till midday, after their search parties double back."

Elara laid her palms flat to the table, posture unwavering. "Listen. We go in pairs, different routes, intervals between. Anyone caught tries for the glade near the southern copse. No less than three fallback places. No one left behind."

He watched her command settle over the room— intent yet hesitant, as if the air itself recoiled from the word trust. Kaelen's hand hovered near the edge of the maps, yearning for certainty. He had learned long ago: trust was the kingdom's rarest coin, easily forged, too quickly spent.

They spoke in turns, argument winding in and out of the lamplight, ideas sparking then sputtering under the weight of imminent fear. Kaelen's mind churned with images that refused to be quieted: flames licking at the inn's eaves, boots thundering up narrow stairwells, the ink of betrayal spreading from one desperate heart to another. He pictured Marek, pressed against a shattered doorway, weapon in hand—would he hold the line if escape demanded sacrifice? Would Lysandra, so sure now, break under the whispered threats of a witch hunter? And Elara— would she keep her promise if her safety rested on abandoning them?

He tried to see another outcome, one shaped by solidarity rather than despair, but the images blurred at the edges. He grasped at hope only to find it slippery, like dew on cold stone. The necessity of reliance pressed tight around him—yet every tentative vow risked becoming a future wound. Noble blood or not, what was he now but a lone man among hunted witches, forced to gamble everything on the weight of words and fleeting alliances?

Marek's voice broke the quickening silence. "Swear it, all of you. If the worst comes—no matter who they go for—you help the rest run. Every soul here gets a chance."

A murmur of assent traveled the shadows.

Kaelen pressed his palm to the brittle maps. The other hands—Elara's, Lysandra's, Marek's, even Seraphine's—closed atop his, warmth trembling with unspoken fear. The candle burned low, light trembling. Around that wobbly flame, their promises mingled in breath: fragile, urgent, impossibly rare. And as the dark pressed in, Kaelen's doubts pooled behind his ribs, silent as blood.

Elara padded quietly through the crowded main hall of the Hearthstone Inn, her boots swallowing the boards' creaks beneath the rattle of tankards and low, suspicious laughter. Light from the stone hearth flickered across the haze, casting trembling shadows atop knots of outcast faces—map-stained fingers, sharp eyes glinting from beneath weather-beaten hoods, the shhh of secret business. She slipped between a table of hedge witches and a crumbling stone pillar, the bitter tang of burning sage and spilled ale winding around her senses. Rowan stood at the bar's edge, one hip cocked, arms folded, eyes scanning the swirling commotion as though searching for a threat—or a way out.

Steam curled from a dented kettle. Elara's hand brushed the edge of the bar as she approached, leery of any glance that lingered too long. Rowan's presence radiated the voltage of a storm contained. Each curl of her cropped hair haloed in amber firelight, chin tipped just so—a challenge simmering beneath that stance.

Elara stopped a stride away, giving Rowan space enough for escape or attack. The hush between them seemed louder than the raucous tavern beyond.

"So," Rowan said, snapping the silence. "Our fearless oath-breaker graces the rabble. Trust running thin out here, is it?"

Elara kept her gaze steady, resisting the urge to flinch. The burn of Rowan's words rooted somewhere deep; she wore the accusation like a bruise already half-faded. People whispered about oath-breakers, and worse, but Rowan's was the kind of cut meant to see if she'd bleed.

"I didn't come to posture," Elara answered, voice low, careful. "But there's a difference between surviving and hiding. I thought you understood that."

Rowan's lips tilted, not quite a smile. "Don't talk to me about surviving. You lead your little rebellion one broken promise at a time. Out here, those get people killed."

Elara found herself measuring the distance between them, weighing whether trust had ever meant safety for any witch in the kingdom of Varric. Every promise —the sacred, the sworn, the accidental—became weight in the air, watched for cracks, for failure. Her own were the chains around her wrists, invisible but unyielding since that night Kaelen had staggered, dying, beneath the Shadowed Wood's boughs.

"Promises aren't armor," Elara said, tasting the bitterness on her tongue. "Sometimes I wonder if they're only traps we build ourselves."

Rowan's snort was soft, edged. "Didn't take you for a philosopher."

More laughter knit the far end of the room together. In the shifting firelight, Elara noticed the tired cut of Rowan's knuckles, the faint pink seam of a scar at her jaw—old wounds stitched by flight and fight. Somehow, these small vulnerabilities gave Rowan's steel a kind of gravity. It was easier to challenge a cynic than a survivor.

"Betrayal isn't new," Elara went on. "You've seen it, too. Otherwise you wouldn't be here."

Rowan's eyes narrowed, weighing, considering. Her hands uncrossed, one finger tapping the wood in a private rhythm. The air thickened with memories of flight through dew-laced fields, the torchlight of witch hunter patrols angling through branches, friend and foe vanishing into blue-black dawn.

There had been a time—before the oath, before Kaelen's blood pooled on moss—when Elara imagined trust as a choice: a gift bestowed and, if broken, easily revoked. Now, with loyalty made brittle by necessity, it felt like walking the rim of a blade. Every ally was both shelter and threat.

Rowan broke the impasse with a sideways glance. "You know they nearly caught me in Belmarsh?" she said, voice quieter now, dulled with something like weariness. "Thought I'd found sanctuary. Somebody I trusted bartered my name for passage. Never saw the knife coming—only the aftermath. Spent two nights neck-deep in the Marshes with hunters at my back. Learned who I could count on. Wasn't many."

Elara pictured it: Rowan slogging through mud and fog, breath raw, the world reduced to footstep and silence, grasped magic seeping away into the fathomless dark. Betrayal wasn't a word, but a wound, crusted and never clean.

"I'm sorry," Elara said, soft.

A hush lingered. For a heartbeat, the warmth of the hearth pressed closer, a reluctant cocoon. Elara's longing for safety—genuine, fragile—shoved against her wariness. She wanted to ask if Rowan trusted *anyone* now, but swallowed the impulse. It would only sound like an accusation.

"I don't owe you loyalty," Rowan said. "But we're all one mistake from the pyres. I'll watch your back. You watch mine. Information moves fast and slow in here. We share what we hear. That's as far as it goes."

Elara hesitated. The desire to believe faith could be conjured like a simple ward nipped at her. She extended her hand, palm open. Rowan's grip was firm, a pact with the roughness of earth and rain. Their fingers tightened—not in friendship, not in forgiveness, but in the wary, precious knowledge of necessary alliance.

Behind them, a burst of laughter rose like birds from a thicket, but between Rowan and Elara, trust stirred —uncertain and new, a green shoot in frost.

Chapter 6

The Broken Marshes

Elara stepped from the dense cloak of alder into the sickly light of the Broken Marshes, air thickening as if the landscape itself meant to lodge in her throat. The first secret of the marshes was the hush—they devoured sound, wrapping every footfall in slick cold and silence. Behind her, Rowan's voice cut that hush, sharp and low. "Step in my tracks. Quicksand creeps where it chooses. It does not forgive."

Marek prowled forward, long stick angled before him, every thrust followed by a slurp or a resistant clump. "Solid," he murmured, and let his boot find the patch he'd tested. Elara's fingers tightened around the carved birch of her staff, pulse flickering against her palm. She would bear them safe across this wasteland if it cost every drop of magic still left in her veins.

In this world beyond hedged safety, risk was unending. Old stories had called these marshes the kingdom's wound: a place neither earth nor water, but something in between, treacherous and wild. Here, in the open and vulnerable, trust was currency. One slip could mean an end beneath the black-green water, claimed by silence and rot.

Elara knelt, skirts dampened instantly, the smell of peat and something older, almost sweet, drifting beneath the sharp tang of decay. She pressed her palm into the yielding ground and exhaled. Elemental currents spun through her: power and burden, both. She whispered, coaxing the air forward—a gentle sweep of wind that peeled thin layers of fog from the moss. Spongy earth responded to her second silent command, arcing up in plaited rise, flecked brown and green, to mark safe-to-step ground. Her magic shaped subtle furrows, a living map visible only to those who watched closely.

Kaelen moved along the borders of her path, his blue eyes restless, bootsteps soft, never straying too far from her work. She caught him glancing back, once —a silent question. She nodded, heart stuttering, and kept leading. Each act of elemental magic carved something from her, renewed a secret fear: that every gift she used risked another betrayal of the oaths that bound and hunted her kind.

When she stood, drizzle clung to her braid, lips cold, jaw set. To care this much for their safety was its own violation—she feared what it meant every time her magic responded less to law, more to her stubborn need. Elara's independence had once protected her like a shield. Now, every pulse of her power pulled her closer to those she'd sworn to help...and farther from old sanctuaries.

Behind her, Marek's warning reached her ear. "We're running low. Dried meat's gone. Water too—one skin's near-empty." He turned bags inside-out, grimacing at the dust inside the last pouch.

Lysandra knelt in sucking mud, bracing herself against a reed, sharp and sure in her movements. "Roots here are sweet enough if you cook them," she said, slicing a tangle of swamp growth with her knife. Rowan waded carefully to a shadow-ringed pool, one hand dipped, voice weaving an incantation—low, measured syllables that laced over the stagnant water, drawing out a faint silver flare. The liquid cleared, leeching the faint scent of rot from the air.

Elara's world was one where magic was necessity and liability alike. The mists might twist a man's sense of direction, the water might poison him, but the kingdom gave no quarter to what it deemed unnatural. Out here, survival demanded more than clever feet; it required the forbidden, the gifted, the hunted.

She felt the effort in every muscle, every flick of her wrist, the knowledge that with every utility spell or whispered breath the kingdom's laws violated, she bound herself more tightly to the people around her. The past weeks had become a lesson. She could not move alone through this world; here, trust was not weakness, but a weapon against a different kind of death.

Elara's voice broke the next silence. "Keep close," she told them all, watching each face—Rowan's stubborn composure, Lysandra's guarded smile, Marek's suspicious reserve, Kaelen's fierce, unreadable stare. She concealed her unease beneath command, but her thoughts turned over and over to the secret oath she'd broken, the old words that could not be unsaid, the consequences still unreachable on the horizon. Guilt pressed as heavily as the marsh's reek.

Mist uncurled across the bog so suddenly that it erased color and space—a tide of gray-green, thick and cold. Sound fell away, replaced by the fainter, more menacing promise of something moving in the haze. Elara raised her hand and gestured. "Hands— now." Rough skin caught hers: Marek's, Rowan's, Lysandra's, finally Kaelen's, warm despite his cold look. Their circle became its own fragile talisman.

Shadows shifted on the edge of sight, suggestion without substance. They could have been shapes made by lavender reeds, or they might have been something with intention, something hungry and half-alive, older than the kingdom's oldest curse. No one spoke. Their feet pressed together on an uncertain trail, hearts a single uneven drum.

When the mist thinned, the group halted on the broad back of a battered stone, scabbed with emerald moss and runic scars. Their hands did not unclasp until the memories of distant, haunted cries —neither entirely beast nor human—echoed away into the deep, invisible places of the marsh.

Moonlight pressed in as Elara crouched at the wind-bitten edge of the hollow, shaping driftwood and reed into a careful pile. Her hands trembled; fatigue, hunger, and the ache of spent magic all sang in her bones, yet she anchored herself in the rhythm of ritual. Quiet words spilled from her lips like smoke, each syllable weaving through the damp air, coaxing a pale blue flame to life. It shimmered at her touch— her secret, fragile defiance—casting shadows on the tangled wall of reeds beyond.

Kaelen appeared at her side, wringing out a cracked tin cup. The water inside was lukewarm and faintly bitter, but he pressed it into her palms as though it were spun gold. "You need it more," he said, voice barely louder than the flicker of firelight. He settled onto the moss beside her with a careful, unaccustomed grace.

They drank in silence, the watery taste mingling with the scents of peat and wet stone. A hush had descended over the marsh—so complete that even their breath seemed to disturb it, as though the world itself was holding its tongue. Around them, Lysandra and Rowan whispered low, their words blurred by distance, leaving Elara and Kaelen alone in the glowing cradle of night.

She found herself speaking of her mother—soft-eyed, bird-boned, lost to the pyres when Elara was still too young to understand the power of grief. One by one, memories unfurled: a lullaby hummed under summer leaves, a quicksilver smile vanishing into shadows. Kaelen listened, the fire engraving his profile in molten gold and blue.

He told her of mist-shrouded winters in the far north, of a sister who braided charms for luck and a father who vanished on an autumn hunt, never to return. His words wove together longing and loss, as if the marsh itself required an offering of pain before granting passage.

A length of bloodied bandage clung stubbornly to Elara's forearm. Kaelen's fingers brushed against hers with a hesitant warmth, unwrapping the cloth to reveal the angry red cut beneath. He rinsed it with marsh water and dabbed it with patient care—gentler than she'd expected, given the roughness that colored so much of the world outside.

Now it was her turn—stoic, uncoiling. She reached for her herb pouch, grinding root and leaf between her nails, mixing mud from the bank. When Kaelen stripped off his tunic to reveal the angry bruise blooming over his shoulder, she pressed the makeshift poultice to his skin. Their hands lingered, movements slow and uncertain, as if both feared what would pass between them should either retreat.

Her thoughts knotted tight around shame and gratitude. The oath she'd broken—the promise never to meddle in a stranger's fate—clung to her like a chill. Magic wasn't meant to be a tether; it was supposed to be a guardian, a guide, never a shackle. As Kaelen's skin warmed beneath her touch, something inside her ached—the fear that mercy had changed her, tainted everything she might become.

Kaelen winced, hissing a breath, but his lips twitched in faint amusement. "Is pain part of the healing process, or just your personal touch?"

A laugh broke from her throat—unexpected, rough. "Only for those who complain." Her hand hovered, gentle now, letting the bitterness drain from the moment.

For a time, they watched the fire's hungry dance, saying little, sharing the weight of a day survived. Rowan and Lysandra retreated into darkness, claimed by the hush, leaving the hollow to Elara and Kaelen alone.

As the fire's glow softened, she began: "When I was ten, I tried to summon wind for the first time. It slipped from my grasp and turned my whole cottage inside out—flour everywhere, my poor cat halfway up a tree."

He laughed, a true and careless thing, broken by the marsh's hush. It caught her off guard, lighting the gloom around them. "Your cat's braver than I am," he said, and she felt the tightness in her chest loosen, just a fraction.

"That cat never trusted me again," Elara admitted, the memory brightening the dark.

In that pocket of warmth, she risked a glance at him —the set jaw, the softening eyes. The marsh towered dark and implacable at their backs, but in the circle of firelight, the world fell away, leaving only shared breath and possibility.

Kaelen's gaze lifted to meet hers, hesitation flickering across the scars at his mouth. "I can't pretend I'm not afraid of what's happening to us. This magic—it feels bigger than I am. Than we are."

Elara inhaled, the night pressing close. She felt the burn of fear and want uncoiling in her chest, threatening the armor she had cloaked herself in for years. "You're not alone in fearing it," she admitted, voice trembling, each word pulled from someplace deep and stubborn. "But I can't help hoping—maybe it means we could be more than what they say we must be."

Unspoken words hung between them, thick as the fog that haunted the marsh. Elara swallowed, letting herself drift, briefly, into a future not yet ruined—one where her choices weren't chains, and love could be a force that made and unmade worlds. But what if hope was a curse too? What if mercy only led to ruin? She didn't know—couldn't say.

When Kaelen turned away, his hand brushed hers, subtle but unraveling. Elara watched the flame dwindle, then spoke quiet words, sending a cool breath of magic to snuff the fire. Darkness swept in, raw and total. She lay back on her threadbare blanket, every sense drawn taut around Kaelen's nearness, exiled from sleep, and unbearably alive.

Marek's fist snapped into the air—silent, urgent. Elara's breath caught, nerves tightening beneath her skin. Somewhere through the low mist, metal clinked: the ring of a buckle, the double-step thump of boots against the marsh's brittle crust. Shouts rode the air in broken fragments, drifting between woolly drapes of vapor. Rowan crouched low beside a twisted alder, eyes wide, and Elara could just make out the glint of armor: five figures, heads bowed beneath helms, advancing along a patch of drier bank where saffron moss curled at their feet.

Her heart leapt, echoing from rib to rib. Memory sharpened in the hush. The last time she'd glimpsed that flash of polished steel, she'd been barefoot in the dawn mist, clutching Lysandra's wrist, hiding from hunters beneath a blanket of bracken. That day, she'd watched a witch's reflection slip across a blade

—a warning that mercy was weakness. Now, every choice pressed against her, thrumming in her palms, as though the echoed threat of discovery might split her in two.

She thrust her staff into the muck, gripping its worn wood in damp hands. "Down," she mouthed, voice swallowed by reeds and rot. Rowan slid deeper, Marek followed, and Kaelen moved with slow precision as if he understood the stakes were more than mortal. Elara pressed herself flat. Cold water oozed under her sleeves. The sour scent of decaying rushes curled into her nostrils; even her magic, silent for now, hummed at the edge of awareness, knotting inside her with quiet dread.

She nodded to Lysandra, who already knelt in the reeds, cloak pulled tight with the talisman pressed rigid to her chest. The dangling sheets of moss hid their faces, yet the weight of every breath felt monumental, terrifying in its fragility. A soft, familiar fear flickered through Elara: not of death, but of failing the fragile trust they'd stitched together in the wild.

The witch hunters reached the edge of the water. Their lanterns, swinging from lengths of iron chain, cast beadwork glimmers across stagnant pools. Muddy boots squelched. A captain's voice cut harshly, searching: "Signs of them—look for burnt reeds, footprints. Report anything that reeks of sorcery!" Nearby, a heron exploded skyward, its cry sharp and lonely in the muted sprawl. Elara's skin prickled with sweat. Water trickled down her brow, following the curve of an old scar carved by a night not unlike this—a memory of hands dragged rough over her arms, of Lysandra's quiet sobs as soldiers pounded past their hollow-tree refuge.

Those months on the run had taught Elara the necessity of silence. Quick wits and quieter footprints. She remembered the shivering patience it took to wait as boots passed inches from her cheek, the desperate discipline of holding a cough inside until lungs ached. Every lesson lived in her now. Feed the group's trust. Do not let desperation crack your composure. Keep them invisible.

Mud shifted at her knee. Kaelen, caked in gray-brown, did not move, as motionless as a shadow. His hand, half-curled, clutched a dagger stained with marsh clay. Elara found herself longing—ache blooming in her chest—to cross the gap between them, to press her fingers to his palm, to reassure not just him but herself that they still existed as more than prey. Instead, she closed her eyes, committing to the moment and to the hush that held them together.

If she fell, she thought, the hunters wouldn't just take her. This was the cost of the broken promise—the secret bond woven beneath skin and sinew and fear. She'd die before handing any of them over. That was the kind of love they did not sing about in the sweet country ballads; the kind born from frostbite nights, bloodied wrists, from hope too stubborn to die.

"Captain, nothing here but ghostlights." A lantern swept dangerously close, its gold glint flickering over Lysandra's boots.

"Press on to the narrows! Don't let the witches slip by again—we answer to Lord Dalen for every hour they remain free!" The leader spat into the water and the squad moved, leaving only the chirr of insects and the tidal suck of boots fading into nothing. Even their curses soon grew faint, replaced by the soft lap of marsh water.

Elara's jaw ached with the restraint of stillness. She waited longer—a learned patience, gifted from all those narrow escapes. When she was certain the only movement left was her own heartbeat, she risked a slender gesture, one finger lifting to signal the group up. Mud streaked her cheek, chilled beneath veils of sweat.

"You all right?" Marek whispered, voice low, eyes tight.

"I'm fine. Stay low till we're clear," Elara breathed.

Lysandra wiped her brow, rune-etched talisman leaving a clean mark in the grime. Rowan exhaled in tiny shivers; Kaelen's gaze caught hers, and in the thin slice of sunlight that peeked through the mist, Elara felt their connection surge—voltage between trembling hands, gentler than hope and sharper than longing.

Elara bent her head. "Spirits of root and reed, thank you," she whispered, prayer carried by the hush. They waited, exchanging glances wordless but unbroken. Every look was a promise in itself: we made it, together.

Mud-streaked, silent, and whole, they pressed on, footsteps brisk and purposeful, holding tight to each other's shadows.

The sun bled gold across the expanse of the Broken Marshes, and the islet of firm ground felt like a refuge torn from another world. Rowan knelt, boots sinking in damp moss, and rested atop a weathered boulder crowned with ancient lichen. Around him, Lysandra picked at her splattered hem, Kaelen prowled the tangled bank, Elara crouched beside her staff, and Seraphine traced silent circles in the tepid, reed-fringed water. Rowan drew a slow breath, tasting the brine-sharp air, and let his eyes turn inward toward memory.

He had always been the keeper of stories, the one who patched silences with words spun from the marrow of the past. Tonight, with shadow cloaking the marsh and every heart drawn tense by secrets and pursuit, the stories pressed against his ribs— demanding release.

"Long before any kingdom marked these borders," Rowan began, his voice threading through the hush, "the first witches shaped the world with language alone. Their words bent fire and stilled rivers, and the cost of each syllable was paid in blood and hope. They feared chaos more than any blade—they were as likely to destroy as to heal."

He saw them listening, the way dusk sharpened the lines of their faces, the way their breath stilled at the edge of listening.

"It was the Oracle of Eryde who gathered them beneath the twin moons, in a clearing not unlike this. Each bound herself to the next with a promise—a sacred oath—woven through with spell and soul. It was said the oath would outlast the world." His fingers absently traced a scar along his wrist, a mark from rituals older than any written law. "To break such a vow was to unpin fate itself. That was the bargain: safety for all, so long as the promise held. The moment one betrayed it, the price would be endless—shame, exile, magic twisted or lost."

Rowan let his gaze wander toward Elara, though he did not speak her name. The forbidden act echoed between them, unstated but ever-present. How many before her had chosen mercy and found only ruin? His mind filled with stories half-whispered in the hidden covens: of Elys the Gentle, who healed a dying child and lost her gift, her hands curling into claws; of Miren the Defiant, whose spirit shattered in the breaking.

He wondered, as he often did, whether fate's punishment was truly justice or whether it was merely the old order's desperate grip on power. The pact had been forged in fear of chaos, but perhaps chaos was simply another word for change. What would happen if they let go of caution and remade the promise? Could mercy be more than a curse?

As Rowan drifted through his musings, Seraphine knelt by a brackish pool, fingers caressing the surface until ripples spidered outward, disturbing a skein of green and gold light beneath the water. He watched her movements, slow and deliberate as any ritual, and the marsh responded in subtle ways—a shudder in the reeds, a hush swallowing birdsong.

"Ley lines run here, deeper than roots," Seraphine said, voice soft but certain. "Magic pools in the cracks between old stones, restless from promises unkept. The runes below warn of a journey twisted by broken words—ours or those long dead."

Rowan pressed his palm to the rough boulder, felt the faintest stir of heat beneath the moss, the memory of ancient hands pressed here long before. The thought landed heavy: their every step now shadowed by a legacy of failings and the chance to forge something new—if only they dared.

Kaelen's restless pacing sent shivers through the reeds. Every so often, his outline flickered against the horizon of dying light, the gold turning his hair to fire. Rowan watched him grapple with a truth now inescapable—there would be price for this journey. For each broken oath, a consequence; for each act of mercy, perhaps doom. He thought of how some promises, even written in the bones of the land, could be bent but not unmade.

Lysandra's voice cracked the silence, brittle as frost. "How many lines can be crossed before we lose ourselves? Do we tempt destruction, or save ourselves from something worse?" She held herself close, the question lingering in the air like mist.

Rowan let the question settle, filled with warnings from a thousand tangled tales—a history shaped by the tight coil of duty and the wild ache of freedom. He felt their fate was a cord stretched thin, ready to snap or sing, and wondered which it would be.

"It is always the ones who love deeply, who risk the greatest fall," Rowan murmured, mostly to the listening dusk. "But perhaps the world fears those capable of grace in the face of cruelty. Maybe what's broken in us is meant to make something new."

He let himself imagine futures: a kingdom unbound from fear, where witches chose their paths without threat. Or a land where oathbreakers paid with silence, burying every hope in the salt-sodden ground. How much pain would it take to shift the balance? Would Elara's defiance herald the end—or the beginning—of a world worth living in?

As the last rays seeped into the water, Rowan saw Elara move quietly to Kaelen's side. The two stood close, speaking in voices too low to carry, hands brushing. Rowan watched the gesture—the promise unspoken in the touch. Tomorrow might demand a price none of them could bear. For now, their presence was enough.

He gathered his ragged satchel, lips moving in a silent plea to nameless gods. Around him, the others readied cloaks and packs, all eyes haunted by fatigue and the thrum of peril. When they slipped from the islet, feet glancing over moss and mud, Rowan carried the stories with him—old wounds and imagined futures threading every breath as dusk bled into uncertain night.

Chapter 7

Secrets Beneath the Moonlight

Crushed underfoot, the moss in the Moonlit Glade yielded in springy silence as Seraphine led the group beneath the gaze of the full moon. Vapor thin, the night air pressed cool against skin, holding in it the metallic taste of recent rain and the faint perfume of moonflowers, their pale petals wide and trembling. Branches overhead laced together in a lattice of old power, every twig and shadow woven with centuries of secrets. Seraphine's stride was measured, her cloak stirring in time with the susurrus of owl wings overhead. At the glade's heart stood the altar—stone polished by rituals unnumbered and bathed now in argent light, pulsing in rhythm with a magic only those bound to the old ways could sense.

She raised her hand, a silent command, and they gathered in the circle. Elara's wariness hung thick as fog, Kaelen's step faltered, and Marek's boots crunched with purpose. Lysandra knelt, pressing her careful fingers to the altar's rough plain, winding threads of silver and blue woodland flowers in intricate knots. Their scent—sharp, clean, almost ice-brittle—rose to mingle with the sweet, earthy aroma of overturned loam where Rowan, determined, pressed sacred stones into the soft, black earth at the altar's edge. Each gesture echoed the reverence demanded by this rare alignment of place and time: the Moonlit Glade, swelling with an energy only the full moon could reveal, its magic deepened by the weight of oaths not yet broken.

Legend whispered that the glade's heart beat in time with the elements, that here the fabric between the world and the raw forces beneath it ran thin and bright. Few sites remained where elemental rituals could be woven with such certainty—where the moon's song tugged at marrow and blood and demanded truth over pretense. A ceremony here was no mere act. It was covenant. It was declaration. Ancient oaths, once spoken in this place, gained the flavor of iron and binding frost, shaping a legacy both beautiful and perilous.

Such rituals defined witch culture, Seraphine knew, even when the world outside sharpened its knives, even when tradition threatened hope. To speak an oath here made the ground itself a witness; to break it would twist the very roots of the land and weather. The shame of a broken promise would ripple through lineage, through breath and bone—its consequences harsh, its redemption rare. Yet tonight, under the silver gaze of the moon, a forbidden bond was being called into being, layered with promise and threat.

She reached deep for the words of the old tongue, letting her voice slip into melody. The elemental names spun through her like threads of storm-light and river stone. The air vibrated—the scent of ozone, the taste of rain-soaked leaves, something sharp as struck flint. Currents spun from her fingertips, visible in the charged hush; wind tangled hair, sparks glittered in the grass, and the world stilled in expectant pause. In her core, reverence warred with unease.

Elara stepped forward, Kaelen beside her, uncertainty hidden behind determination. Their fingers pressed together on cold, unyielding stone as the chant gathered force. Power lapped at the edge of

Seraphine's senses, heady and bittersweet—a music both familiar and new, flickering with risk. The glade grew brighter, auroras blooming atop Elara's skin, blue-white and fluid as breath, wrapping Kaelen's hands in radiance. Where their palms met, light unfurled—a blooming fusion that crackled and braided, the air around them rippling with living color.

Seraphine's lips shaped the final syllables, old as dawn and twice as dangerous. Her heart knocked hard against her chest. She remembered every lesson etched into her bones—tradition was shield and chain, both haven and prison. The weight of history demanded obedience, but some part of her— a secret, hungry part—thrilled at the unraveling underway.

She watched them, saw the cost etched in the shadow under Elara's chin, the stiffening in Kaelen's spine as the energy surged. The forbidden magic knitted them tighter, invisible threads burning gold and frost into the air. Seraphine inhaled sharply; the world narrowed. She suspected what legends would declare abomination, yet she could not deny the beauty in their joined light, a beauty threatening to unmoor everything she had sworn to protect.

Behind duty, Seraphine nursed her own secrets. In the old tales, a witch who mediated a forbidden bond risked the moon's curse—her soul marked, her fate unsettled. She knew the danger yet pressed onward: something in this union tugged at her, a puzzle that gnawed at the edges of her composure. Was it prophecy or pride that drove her? She wondered if the rules she honored had been fashioned for protection—or for control.

The chant reached crescendo. Kaelen jerked, eyes wide and hollow, gasping as though he'd plunged beneath ice. His gaze fixed on a place beyond sight—

and for an instant, the glade seemed impossibly vast, shadow-rippled, rows of spectral shelves and a trembling candle's glow glimpsed beyond the mortal world. Light whirled about Elara and Kaelen, unspooling into the spaces between the trees, illuminating bark and leaf and every sharp line of uncovered skin, before guttering slowly, as if the ancient altar itself had exhaled.

The air stilled. No one dared break the silence. Seraphine drew back, the taste of copper lingering on her tongue, and surveyed Elara and Kaelen. Between them shimmered something new—visible, electric. The glade, for one quiet heartbeat, seemed to breathe in witness.

Elara slipped between strands of willow-shadow and blue moonlight, boots ghosting over the moss. Each step bred more distance from the circle gathered at the heart of the glade—their murmurs finally faded into the velvet hush of leaf and night. She found herself beneath an ancient birch whose coiled roots upthrust from the soft loam like half-buried arms. The silver bark drank the light; her own reflection returned in every shallow scar across its trunk, fractured and doubled. Elara folded her arms tight, hugging the cold to herself, stance edging toward invisibility. Here, on the ragged edge of the glade, she forced her ragged breath to slow.

She let her eyes slip closed. Behind their darkness, the memory lurched and spilled forth, crystalline and treacherous as a freshet after ice-melt. The shriek of the sacred oath snapping in her mind rang cruel as any hunter's hound. She saw Kaelen, his blood slicking her trembling hands, eyes fogged and body slackening against her. She tasted the metallic tang of his life threaded with magic, touched the jagged heat, smelled the salt of his skin. For a heartbeat longer, the memory held her in its vice—her breath wild, her lips parted in denial, the compulsion of the oath burning in her chest and the desperate knowledge that to save him was to destroy herself.

Beneath the birch, guilt chewed through her like root-rot. Witches before her—bold, cautious, cunning or kind—had honored the old bargains. Their fates mutated into legends, warning stories, silent graves. Elara could name too many lost to the hunt: Morrin, whose laughter once split the autumn fog; Danika, whose songs Elara still caught herself humming while twining sigils; the nameless bones buried where flowers dared not grow. She imagined their ghostly faces, pale as the moon, watching and weighing, marking her betrayal. The faces circled Kaelen's body hunched in her arms, the forbidden magic coiling around them like a serpent biting its own tail. Every memory pressed down—a burden both searing and sacred.

She opened her hands, then pressed them hard to her heart. Night air laced with petrichor invaded her lungs, clearing the stale ache. She told herself it was mercy—what she had done—no more and no less. But the ache stretched beyond mercy, deeper than guilt, into longing and defiance. Duty had once been as simple as silence and secrecy, a solitary garden cultivated at the kingdom's cruel margins. But Kaelen's life, his pulse steadying beneath her spell, had transformed that rough simplicity to something sharpened and double-edged.

Elara's instincts, always tuned for flight or cunning, now smoldered with something far more combustible —a fierce will to shield these people at any cost. Lysandra's worried glance, Rowan's wild certainty, Marek's tense vigilance, even Seraphine's unreadable poise—each face anchored itself to her choice. The oath-breaking had not only chained her to Kaelen, but to a perilous kinship. No one else could bear the consequence; the bond had to be her cross. She inhaled, feeling the herb-sweet air catch in her chest before unraveling her resolve.

Could she stand as both shield and witch, both oath-breaker and protector? Was it possible that in defiance lay not only ruin, but the slender hope of something new? Whenever she tried to untangle what they might become—she and Kaelen bound by forbidden threads, shadowed always by the threat of discovery—her thoughts ran wild and stubborn as blackberry canes. She pictured a world remade, a day when promise broke the hunters' grip and allowed witches to heal in sunlight. But every time, fear stalked behind hope: if she faltered, if she let herself need too much, the ruin could devour more than herself.

The scent of moss and night flowers enveloped her, and a pulse of energy seemed to tremble beneath her boots, the lingering residue of the ritual. Was this what transformation felt like? A jagged coil of risk, of yearning sharper than pain, a promise made in the hush between heartbeats—one that might save or shatter. She ached to choose her own fate, yet understood now that freedom always bartered with sacrifice.

Her lips shaped a promise, silent and slippery, never meant for the ears of gods or ghosts. She would protect Kaelen. She would protect them all— Lysandra, Rowan, Marek, even Seraphine whose secrets shimmered like moonlight on ice. It did not matter what it cost. If she must become the knife and the balm, so be it. Let whatever gods watched from above know her choice.

The bite of uncertainty remained, but it was no longer paralyzing—it stoked a dangerous joy, a conviction that shimmered beneath her skin. Duty was no longer a solitary path, but a joined one, lined with risk and wonder and the slow kindling of trust. She wondered, just briefly, if love—whatever that wild thing was—could really exist alongside duty. If they could all endure the collision, or if the fire she started would consume them. Only time and courage would answer.

She turned from the birch, letting the hush and shadow trail her back to where the others glimmered around the altar, the edges of their bodies wreathed in the low blue-white sheen of residual magic. Kaelen's shape drew her gaze first, his silhouette as fragile as glass and as dangerously bright as the full moon. Elara's steps grew steadier as she joined them, a new light sharpening in her eyes. She glanced at Kaelen—he met her with quiet understanding, though nothing was spoken. The afterglow of the ritual thrummed in the earth and within her, a low, resonant promise forged beneath the skin. The night thickened with possibility as she stood beside him once more.

Moonlight bathed the glade in an argent wash, scattering the world into shadows and silver. Kaelen stood among drifting motes, his pulse still thrumming with the vestiges of ritual magic. The air hung thick with ozone and the tang of crushed grass, the altar's cold weight an anchor beneath his hand. He could still feel Elara's touch—her warmth flowing into him, her breath caught between defiance and doubt—and for one suspended moment, he believed the world would never change.

Then the ground tilted. Kaelen's vision warped at the edges, moonbeams contorting, the ancient trees bending above like watchful sentinels. Sound swelled and dimmed, all voices falling away. In the span of a heartbeat, the glade was gone.

He staggered, head bowed. The scent of old parchment and melting wax wrung the night air, so vivid it drowned out the earthy richness of woodland moss. Kaelen's sight unfurled into a place that was not the present—a long, vaulted chamber where dust loomed thick as mist. Shelves, carved from petrified wood and tangled with glyphs, stretched beyond sight. Scrolls spilled from open cubbies, their ink faded to indigo and sage green, each one whispering secrets into the hush. Light trembled in thin, golden filaments, each born from the flame of a solitary candle perched on a distant desk. The candle bled orange through shadows, illuminating nothing in full —only fragments of curving script and the glint of a steel seal pressed deep into wax.

A tremor ran through Kaelen's frame. Words tumbled from his lips, spun from a tongue that belonged to myth and bedtime warning.

"Selenar... Caelum... the Tower."

His voice rang out, brittle as spun glass, lost beneath the tapestry of night music. The syllables slid over his tongue, alien yet achingly familiar, as though the bones of those words had been buried in him since before his first memory.

He gasped, hand poised midair, searching the dark for purchase. Shadows recoiled from his palm. Behind him, someone's foot scraped over damp leaves. There was a hand—Marek's—heavy and grounding on his shoulder. The warmth of that touch barely made it to him, but it was real enough for Kaelen to clutch at the world.

"What did you see? Kaelen. Speak."

He blinked, eyes refusing to focus. Marek's tone was grave, every syllable clipped with a soldier's urgency. Kaelen's lips parted but found only a hush at first, as if the chamber from his vision clung to his throat with cobwebs.

"The library—shelves forever. Scrolls. A candle, burning. I said..." He tasted the words again, rolling them over in his mouth, their power thrumming through his teeth. "Selenar. Caelum. The Tower. I don't know how I know the names—but I do. Like waking and remembering a dream that isn't yours."

Two shadows moved—Lysandra and Rowan—faces ghostly in the moonlight, meeting each other's gaze in silent question. Around Kaelen, the magic's aftertaste still pulsed, bitter and sweet, like sap left too long in sun.

He drew breath, willing the vision to let him go, but fragments clung to him—books written before the kingdom bore a crown, promises carved in gold on split marble. He saw hands, gaunt and young at once, pressed to stone—felt the pulse of a vow unwinding from his chest, binding him both to earth and sky. The sacred oaths: he'd heard their stories, spoken under cover of night as a boy when magic was only fear and fairytale.

They had once shaped every corner of the realm. Each oath: a contract of will and magic, breathed into being atop the threshold of the Forbidden Tower. It was said the first witches went there to bargain with ancient powers, striking pacts for rain, harvest, love—sworn on pain of soulburn if broken. The Tower's stones kept the blood-price; its doors opened only for those with the means, or the madness, to offer everything. Some called it hallowed, others said it was where magic had been fettered and twisted, the start of the kingdom's unending hunt.

Kaelen's own connection to those stories had always felt like a parlor trick, a half-memory lost in fog. But now—the vision, the words—he wondered if his past was not just marked by them, but written into their very binding.

What if he was not simply a man without a past, but a link in a chain of broken promises? What lay in that vaulted library—was it knowledge to sever the spectral band between himself and Elara, or some curse set purposely to punish mercy? He felt the weight of all the old stories—the ones about lost heirs and forgotten bargains—pressing close about his heart. Did they hold the hope of freedom, or only deliverance into a different kind of captivity? Did his own hands help forge the shackles, long before memory faltered?

He looked to Elara. The silent question in his eyes needed no words. Her face, luminescent and grave, hovered at the edge of his clarity. Her magic was in his marrow now—her touch in every breath.

"No one here recognizes that language," Seraphine said, voice carrying an echo of wind against limestone, inscrutable and final. She curled her fingers until blue fire crackled at her wrists. "Visions do not follow accident. The Tower, the library—your past—may decide the cost for all of us. Whatever was bound can be undone or renewed. We must seek your memory's door."

Rowan's voice cut through the gathering hush. "Then we seek the library. If Kaelen's vision holds truth, it could tell us how to break this bond or—save it."

Lysandra and Marek exchanged brief, silent nods; Seraphine's gaze lingered on the moon's shrinking disc.

They gathered close, as if the light that lingered upon their faces might stave off doubt. For the first time since waking in the shadow of the woods, Kaelen felt the shifting sands beneath every vow— and wondered if hope and fear together would be enough as they stepped toward the unknown.

Thin clouds drifted over the waning moon as Lysandra lingered on the edge of the glade, her boots sinking into velvet moss. Soft murmurs flickered among the circle; tension pulsed like a second heartbeat beneath the hush of wind and distant night-owl calls. She tracked Rowan's movements—the set of his jaw as he caught her gaze, tawny eyes glinting. Lysandra answered with her own steady look, braced and unblinking, and in that silent span, she read the shadow behind his brisk nod. It was the secret wariness that had crept into them all. Beneath the silvered leaves, even Seraphine's hands trembled a fraction as she withdrew from the altar's fading glow; the threads of composure in her face looked ready to snap. Against the half-light, every flaw in their trust was thrown into sharp relief.

Lysandra caught the air of unease parting around Seraphine—the subtle clench of her fingers, the guarded tilt of her head. The ritual had cost more than anyone wanted to admit. Rowan shifted beside the altar, brushing dirt from his palms, but his bravado held a brittle edge. Marek's heavy sigh carved the silence.

"This isn't how it's meant to go," Marek said, voice gruff, slicing the night's stillness. "No one knows what comes from mixing blood-oath magic— especially not old promises broken in the heart of witchlands."

Rowan's lip curled, quick with challenge. "Doing nothing guarantees the hunters win. We can't sit and wither under fear because the path ahead is uncertain. Elara took a risk and so did we." He glanced around the ring, daring any to argue.

"And what happens when the risk turns on us?" Marek cut in, his words low but shaking with force.

"You saw that light. You felt the air snap. Magic that old has claws—who here pays if things go wrong?"

Rowan squared his shoulders, refusing to bow. "If we falter now, all this is for nothing. We're hunted whichever route we choose. I'm tired of letting their laws bind our hands."

Lysandra pressed closer, eyes moving between them. "Enough. This circle will only fracture if we fight amongst ourselves. Whatever doubts you have, keep them from poisoning what little safety we have left." Her tone carried a gravelly resolve, but her lungs felt tight, as if the charged air lingered inside her ribs. Elara's return pooled at her periphery—a slender shadow, chin high, but Lysandra noted the tremor when her friend slipped beside Kaelen.

Lysandra's mind wandered—darting between Rowan's defiance and Marek's stubborn dread, to the cool certainty in her own hands as she'd wound the flower chains for the altar, desperately invoking old protections. These woods had sheltered witches for centuries, and the Moonlit Glade belonged to their people's oldest roots—a place where truth usually felt simple. Tonight, nothing was simple. Old oaths snapped like dead branches; in their place, uncertainty bloomed, scenting the night like crushed fern.

She blinked, considering Seraphine. A woman cloaked in riddles, who masked her hesitation behind ritual words and sly half-smiles. Lysandra had trusted her once, years before the world began eating itself with suspicion. Now, she saw the fissures in Seraphine's certainty just as she saw the funeral shadow that clung to Kaelen. She wondered how much any of them truly knew about the bond that pulsed, living, between Elara and the stranger. If Seraphine doubted—even a little—what could it mean for the rest?

It pained Lysandra to see cracks thread through their unity, to taste bitterness where once there had only been fierce loyalty. Her love for Elara was a force greater than the spells they worked; it had shaped her childhood, taught her where trust could be found when the world forbade such luxury. She wanted to believe in the beauty of what they'd done here—the altar crowned in blue petals, the lilt of old magic interlacing their breaths. But she could not ignore the way her heart hammered warnings: every promise forged tonight could also become a blade.

Lysandra's thoughts bent inward, twisted by dread and longing. The kingdom's hunters haunted her dreams, sharp-toothed and relentless. She'd watched too many sisters fall, lost to betrayal and the relentless march of hatred masquerading as law. All her instincts demanded she protect Elara, shield their circle, keep Kaelen at a distance. Yet the vision that had seized him—the ancient library, those burning shelves—hinted at secrets that might save or destroy them. He was both a threat and a key, and Lysandra despised how her wariness flared each time his fingers brushed Elara's.

Stillness fell, broken only by the distant chirr of insects. Rowan looked away, fist tight at his side; Marek glowered at the altar's ghostlight as if daring it to answer. Elara drew a shaky breath, fingers trembling in the moon-softened dark. The hush deepened, thick as velvet, as the others retreated into their own shadows, no longer seeking comfort in nearness. Lysandra's heart thudded with the knowledge that their alliance, once seamless as stitched silk, was coming undone thread by thread.

Above, the moon slipped behind cloud. Darkness swelled in the glade. They stood shoulder to shoulder, yet felt landscapes apart, wary and uncertain. Shadows stretched from the altar, bending long and cold over the circle, silently warning how easily faith could fracture and be lost.

Chapter 8

Beneath Enemy Eyes

A mist clung to the trees, pale and searching, shrouding the Shadowed Wood in an uneasy hush that broke only with the jangle of armor and the heavy tread of boots. Elara pressed her palm against the rough, living skin of an ash tree, feeling its reluctant pulse answer her own, both hearts galloping under threat. Beyond the trunks, steel glinted between wet leaves—a disciplined line of soldiers, their helmets wreathed in white vapor, the red banners of the king trailing behind them, ragged as a wound. At their head walked Lord Dalen, dark-eyed, sword unsheathed, his every stride a promise of ruin. Breath and hope cinched tight in Elara's chest.

Whispers flickered through the sanctuary: a shivering spell, a frantic prayer. "Circle up!" Elara shouted, her voice tearing the hush. Witches gathered, hands reaching for each other, the air thickening with the copper tang of fear and the electric prickle of collective magic. The sibilant mutter of runes knitted together; blue light spilled across the others' faces, carving deep shadows, trembling at first, then strengthening as Elara moved among them, biting her thumb until the taste of iron flooded her mouth, and smudging protective sigils across foreheads, hands, the ground.

A wind rose—the work of Kaelen, who stood on the clearing's edge, hair wild, coat billowing, eyes storm-bright. His whisper wove air into a spinning wall, scattering dead leaves, rattling loose-armed branches overhead. Elara's own magic—earth and bone and blood—answered his, knotting their fates tighter. She crouched, tracing the ancient runes into the loam, each glyph glowing, humming beneath her fingertips.

The sanctuary, once hidden in twisting roots and crown-high ferns, now burned with a stained-glass beauty—fragile, and altogether too exposed.

"Focus," she hissed, catching Lysandra's arm as the younger witch faltered. Lysandra's inhale trembled in the cold; only hours before, her laughter had warmed the undercroft, the two of them teasing Kaelen over his mangled attempt at the binding ceremony. The memory stung, sharp and unbearably sweet.

"Keep the lines strong," Lysandra whispered. Elara squeezed her friend's hand, unable to promise anything.

The kingdom's hatred for witches ran deeper than poison roots. Laws laid bare the cost of existence: For magic wrought, a hand severed. For spell spoken, a tongue cut out. For mere suspicion, a neck stretched on the king's gallows. Elara knew these rules as intimately as her own bones—words taken in childhood, a cage built with every tale shared hush-hush by candlelight. Even here, hidden, every hour was thickened by the threat of betrayal and the violence lurking just beyond the sanctuary's dew-wet bramble. That violence was coming now, a black tide cresting at the sanctuary's edge.

Metal clashed—a battering ram swung; branches blazed as arrows choked the sky. Soldiers roared, boots snapping twigs and ferns—unnerving in their unity, terrible in their numbers. Magical wards shivered, ruptured, exploded into shards of sapphire light. Men poured through the breach, loosing volleys of bolts that thudded into tree bark and spun moss into the air with red mist and splinters.

Elara's voice rang higher—words not her own, words older than memory. Sparks leapt from her fingers as she threw up a shield, the suction of it tugging at her core. Kaelen's wind bent, deflected, howled against the invaders, tossing them back like toys, but more surged forward, undeterred.

She heard the scream of a branch above—the sound was sharp as shattering pottery—and saw Lysandra, cloak silvered in blood and dew, duck beneath. Elara's heart lurched, feet rooted where fear and duty met. Crossbow bolts sang, spells exploded in jets of color, the air ripe with burning resin and the harsh sweat of men.

"Tunnels!" Lysandra shouted, staggering toward the half-buried door wedged between roots at the clearing's farthest edge. Two soldiers broke from the throng, reaching for her, red-stitched tunics slick with morning rain, boots churning mud. Lysandra dove, slipped through, vanished in a smear of dark cloth as greedy hands snatched empty air.

"Lysandra!" Elara cried, but the name was torn away by a volley of arrows, Kaelen's wind, the sluicing shriek of fire as another ward failed. Elara wove another line of runes, every letter scraping her soul raw. Kaelen dropped to one knee beside her, wincing, hands raised to steady the barrier where it sheared under steel spearheads.

"We have to hold the line," he growled, voice bruised with exhaustion.

Elara's mind reeled with the knowledge that every heartbeat was a coin paid for time. If Lysandra fell, if any witch was captured, it would not be mercy that awaited them. She carried the weight of a broken oath stabbed like a thorn in her chest, binding her not only to Kaelen, but to every frightened soul clustered behind her—her love, her guilt, her hope braided impossibly together.

A sudden rush—the witch hunters surged forward, filling the sanctuary with the raw stink of oil and steel. Elara glimpsed, over the collapsing wards, Lysandra's narrow figure tumbling down the secret passage, hair swinging like a banner, swallowed by darkness. Then the enemy crashed through, separating Elara from everything and everyone that mattered, and the world shattered into smoke and blood and light.

Cool mud slicked Lysandra's palms as she dragged herself from the narrow tunnel, breath sharp and hot in her throat. Dawning grey filtered through ferns; above, brambles tangled with dew and clots of last autumn's leaves. Every inch of her stung—a line of blood trickled from her knee where stone had bitten deep. She tore a patch of moss loose to press against the scrape, barely registering the pain beneath the roaring in her ears. Just beyond the veil of trees, dogs bayed, throats guttural with excitement, and boots smacked the loamy ground in a drumbeat of dread. The witch hunters had fanned out already, their shadows flickering across the damp world, searching for any sign of her.

She pressed deeper into the vegetation. Each heartbeat seemed to echo in her chest, braced against the memory of a night in Siren's Hollow years before. Moonlight on slick flagstones, the scent of old rain, a whispered warning from her mother—Lysandra, stay low, stay silent. Even then, her mother's trembling hand had taught her the art of holding still, of listening to the twitch of every leaf, the meaning behind every broken twig. That memory lived in her skin now, guiding her hands as they gathered brush to hide the tunnel's exit.

A man's distant command crackled through the shrubbery—"Drive west, circle the glade!"—then another, even closer: "Tracks here!" Panic wanted to claw up her throat, but she bit it back. There was no time for fear, just movement—silent, deliberate. She forced herself upright, pressing into the dark perfume of crushed bluebells and the metallic tang of her own blood.

The world had collapsed to essentials: hide, mislead, survive. She whispered a word under her breath—old Essexian magic, stolen from the root song of the forest. Her fingers sketched a sigil in the air, weaving threads of compulsion around something so simple as a trail. Leaves tumbled, snapped and fell, the story of her passage rewriting itself in a gentle arc northward. Bark scraped beneath her nails as she arranged broken twigs. She remembered her first near-capture: the way torches turned the marsh fog gold, the suffocating press of a hound's body when it bowled her over, jaws snapping inches from her throat. She survived by doubling back, wading blind through river weeds, trust placed not in her power but in the disdainful patience of her heartbeat and breath—always breath, slow and deep.

Now, worn from the run, she edged toward the stream. Its water ran chill, sliding over soft mud and clattering stones, frost still clinging at the banks. Lysandra waded in, teeth gritted. Cold knifed up her legs, numbing tenderness and the fire of exhaustion. The current washed away the sticky blood, swept her scent downstream, and she tucked herself low, mindful of each step. She kept to the center as long as she dared, only leaving the water when the barking drifted off behind her like a half-remembered nightmare.

Branches scored her arms as she wove through brush, guided by little more than hope and the ragged sound of her breathing. With each knee-high root and clutch of nettles, she forced herself to recall the countless times she'd eluded capture. All those narrow escapes— the time she hid with a half-starved fox beneath a fallen log as soldiers trampled past, the snow-muffled dawn when she trusted that birdsong would cover her cough—had sculpted her into something both fragile and remarkably durable. That blend kept her from despair now, steadied her nimble movements, reminded her that to survive was more than instinct. It was a promise.

Her mind spun with Elara's face. That wild flicker in her friend's eyes when spells flew and the old trees burned. Lysandra's pulse quickened less from fear, more from the press of loyalty—a fierce, aching need to protect what few treasures this world left her. She rehearsed alarms and message codes beneath her breath, smoky strings of syllables she had woven into ritual through sleepless nights. Even as she pressed on, fear pinched beneath her ribs, urgent with questions she dared not ask: Was Elara safe? Had Kaelen made it to the glade? If she failed, what scraps of hope did their cause have left?

The woods grew denser, shadows thickening, the air struck through with the spicy scent of pine needles and moist earth. Somewhere ahead, a shape—stone veiled in moss, hunched beneath willows—caught the faint light. Lysandra pushed harder, branches snapping. She stumbled to the squat door of the outpost and rapped twice, the coded rhythm echoing in her bones.

A hooded figure slipped the door open and drew her inside. The chill of the forest yielded to the humid closeness of earth and straw, fireless for safety, lit only by a single enchanted orb. Lysandra's voice came out cracked, urgent. "The sanctuary's fallen. They're everywhere—dogs, steel, spells. Warn the others. We're not safe here."

She dropped onto a battered crate, uncapping a brass inkwell with fingers only just steady. Paper—already ruled with the cryptic markers she'd memorized years ago—trembled as she wrote: South breached. Hunters converging. Trust no roads. She wound the slip around a slender hawk's leg, her hands careful but quick. The bird clicked its beak, eyes glimmering with borrowed magic, and Lysandra whispered, "Find Elara. Now." The hawk vanished into the thin grey morning, wings brushing dust from aging beams.

Lysandra's knees buckled. She knelt onto the straw mat, cheek pressed to scratchy fibers, chest rising and falling. Her fingers shook—residual dread, relentless hope—and she let her eyes close, willing strength she hadn't known she possessed to carry her one heartbeat further.

Marek crouched on the spine of the watch post, dew chilling the leather along his shins. The ravine below vanished into bottomless grey, the wet air thick with the quiet hush before disaster. Smoke unfurled in curls over the distant trees, veins of ash winding through the leaf fog where the sanctuary burned. Far off—close enough to raise the fine hairs at the nape of his neck—magic snapped against steel, the peal of crossbow bolts ricocheting from iron bark. Shouts echoed, hoarse and panicked, too many voices—his countrymen—hunting.

The sword at Marek's side felt heavier than it ever had in years of campaign. He wrapped his fingers around the hilt until his knuckles blanched. Duty demanded this grip, the tenet of loyalty forged by Dalen's iron will and signed in the blood of countless traitors who clung to the old ways. But even now, Marek's breath snagged against the remembrance of eyes wide with terror, wild with the animal instinct to run. Witches—women and boys and old men—coiled in defense circles, faces lit by the sickle glow of rune shields, not much older than his own sister before fever took her. Smoke stung his eyes; he blinked hard, but the ghosts called to him anyway.

Honor had once seemed simple: serve the banner, obey the oath, hold the line. Yet beneath the black-and-crimson tabard, his chest ached with shame. He'd seen a child clutching her mother's skirts as the ward shattered—too small, too new to the world, pressing petals into her fists as if flowers could barter peace from the Fates. Marek had turned away, tightening his jaw, trying to become another cog in Dalen's ever-grinding machine. But today, with his palms sweating and the clash of war driving splinters beneath his skin, the veneer of obedience shattered.

A memory surfaced, unbidden—one winter, years ago, Dalen had decreed a village's razing for harboring a hedge witch. Marek remembered standing behind the line of torches, watching flame curl over rooftops—a lesson taught in smoke and agony. Afterward, the men had drunk and toasted the Lord's ruthless wisdom, but Marek had lain awake, listening to the wind worry at the charred beams, heart thundering with doubt.

He had heard the muttered stories too, those traded in corners after the barracks fires burnt low: how Dalen had broken the covenants of mercy during the Siege of the Northwood, how unexpected acts of kindness became cause for execution. A man so devout in his cruelty that even those sworn to him walked soft in his shadow. Marek's loyalty splintered, each tale a wedge driving into his faith.

A gust rattled the watch post. The embers glimmered on the horizon—a wound on the kingdom's face. He had never been one for wishing, but tonight he craved the impossible: that he might silence the shrieking in his conscience, that he could carve his own fate from the welter of violence and law.

He waited until dusk bled purple through the spindles of cloud, until the last of Dalen's hounds had swept through the trees and the immediate carnage faded into echo. Marek picked his way down the ravine's zigzag path, boots caked in mud and guilt, every step away from the post tightening the knot in his gut. The sanctuary's ruin lingered behind his eyes— starlight catching on rents in the earth, the taste of panic metallic on his tongue.

At the edge of a silver-barked grove, he halted. The world here smelled of new rain and old moss, a quiet lushness, untouched by fire. Shadows shifted and a figure glided forward, cloaked in forest-dark green.

"You're late," the contact's voice hissed through the gloom.

"It was chaos," Marek whispered, breath smoky. "The hunters overran the wards. He'll send men to the villages by dawn."

A gloved hand extended a slip of oil-crackled parchment. "You'll want this. It tells where Dalen's next purge will fall. He's growing paranoid. The King suspects nothing, but there are... doubts among the barons."

He tucked the message into the lining of his jerkin, pulse thrum heavy in his ears. "How many survivors escaped?"

"Hard to say. More than Dalen would prefer. Fewer than the world requires."

Marek hesitated. "Tell me, these raids—they've grown worse since Dalen—" He faltered, voice raw with hunger for answers. "Why does he relish it? Has it always been like this?"

A brittle laugh. "Some men need monsters. Dalen makes them—and then hunts them. He's been at this since the old peace was broken. They say he keeps a ledger, marks every act of mercy in black, as failures. Be careful, Marek." The figure faded back into darkness.

Left with the pouch and a soul unmoored, Marek let silence claim the grove. He thought of those hunted, of every plea that had met only steel. The oath sat sour in his mouth—a bond once sacred, now poisoned by what he'd witnessed.

He turned toward the kingdom's border. The wind tugged curls of smoke toward the setting sun, where the Shadowed Wood burned against the bruised sky. Marek stood unmoving, the embers marking loss and the flicker of something fierce inside—his fear, close companion to the shape his courage must now take.

The palace of the Capital City swelled with whispers. In the rose-gold wash of afternoon, news of the Shadowed Wood raid seeped beneath every carved arch and along the veined marble floors. Their majesty's halls—a place of crisp banners, onyx candelabra, and polished stone made for echoing secrets—had gathered knots of nervous men and women. Scribes, their ink-stained fingers wringing scrolls tight, circled among the lower courtiers. Each face reflected uncertainty, the air salted with fear. The scent of overturned parchment mingled with the perfume of hothouse lilies, heady and close within the windowless corridors. Soft footfalls flickered between columns, carrying rumors: blood in the woods, sanctuary lost, sparks and ashes carried by the wind. A single bell tolled somewhere beyond the palace walls.

King Varric moved through his world as if it hovered outside himself, every marble step carefully measured. The guards who lined the approach to the gilded war chamber stiffened at his arrival, but he saw only the glimmer of sunlight on their breastplates, faceless and still. He entered the council chamber—ceiling arched and veined with gold, table lacquered to a glass shine—and took his seat beneath the obsidian crest of his line. The chair to his right, draped in a banner of red and black, remained empty: Lord Dalen, absent on campaign, his deeds carried as shadow and threat in his stead.

Varric's face held no tremor, but within him tides surged. The council gathered around, their eyes darting as light danced across crystal decanters. Lord Branth, Dalen's chief supporter, slammed his fist to the table. "Mercy breeds defiance, Your Majesty. The unrest festers. We must act—swift, unyielding justice, before rebellion can take root."

Across from him, Advisor Halden, white-haired, voice lined by years, folded his hands. "My king, blood breeds nothing but blood. Even now, talk of new uprisings stirs the heart of the city. We forget the lessons of past purges at our peril."

Lady Brienna, the head of the merchant guild, swept forward—her sleeves trailing, voice rich with smoke and iron. "If Lord Dalen's men keep razing our borders and snatching folk from the docks, my merchants will bolt. The city's lower wards simmer. Bread riots are not far off."

Lord Malthus, accent curved as a scalpel, leaned forward, the flicker of ambition bright in his eyes.

"There is a path between chaos and leniency. Let us convene a tribunal. Special courts, chosen by the crown, to judge all suspected magic-wielders. The people crave security—yet too many burnings fuel only sympathy for witches."

The debate unfolded like a fever. Varric kept his gaze fixed beyond the flash of gestures and harsh light, hands pressed together so tightly the knuckles whitened. He listened as voices rose and fell, as the scent of bee's-wax drifted from the chamber's heavy door, as gold caught the pulse of torchlight in the mirrored surface of the council table. He thought of Dalen's red banners advancing through blue shadow, of ashes becalmed in a forest glade, of names erased from every book but never from memory.

Varric remembered the earliest days of his rule, when he was a younger king, hungry for certainty. The first decrees he signed had swept through the kingdom like winter wind—witches branded, sanctuaries razed, magic spoken of in only half-whisper and prayer. Those laws, authored by men eager for legacy and safety, were forged in fear: fear of the drought that followed the last rebellion, fear of the prince—his brother—struck down by unnamed sorcery, fear of the unknown. But even then, blood turned the people restive, their loyalty brittle. After the fifth uprising, Varric's seal had turned colder, inked instead with compromise. Tolerance, then: witches registered, elemental circles monitored, healers paid tribute and worked beneath a banner of peace. The peace was never more than a hush. Every spring brought fresh rumors of wild magic, dark eyes watching, a baker's wife with rain-soaked fingers and frost curling on her lips.

Now old men called for iron, young men for patience —every voice reflecting a kingdom fractured by the consequences of its own myth and memory. There was no true safety and no justice untouched by sorrow.

His chest ached with the weight of each word, as though every councilor's speech spun another invisible thread that wound around his ribs. Cold, measured, he turned a gold signet on his finger. To decree another purge would be to drown his people in the very hatred that had nearly broken the realm before. Yet every hesitation was counted as weakness; already, Dalen's loyalists spoke in taut, urgent circles, torching any glimmer of mercy.

He gripped the shape of his own reflection in the table's dark glass. His father's hand was not gentler, Varric remembered, and yet the world he had inherited was a kingdom of fear and shadows. Was this the only inheritance he could leave? Each moment stretched, another breath freezing in his throat.

Twilight pressed its violet hand to the stained-glass windows, shedding fractured light onto the anxious chamber. Everywhere, quiet alliances yawned wider in the crevices of the council's despair. Missives passed behind raised fans; secrets hissed where torchlight failed.

"You disagree," Lord Branth challenged, voice sharp as the crack of a whip, "Your Majesty, we cannot hesitate. The witch threat burns at our doorstep."

Varric's forearm tensed, his gaze fixed and iron-willed.

"Order built on terror will not hold. We must not drive the kingdom to open revolt."

Lady Brienna's eyes glistened. "Then we beg you, demand restraint."

Lord Malthus interrupted, "Or is it your intent to let the embers catch, Majesty—until there is nothing left but ash?"

He let the silence linger, watched by every hungry, fearful, and hopeful eye. The empty seat at his right loomed, a wound and a warning.

With a single gesture, Varric raised his hand—voice ringing low and final.

"Enough." The word cleaved the chamber, heavy as prophecy.

The council stilled, and he let his gaze settle one last time on Lord Dalen's vacant place, the echo of undecided fate hovering in the thrumming dusk.

Chapter 9

The Forbidden Tower's Secrets

Elara pressed gloved fingers to the Forbidden Tower's outer wall. The stone beneath her touch bit with ancient cold—an old, bloodless chill that had seeped through centuries, that even the moonlight feared to disturb. Patterns of warding glyphs, carved deeper than memory, shimmered faintly across the wall's pitted surface. With a careful exhale, she guided a filament of wind between her skin and the stone, coaxing the dormant glyph awake. Earth's patience mingled with wind's subtlety as she spun magic into silence, wrapping the glyph's alarms in frost and gentle dust. The rune faded, its warning snuffed, and she felt the sting of magic recoil up her wrist, lingering like a whispered dare.

The Tower loomed above her, scalp-tingling in its presence. No sanctuary—never that. It was the place mothers threatened in lullabies, the spire that shadowed the city's heart with unspoken dread. Witches, whispering beneath bramble roofs, locked eyes over veiled candles when its name was spoken. The Tower was where the first oaths had lashed magic into service, where betrayal echoed endlessly through stone. The pulse of old pacts still lived in its mortar, feeding the kingdom's balance with secrets too dangerous to bear aloud. She'd heard children dare each other to touch its doors, and seen the haunted eyes of those who'd walked its halls for royal coin. To breach these wards tonight was to test the roots of the kingdom's fear—a trespass against memory itself.

The cost of secrets collected here weighed heavier than any jailor's chain; in the Tower's breathing dark, even promises might bleed. Elara's own oath— broken for mercy—seemed to vibrate in her bones, a living thing hungering for consequence. Each step closer to the heart of the Tower was both a rebellion and a confession. What she risked was not only her flesh, or her magic, but her last claim to belonging among those who had survived by vanishing. But there was Kaelen—her defiant, wounded stranger— whose throat she had healed, hands trembling as she broke the one rule that mattered most. She steeled herself, drawing purpose from the line of scars across her palms, each a reminder that her life was her own to spend or to squander.

On the other side of the entrance, Kaelen's silhouette flickered through fractured torchlight as he pressed along the corridor's edge. His boots made no sound against the carpet of dust—the dust itself a hush, preserved out of superstition, as if loud footsteps might wake the Tower's sleeping anger. He stopped, a sliver of worry tightening his brow. The corridor twisted in a way that made sound slippery: every creak, every intake of breath, seemed carried away by the angled walls and arched shadows. From her vantage at the threshold, Elara watched him skirt the flagstones, moving as if the very air threatened to betray him.

He bent low, fingers nearly brushing the floor, and paused, shifting to avoid invisible thresholds where spells might wait coiled and venomous. There, at the edge of a torch's sputtering reach, the stones pulsed. Not light, but sensation—a crawling tingle, gone as quickly as it arrived. Elara's skin prickled in sympathy, recalling the whispered warnings of traps that could strip a witch of words, or soul, or shape, and leave only a rumor in the morning.

They converged at the central archive, exchanging no words. Kaelen's gaze met hers in the half-dark, the colored moonlight through stained glass carving both of their faces in emeralds, sapphires, and old blood reds. Here, words felt dangerous—unnecessary when purpose hummed between them. Moonlight scattered across Kaelen's cheekbones, catching a hint of gold at his temple. Dust motes turned hypnotic in the beams overhead, swirling in the air with the soft grace of moths that had survived decades without light.

Elara reached for the archive's crumbling shelves, careful to avoid the carved wards that lingered like spiderwebs between books. Her fingertips left dark lines in the layered soot and age, marking her passage with undeniable presence. She scanned the bindings—midnight blue, velvet black, faded leather tattooed with forbidden scripts. Some tomes practically twitched beneath her touch; others sent a whiff of dried violet and old candlewax into her lungs, conjuring times before oaths had devoured kindness.

Kaelen moved with quick logic, his hands steady as he examined each spine. He lingered on a folio edged in silver, gently prying at its edge before setting it aside, brow furrowed. Elara caught the careful way he traced the deep geometric cuts in the next binding. She knew those patterns: code-spells for either sanctuary or doom. She nodded once—barely more than a breath—and Kaelen left that book untouched.

With each minute inside the archive, tension thickened the air. The silence was oppressive, broken only by their near-silent breathing and the faint click as Kaelen drew a heavy volume partway from its place, then pushed it gently back. Elara's sense of time wavered; urgency bled in, slow and sure, as if the Tower itself counted heartbeats.

Behind them, the door's battered hinges groaned, a draft urging it nearly—but not quite—shut. The temperature shifted by degrees, the first warning that the Tower's patience—like its secrets—was never infinite.

The silence pressed in, heavy as velvet and thick with the residue of old magic. A thousand tomes huddled on crumbling shelves, their spines etched with cryptic symbols, the scent of dust and ancient ink coating every breath with the dry tang of yesterday's secrets. Elara's palm hovered over a scroll that seemed to pulse with its own heartbeat, its parchment as fine as shed snakeskin, coiling restlessly beneath her fingertips. She whispered an incantation, voice barely more than a sigh, silver mist streaming from her lips and receding into the brittle surface. The runes awakened, iridescent, flickering in patterns that shifted like water under moonlight, their curves unfurling and knotting with each slow inhale.

She seated herself on her heels, the cold stone biting through her cloak, and coaxed the scroll wider. Its pictographs blazed briefly in shades of blue and violent gold, the ink raised against the parchment as if it had never truly dried. Moonlight, filtered through a shard of stained glass, traced wavering bars over the writing as if eager to keep its wisdom imprisoned. Kaelen knelt at her side, close enough that she felt the tremor in his body, close enough that his warmth mingled with her own, soaking through the air that tugged restlessly at the strands of her hair. His breath stirred the dust, deep and measured, a rhythm that mocked the frantic flutter in her chest.

He reached out but held his hands above the scroll, the ghost of a touch, reverent and uncertain. For a moment the silence between them felt dense, undisturbed by the outside world—only the beating of their hearts and the occasional drip of condensation punctuated the hush. Kaelen's gaze traced the runes, lips parting as if on the cusp of speech. An uneasy familiarity flickered across his face, a haunted recognition, eyelids fluttering as he gathered fragments of memory from some shadow-soft corner of his mind.

His voice, when he finally spoke, rumbled low and uncertain. "These are oaths, binding as iron. The language is—" He faltered, half-wonder, half-dread curling at the edges of his words. "Older than the royal creed. It warns of a bond formed in mercy, one that cannot be severed by blade or spell." His finger hovered over a pictograph of two figures, their hands entwined, roots lacing around their wrists, thorns pressed to skin.

Elara swallowed back the copper taste of fear. The room pressed tighter, as though the tower itself bent to listen, and she could not stop her mind from leaping back, racing through the lonely fragments of her life. Lysandra's warnings echoed: Trust is a thorn —it will bleed you if you hold on too tightly. She had lost too many friends to silent betrayals, to the crackle of fire in the night and the slow, choking hush when promises died on the tongue. The scent of burnt heather, the memory of splintered wands, the memory of Lysandra's hand clenching hers until their knuckles blanched—reminders that witches born under hunted stars did not gamble with oaths lightly.

She forced herself deeper into the text, mouthing each word as Kaelen read, breath frosting cool against his cheek. The scroll's gloom-wrought ink revealed its warning, coiling through her spirit with every syllable. Mercy, the runes proclaimed, is not without price. Should a witch break the sacred vow and bind her fate to that of another, the curse will awaken—bone-deep, marrow wrought, spreading its torment through the flesh and the soul of both. The doomed lovers, as the script called them, would share agony and ecstasy, cursed to mirror each other's wounds and longings, unable to loosen the knot that entwined them. The curse would neither yield to death nor reason; it would only tighten, day by day, until both natures—witch and bondmate— became one, for good or for ill.

Panic wormed through her veins. She remembered every forced retreat, every frantic flight from city to glade, always with the scent of torch oil in the air, always with ashes gritting her palms. The cost of a broken promise—she had recited the lesson like a prayer since childhood, swearing she would never bring doom to another as so many had before her. Yet Kaelen's blood had stained her hands, and in her defiance, she had breached every warning whispered in the dark. A life exchanged for a curse—her independence shackled to someone she barely knew, someone whose voice already wound through the hollows of her mind.

"What does it mean for us?" Her voice trembled. She hated how small it sounded in the vaulted gloom.

Kaelen's jaw tightened. "We are bound—the spell has seen to that. I feel it, as sure as I feel my own heartbeat." He traced a line down the scroll but did not look away from her. "Every torment you bear, I will share. No blade, no mage can undo it. Not even death."

Elara's lips parted, words failing her. The urge to run clashed with the need to understand. Freedom—her independence, the fierce solitude she clung to—shriveled in the light of what she had done. The scroll still glimmered in her lap, cursed runes branded upon her memory, their song a dull lament humming beneath her skin. How could mercy turn so quickly to doom? Was this the fate she deserved for daring to care, for believing—if only for a moment—that she might overcome the kingdom's relentless cruelty?

She met Kaelen's gaze, saw her own fear mirrored back in the way his hand fisted on the ancient wood. The moonlight, their only witness, slipped behind a cloud, and the shadow in the room thickened. Elara let the scroll slide from her hands, parchment whispering against stone as it settled between them. For just a heartbeat, they sat in that hush, the certainty of their entwined destinies settling like ash.

Rowsan had waited in the creased silence for the moment when shadows, thin and elongated by fractured moonlight, would shroud his movement. When he emerged—gliding from an alcove lost behind a collapsed stack of ledgers—Elara's gasp broke the hush, her fingers tightening around a brittle scroll. Kaelen spun, reaching instinctively for the knife hidden in his boot, but Rowsan's gesture stilled both: two fingers pressed to his lips, the faintest hint of a smile revealed within the hood's gloom.

He glided closer. Cold stone pressed at his back, whispering with the secrets of centuries. His voice, barely more than breath, threaded through the dust and the pale blue shimmer of lingering magic. "I have been listening. The patrols circle, drawn like storm-crows by the scent of change. Dalen's men do not wander—tonight, they sweep for prey."

The chamber pulsed with warnings—the prickle of old wards tickling the edge of awareness, the scent of charred parchment where some careless hand had unleashed magic unmeant for these halls. The air thickened with urgency, but Rowsan took measure, letting his gaze travel between the glint in Elara's eyes and the hard line of Kaelen's jaw.

The Forbidden Tower had always felt living to Rowsan —a thing built to remember, to record, not merely to contain. In ancient days, he had learned, it had been the heart of the council's covenant. The sacred oath had not begun as a chain, but as a mutual shelter. Before the royals hungered for the secrets of flame and wind, before court witches were dragged in daylight to silent deaths, it had been a pact to hold the wildness of magic fast, so none—not witch nor king—could unmake the boundaries between the known and unspeakable.

He remembered stories whispered at his mother's hearth, of witches whose voices braided together in the stone amphitheater beneath the first council. Sworn secrecy had not been fear but promise—magic would remain unbent, safe from a world eager to turn it to famine or war. Yet even as those words had kindled protection, doubt had entered the circle. There had always been those—restless, bright-eyed —who saw the oath as suffocation, not sanctity. Why must power hide, why should witches bend before a pact devised to dampen their brilliance simply because kings and lords trembled at what they could not summon?

Rowsan knew the tale by heart, each turn echoing the fractures that still haunted them all: split councils, exile, rebellion wound bitter with regret. Some wore the oath like a banner; others bore it as a yoke that pressed every choice to the dust of old fears.

His own loyalty, ever splintered, had been shaped by these legends. He had learned the oath's price in the hush of hidden meetings, in the stone-banked flames of council chambers and the tears of those who'd lost daughters to loyalty's mistaken zeal. He did not believe in blind silence, nor in surrender to the whims of royal greed. Yet without the pact, what shield would the world hold against the greed of kings or the recklessness of the gifted?

Tonight, that old split breathed again in the chamber's gloom, in Elara's wild courage, in Kaelen's wary gaze. He felt the council's burden settle onto his shoulders: to warn, to guide, to gamble with the fate of those who dared love across the fault lines drawn by blood and promise.

He pressed close to them, urgency burning through restraint. "Listen. The tower's pulse has changed. I watched Dalen's hands—counted three times the patrol to these halls. The glyphs at the outer stones trembled when you passed. They will know soon who has come, and they will guess why. We have no more than minutes. Perhaps less."

Kaelen's mouth was a taut line. Elara barely breathed, shards of moonlight painting the curve of her cheek and the gold spun through her hair. Rowsan's voice softened despite himself, the space between them fraught with something he could almost name—a danger that felt too much like hope.

"We need every chance. Kaelen—those ledgers by the third pillar, search for the mark of the sleepless owl. Elara, gather nothing that gleams with fresh spellwork. Take only that which is old, untouched by recent hands."

He pulled back a trembling tapestry, its velvet rotten, revealing the dim suggestion of a hidden door. Beyond, the narrow passage breathed out cold that tasted of deep earth and lost seasons. The scent mingled with Kaelen's sweat and Elara's faint trace of wild thyme, sharp and grounding.

Rowsan knelt by the wall, fingers splayed on ancient stones now alive with memory. "We will split the scrolls. Elara, you lead—shield if you must. Kaelen, carry the council records." He pressed the scrolls against Kaelen's chest, their weight no less than the force of centuries. "I'll hold the way until you're clear."

A thundering of footsteps down the distant hallway seeded urgency through the hush. Rowsan fixed his hood about his face, shadows swallowing his expression as he gestured wordlessly to the concealed doorway. The hush that followed was electric, their shared fate hanging a heartbeat before flight.

Torches hissed alive, gold light flickering through the library's half-rotted doorframe and spilling onto the fractured mosaics underfoot. Elara's breath wove frost into the air as she pressed her back to a shelf, fingers smeared with ancient dust and ink. Soldiers moved on the other side of the walls—she felt the grind of their boots reverberate through the flagstones, a predatory pulse, slow and relentless. She tasted the iron of old sorcery in the air: a sharp tang electrified by fear.

The Forbidden Tower was rumored to consume the hearts of careless witches. Oaths had been whispered in these corridors for centuries, each binding a thread of power to the throne above while tearing another from the wild magics meant for freedom. Elara felt the weight of these betrayals accumulated in the claustrophobic hush—the very stones seemed to shiver with warnings. Her own defiance echoed back to her in the tap of every boot

—each sound like a verdict handed down through time.

A harsh voice murmured orders, growing nearer with the oily promise of violence. A sliver of torchlight licked over Kaelen's jawline where he stood at Rowsan's side, framed by racks of brittle parchment and glass-eyed beasts painted on the walls. Elara risked one more glance at her companions—Kaelen's urgency flared from the set of his mouth, the restless tightening of his hands around scrolls bundled at his chest; Rowsan's calm radiated outward, steady as riverbed stone. For a heartbeat, suspicion twisted beneath Elara's ribs. Could she truly trust them, or was this alliance another illusion, a temporary truce destined for betrayal? Yet a deeper need knotted in her—she could not do this alone, not now, not ever again.

The door screeched inward as soldiers poured in—shadows made real by steel and iron, their faces blank as death masks beneath their helms. Elara lifted her hands, channels of power unfurling from her core. Words slipped through her teeth, the old tongue that woke primordial elements, summoning wind and earth to her aid. Threads of light spilled from her wrists, spinning with fierce intent.

A wall of swirling ember and dust, dense enough to choke the torch flames, bloomed between the trio and the oncoming guards. It smothered the first arrows, sending them clattering harmlessly to the broken tiles. Kaelen darted to the battered desk to her left, his body a study in haste—muscle and instinct as he seized the most damning scrolls, eyes flicking to Rowsan. Rowsan, in the cool hush behind the barrier, moved like a river current—fast, silent, holding his own secrets behind steady hands as he tugged at the sagging tapestry concealing the escape.

"Go! You have seconds!"

Rowsan's voice sliced through the chaos.

"I'm not leaving you pinned—"

Kaelen tossed the scrolls into his satchel, his gaze fixed on Elara, defiant in the stormlight.

They clustered—shoulder to shoulder, only inches between their bodies—the shared terror almost intimate: breath, touch, proximity. Elara caught a trace of Kaelen's scent—stone and wild grass, rain lingering in his cloak's folds.

The burning shield flickered as a spell struck it from the other side, pounding with a force that reverberated up her arms.

Soldiers advanced, weighted nets laced with runes flying in arcs above the embers. Steel-tipped spears flashed, whistling just over her head. Elara locked eyes with their mage—his gaze hard as obsidian— power lancing out, raw and foreign, searching for a seam in her barrier.

Her hands trembled. Magic strained at her, hot and wild, desperate to obey but shuddering under so many conflicting oaths—her own, the kingdom's, the ones inked in her blood. The oath she'd broken threaded through her now, biting into flesh and soul alike.

For one split instant she faltered. A net grazed past her, and a spear crashed into her barrier, narrowly missing Rowsan's shoulder. Sweat blurred her vision; the taste of her fear merged with shame. She didn't want to depend on them. She was the independent one, the self-sufficient witch—stories warned against letting anyone else become your shield. Yet without Kaelen's urgency and Rowsan's unflinching steadiness, she would crumble.

Kaelen's arm brushed hers as he smashed his fist into the hidden latch. "Now, Elara. I have you."

Their eyes met—something electric sparking between warning and promise. She let herself lean, only barely, into his side.

"I'm ready."

The pressure built—then shattered as the barrier cracked and rippled with the echo of her failing concentration. The soldiers surged forward. Elara chanted a final word, and the last of her energy burst outward, blowing the nearest guards back, their curses muffled beneath the thunder. Another spear, jagged and impossibly cold, found her shoulder, slicing through cloth and grazing skin. She gasped, vision narrowing.

Rowsan pulled the tapestry aside. Cold air howled from the black mouth of the passage. Kaelen seized Elara's uninjured arm, half hauling and half guiding her through the gap. Together with Rowsan, they tumbled into the chill, her pulse thrumming with the echo of old magic and new trust.

The stone door grumbled shut above, sealing them into darkness. Silence, save for the hard pound of three hearts, pressed close; relief swelled unexpectedly in Elara's chest, thick and terrifying as longing.

Chapter 10

Crossroads of Choice

Silver mist hovered in the hollows of the Shadowed Wood, painting every root and briar white beneath the too-bright moon. Branches bowed overhead, their tips trembling in a laden hush. Elara stood at the rim of the glade. Her bare feet pressed into cold, moss-strewn earth, its pulse thrumming faintly with shards of magic she no longer trusted to answer her. The night's silence pressed at her throat, thick as unshed tears.

Kaelen waited in the open, cloak flung back, pale from their flight and the wounds yet healing. He stood where the moon spilt itself across his boots, defiant and alone amongst the whispering shadows. His gaze never left her. She forced herself to match it, though her jaw burned from the effort.

"You can't see it, can you?" Her voice was splintered glass; the words quivered before they found him. "Every promise has a price. Magic always claims what it's owed. If we don't break this—" She swallowed; even the air seemed to flinch at what might be spoken next. "If we don't find a way to end this bond, Kaelen, it will end us."

He stepped forward, boots crackling softly in the undergrowth. "Elara, we're bound whether we wish it or not. That's already done. What matters now is turning it into an advantage." A flicker of grim amusement crossed his face, hard-edged and fleeting. "Would you have left me to die in the snow and pretend none of this was necessary?"

"I'd rather you alive and free than both of us cursed," she retorted. Her magic surged hot beneath her skin, restless and wild. "You think you know what you're asking—this isn't a sword you draw or a shield you lift. It will cut deeper than that, for both of us."

"That's fear speaking," he said, low. "If we run, Dalen's hounds will find us, leash or no. But the bond —your magic, whatever's between us—it's the only weapon they can't see. Why not wield it?"

She folded her arms, hands pressed hard to her ribcage as if she could hold herself together with nothing but her own trembling resolve. The woods hemmed them in, branches crowding at the edge of her vision. Her chest ached as she met his stare, sharp with the memory of ancient stories—every one ending with a witch made to pay for the sins of love, for the sin of trust.

He drew a shaky breath, hands curling into fists at his sides; the white scars ringed his knuckles, stark as confession. "You saved me, Elara. I won't regret that bond and neither should you. We survive together or not at all."

"And what if that's not enough?" Her voice cracked, a surge of panic searing through. "What if together means we draw fire not just to ourselves but to everyone who ever sheltered us? My people—" Her words faltered. She saw, as if split by sorcery, their whispered stories around firepits, her mother's soft eyes pinched with foreboding, warnings that oaths make cages of the soul.

She tried to imagine the path ahead. Would she become a legend scorned, the one who broke the sacred promise for a stranger's life, unraveling the safety her sisters bled to protect? Or was there still some future where Kaelen's haunted eyes softened for her, not in gratitude, but in the bone-deep knowing of chosen love? Both futures spilled out before her like twin rivers running cold and uncertain in the darkness. She could not see where either led.

His shadow stretched long and sharp on the grass. "Then we fight smart, not scared. Let go of the past —just for now. Use what we have."

A shivering silence fell. Elara felt the world pivot on the strain between them, the glade shrinking until all she could hear was his voice and the pulse of her own blood.

"You think recklessness is courage," she spat, voice rising, "but you have no idea what these woods hold, what this bond demands. You don't know the names or faces of the ones I've already lost because I trusted too quickly—"

"And I've nothing left to lose but my own future!" He snapped, the words crashing between trees. "This is my only chance to make something right, Elara. Don't ask me to turn from it."

A storm of words swelled and died in her throat. She spun away, shoulders rigid beneath her cloak, the delicate thread of their magic tightening until she was certain it would snap. Branches clawed at her arms as she pushed deeper into the shadows, the night's secrets swallowing her footsteps.

Behind her, Kaelen's breath came ragged. She did not look back. Each step away from him bled a fresh wound beneath her ribs. Her heart warred with every lesson learned in secret—never love what might be taken, never bind yourself to the doomed. If this bond shattered, would it free her, or only leave her diminished, neither wholly herself nor wholly his?

When the glade fell silent, only the wind's breath and the scent of frost remained. Elara and Kaelen slipped through the web of roots in opposite directions, moonlight cleaving their paths. The darkness seemed endless, uncertainty carrying them forward, each alone in the wide, sorrowing night.

Lysandra chose the far corner of the Hearthstone Inn, where the stone walls muffled the noise of travelers and the crackling hearth cast wavering amber across their faces. Outside, a drizzle stitched watery patterns down the wavy windowpanes, but in here the scent of spiced ale lingered, and the flicker of firelight scattered the gloom. She watched Elara settle opposite, cheeks drawn and mouth set, with Kaelen beside her—tense, hands pressed flat upon his knees. Rowan claimed the stool beside Lysandra, eyes bright and green as spring grass, brisk with some barely withheld energy that made Lysandra's nerves prickle.

The mug before Lysandra steamed between her clasped palms, heat seeping into her skin as she waited for the others to adjust to the hush, the close-in warmth. She measured the lines of strain etched deep in Elara's brow, the way Kaelen's jaw worked restlessly, and the silence that pressed between them—sharp, oppressive, dangerous. Too many wounds, freshly bared, and not yet begun to heal.

"There will be nothing left to fight for if we lose each other," Lysandra began, her voice low but steady as she met Elara's eyes and then Kaelen's. "We escaped with luck, not unity. Whatever binds you—us now— must not tear us apart." She let the words settle, aware of every fast breath, every shuffling movement on the battered wooden benches.

Rowan slid forward, elbows on knees, and for a moment the fire's gleam caught the shadow of freckles dusted across their nose. "Ancient magic has always cost witches dearly. What Kaelen and Elara share—none of us fully understand it yet. But we do know what it threatens: who you are, what you could lose. If you keep giving in to fear, or pride, it will hollow you out until you're both strangers." Rowan's words, so crisp and clear, drew a shudder through the little group. Their gaze settled on Lysandra, and she felt the old ache—responsibility, and fierce protectiveness—stirring beneath her ribs.

Lysandra remembered childhood years spent tracing sigils in damp earth, how Elara had taught her that trust and survival were threads spun from the same magic. Tonight, those threads seemed so frayed she feared they'd snap under the strain. She thought of promises—old, bitter, sometimes broken—and what it meant to lead, not just as a witch, but as a friend.

"Speak, Elara." Lysandra softened her tone, coaxing but not pleading. "Let us hear what's truly at the heart of this. We can't make peace with shadows."

Elara's hands curled tight in her lap, knuckles white as candle wax, and her words slid out brittle, dragging years of secrets behind them. "Magic chose him to bind with me, not mercy. I did not want to curse us both. Every day I'm afraid I damned you along with myself." Her voice broke on the word "damned." Kaelen shifted, but did not move to touch her.

Rowan tilted their chin toward Kaelen, a silent urging. Kaelen scowled, then looked away—the muscles in his throat working until, at last, he spoke, each word like stones grinding together. "I fear what I've become, bound to power I never wanted, unable to leave you—and yet, I fear losing myself to it more." He exhaled roughly, shoulders slumping as the last resistance fled.

The air heated, trembling with revelations. Soot drifted in lazy curls up the chimney, and the golden light licked along the curve of Elara's jaw, the line of Kaelen's cheek. For a heartbeat all Lysandra heard was the spit and pop of fire, the hiss of ale cooling in untouched mugs.

She mourned what was lost: simple belonging, uncomplicated trust. Lysandra had wanted to be unyielding—Elara's shield, unwavering as the old oaks of the Shadowed Wood—but she recognized the futility now. The group's survival depended on its own kind of magic: vulnerability shared like breaking bread, truth spun out in trembling strands.

"Consensus," Lysandra said at last, her voice firmer. "We decide together—from now on, no one moves alone, no one bears secrets." She sought Rowan's eye and found agreement there—a quiet nod, the flick of a smile. "Major plans require all of us to agree. The witch hunters thrive on our weakness; let them find us united instead."

Rowan straightened, speaking for all. "If we want freedom, trust must root deeper than fear. None of us will last long otherwise."

Lysandra's heart steadied, anchored in the fragile hope growing around the fire. She felt the weight of her choices: remain fiercely loyal, or accept that new bonds must be woven, even if it meant letting go of her old, protective certainties. She sensed now that the confessions tonight were not weakness, but the beginnings of something sturdy—hard-won, but necessary. What Elara risked in admitting her terror, what Kaelen laid bare in his dread, became offerings. Lysandra cherished the hush now, heavy yet buoyant, as if new magic had taken root in the ashes of their discord.

They sat together, unmoving, as the flames subsided to a mellow glow. The scent of smoke mingled with spiced ale; untouched mugs steamed faintly, curls of vapor drifting into the hush. For this moment, their fragile unity held.

The chamber beneath the Capital teemed with trapped heat and secrets, stones clammy beneath the silver-haired woman's palm. She entered first, the hush following her as the others glided in—robes brushing worn flagstones, hoods rendering faces both intimate and unknowable. Wax pooled across the center table, whispering smoke into the low beams, burning away the chill that haunted even this deep heart of the city. Beyond the walls, the political district's midnight clatter faded, this clandestine hollow insulated from the city's pulse.

She waited until the last member took their place, shadows knotting thick around them. Her hair shimmered bone-white in the thin glow, an anchor in a sea of shifting darkness. She did not raise her voice; the room pressed closer to catch her words as she began.

"The oath was broken. The ripples have reached us all." Her tone barely disturbed the candle's flame, yet the statement settled over the chamber like a frost. "One witch. One vow shattered in the dark. Now the city stirs with whispers—of forbidden mercy, of power loosed that does not heed our laws."

Somewhere in the upper city, bells chimed the lateness of the hour; here, breath gathered and held, as if collective silence could spare them the truth: fear and desire fed each other in this kingdom, and the witch's folly had become an accelerant.

She leaned forward, hands steepled, and surveyed her companions. There was always one among them who flinched at the word witch, conditioned by a lifetime of sermons and suspicion. The rest wore practiced indifference; they knew she would do what was necessary, that hesitance was rarely rewarded with more than a knife in this marble labyrinth.

Across the kingdom, distrust festered like rot beneath gilded floors. They had cultivated that rot—tending rumors that painted witches as monsters, as seducers corrupting hearth and bloodline. It was so easy to let the people's dread metastasize, easier still to propose protection and order as the cure. And every time a witch stumbled, whenever a promise was broken, that mythology renewed itself; each misstep became not an aberration, but proof of some ancient, hungry malice.

But beneath her calculation was old resentment, never voiced. She had seen the old city before the purges, when magic drifted street to street like the perfume of wild honey, when children chalked charms upon doors and no one bled for it. She could not say if she mourned magic's loss or if she resented the witches' weakness—that they insisted on surviving only in shadows, brittle and secretive, forcing all the world to become their jailer.

"Violence keeps the city afraid, but fear alone cannot break their alliances." Her fingers tapped the scarred wood beside a blank scrap of parchment. "We will sever them at the root. Doubt is a sharper blade than steel—one does not feel its cut until it has gone marrow-deep."

She named her plan quietly, as if confession was a sacrament. Whispered testimony from the marketplace, thinly veiled accusation in the public squares, secret pay to a scribe here or a midwife there—stories spinning like moths around flame. All fueled by the kernel of recent truth. Elara, the oathbreaker. Kaelen, the stranger bound by her sin. The danger that they would unite those who should be rivals, unless someone poisoned the bond between them.

There was yearning, too, twisting close to her resolve. She longed, in brittle moments unobserved, for a future not braced on lies. But the present was a tangle of needs—her faction's, the city's, her own. Hope was a luxury, let to wither in the root cellar of her heart. For now, all she could do was sharpen suspicion into a blade.

A wiry man at her right coughed delicately and withdrew a slip of blue-tinted paper, creased small as a feather. He offered it across the flame; she accepted, skin prickling with the thrill of new intelligence. The wax seal, pressed with the sigil of a heron, broke beneath her thumb. She scanned the crabwise script, savory anticipation on her tongue.

"They quarrel," the man murmured, as her eyes passed over the code. "Our asset near the Shadowed Wood claims the witches' bond is fraying. Their tempers run high enough to spark a fire." He paused, gaze flicking briefly to the others. "Perhaps a well-placed rumor could fan that spark."

She considered this, the message a balm and a goad alike. If Elara's circle fractured now, their movement might collapse before it grew teeth. But if the witches managed to draw together in adversity—if fear welded them to resolve—they might birth something unstoppable, a fever that could not be contained by walls or flame. Trust, once ignited, could be as perilous as any spell.

Her mind chased the possibilities: half-truths woven into rally cries, forged confessions delivered to the wrong ears, double agents worming their way inside council fires. Dolorous work, but necessary. She closed her eyes for half a heartbeat, letting herself imagine a world where unity was not subterfuge's enemy.

A dialogue block:

"He saw Elara and the boy. The argument. They think themselves safe in the wood—what if we remind them how isolation breeds traitors?"

"We sow seeds, yes—but not just among the witches. Let the city hear of Elara's recklessness. Let every ally wonder whose promise will break next."

"Yes. We feed them truth, but twist it just so."

They agreed, voices brushing together like a spell cast in secret, to release word in the underworld's alleys and over sweetmeats in the courtyards— stirring unrest, releasing agents sewn with silver coins and coded words.

Another dialogue block:

"You're certain our man can get close enough?"

"He's already among them. The wood is thicker with spies than trees."

"Then tonight, we strike at certainty. Let none of them know where loyalty whispers or lies."

Candlelight danced against stone as one by one the conspirators slipped into the city's maze,, the leader's pulse echoing with hope and dread in equal measure. Their scheme threaded through flagstone corridors, the scent of tallow and intrigue lingering after the last cloak vanished into the night.

A chill seeped through the smooth stone beneath Elara as she sat, knees drawn up, by the sanctuary's battered threshold. The late hour leached warmth from the air—even the steady perfume of moss and wild mint, usually a balm, stung nostrils raw tonight. In her fist she gripped the charred scrap she'd found at her bedroll: the parchment crisp with fire, its corners flaked away as though it barely escaped a pyre. Black smoke-stained script coiled across the surface, etched with fevered care and sigils she could not place—circles wrapped in crosses, lines dividing points, all warning of a traitor within. Her pulse thrummed through the tangle of her fingers, sweat beading along her knuckles despite the cold. Each word on the note opened a trapdoor beneath her, and every whisper outside the sanctuary walls now sounded like someone else's foot pressed against dead leaves.

Betrayal, Elara thought, could unwind a tapestry faster than fire. She imagined how it might begin: someone murmuring secrets in the dark, a glance lasting just too long, trust leaking away drop by drop until nothing was left but ash. If promises could twist and break as easily as spells, what use were oaths or whispered assurances in this woodland shrine? Had she known, the night she'd broken faith to save a stranger, that the curse of forbidden magic would bind her not only to Kaelen but to peril festering within their own circle? The pain of it thrummed fresh—a wound reopened every time she wondered if the cost would someday be paid in blood.

She pressed the parchment against her thigh, bruising it harder to convince herself it was real. The scent of burned paper clung to her, warring with the clean green tang of the sanctuary's living walls. Uncertainty—it crept inside like the chill, rooting in her bones. To trust was a greater risk now than any enemy blade. Yet what was survival if she surrendered herself to suspicion? Even as her magic burned in her blood, promising answers to questions she was afraid to ask, Elara ached at the thought that one misplaced faith might doom them all.

From the gloom beyond the iron-banded door came a dull clatter: Kaelen, crouched near the embers of their fire, was dragging a whetstone slow and steady along the curve of his blade. Sparks flared faintly, lighting his jaw and cheekbones in relief before fading into shadow. The fire spat, licking at some half-burned map, scenting the air with singed ink.

Then movement—far too abrupt to be idle. Marek, Kaelen's ever-watchful guard, stooped at the edge of the fire's glow, hands deft as he eased a slip of parchment into the pocket of his deep blue cloak. The action was careful, but not quite hidden. Kaelen's head shifted in that direction. The flicker of Marek's eyes met his, something taut stretching between them. Then, as if rehearsed, Marek turned away and faded into the mantle of smoke and night.

Elara swallowed, gaze locking for a moment on Kaelen. His profile was all intent watchfulness, muscles wound for warning. The knife's edge flashed silver in his hand, a wordless promise to harm or protect. Was he thinking what she was? The note—the furtive glance—were signs stacking atop each other, fragile as frost in sunlight.

She rose, dust motes whirling in her wake as she slipped out of view and skirted the sanctuary's interior. Lysandra and Rowan, tight-shouldered with fatigue but wide-eyed, hunched together on a carved bench, their voices a low binding thread. A soft clink: Lysandra poked a hollow log she'd drawn from the woodpile, dropping out a crumpled fold spattered with wax.

"Again?" Rowan's whisper threaded the silence. "That's the third tonight."

"Too many footfalls, too many messages," Lysandra murmured back. "It doesn't feel right. Ever since we left the glade, something's watching us. I wonder if one of ours..." Her words trailed away, the unspoken accusation tasting of nightshade.

Rowan's fingers drummed an anxious rhythm—one-two-one—over a pewter locket. "There's nothing but trouble brewing. Someone's feeding Dalen crumbs, I know it."

The undercurrent of their words unraveled any security Elara pretended to feel. The idea curdled her stomach: a traitor, not faceless but known, maybe loved, choosing Lord Dalen over them. It felt impossible. It felt inevitable. Elara's mind spun through faces, pauses in conversation, sudden aversions to meeting gazes. She pictured scenarios— Rowan deceived by hope, Lysandra turned by fear, Kaelen undone by promises once made. Each vision left a bruised ache in her chest, a longing for a time before suspicion set roots.

"Torch the traitor when you find them, I say," Rowan's voice sharpened to a knife's edge, slicing through the haze.

"We can't," Lysandra replied, steel under velvet. "Not without proof."

Elara stepped closer. "We keep watch. No secrets outside this circle. Until we know more, trust needs limits."

Kaelen's boots scuffed the stone behind her as he joined them, the draught from his passage swirling the ashes at their feet. Rowan straightened, bracing elbows against knees. Lysandra's mouth tightened around a silent prayer. Together, the four of them ringed the last gasps of the fire, shadows flickering higher on the curved walls.

Tension wound through the group, silent but palpable, as if the air carried tiny invisible wires between their hearts, set to snap should one tug too hard. The possibility that any word, any tired glance, could become a weapon—Elara felt its weight settle beside her like an unwelcome familiar. Once, she'd relied only on herself; now, the luxury of solitude was just another memory she might never reclaim.

The urge to protect clawed at her, but so did isolation, her past wounds rasping at the bond she fought to keep alive.

She let the note brush her fingertips as she crossed to the narrow window, the ether-lit walls shimmering blue and ghost green in the moon's trickle. Outside, shadows grew bolder, gathering beyond the fragile perimeter, as if fate itself crouched between the trees. Elara pressed her palm to the glass, cold cutting through her skin, and vowed she would not let the threat inside break them—not without a fight.

Chapter 11

Echoes of Betrayal

Shadows bent and flickered in the narrow attic room above the Hearthstone Inn, flames clinging to stubby wax, breathing a fugitive warmth over threadbare rugs and peeling papered walls. Marek's heart beat a discordant rhythm, each thud echoing through his body as he faced Lysandra in the wavering candlelight. Her arms wove a barrier across her chest. Behind her, Rowan lingered, their quicksilver eyes threaded with suspicion, fingers tracing the edges of the battered strategy maps left from the tense council. The closeness of their presence was a pressure—disapproval thickening the air, extracting marrow from his resolve.

Lysandra stepped forward, boots whispering over warped boards. "Where were you, Marek, during the last sweep of the outpost?" Her voice carved clean lines through the room's muffled quiet. "Not just then. Every time things go sideways, you're missing. If you're with us, prove it now."

Rowan's hand stilled on the table, their gaze hooking into him. "It isn't just absence," they said, voice softer but no less sharp. "Back when Elara nearly fell to Lord Dalen's men in the Marshes, you vanished for hours. You haven't told us how you know the witch hunters' movements before they strike. Are you running messages behind our backs—?"

Marek's hands curled and uncurled at his sides. "You think I'm a traitor."

"Convince us otherwise," Lysandra shot back.

The walls leaned closer. The smell of lamp oil and old dust caught in Marek's nose, anchoring him to this precarious reality. For a long, slow moment, he stared at the wax pooling on the chipped sill, its warmth impossible to grasp. He dragged in a breath, tasting the bitter tang of fear and memory.

"I... wasn't always who I am now." His voice rasped out, rough and unwilling. "Years ago, I was one of them. I served among the witch hunters. That's how I have their codes, know the ways we're watched." He saw Lysandra's lip twitch, Rowan's mouth part wordlessly, but no one interrupted and so words crawled on, resistant. "They pulled me in when I was fifteen—took me from my village after showing what happens to those who shelter witches. You can't imagine how convincing a fire can be, when it eats your neighbor's house and you're told it's witches who made the flames dance." Marek pressed his palms together, knuckles white. "Indoctrination. We were kept apart from the world, fed stories until hate became as reflexive as breathing. Loyalty was the only thing that earned you bread or sleep. To doubt was a punishable offense; I've seen good men turned on, exposed by friends craving pardon or coin."

The candle guttered, throwing monsters onto the walls. He remembered cold stone corridors, the weight of a saber at his hip, bloodied hands flexing by torchlight. In training halls, they stripped boys of their names and rebuilt them in the kingdom's image: you are a weapon, and mercy is treason.

"I saw things," he continued, the words now thinner, "things that never left me. But I changed. There was a witch—a girl no older than my sister, hunted for a spell she never cast. The orders were to root her out. But when she pleaded, I... turned away. The price was exile. I started passing whispers to those running—routes, patrol patterns. It wasn't redemption, but it was something. I'm not proud. I lied to keep us alive." His confession hung in the stillness, veins thrumming.

Elara stood in the corner with Kaelen, their shadows stretching long over the patchwork rug. Through Marek's eyes the candlelight spilled over her cheekbones, silvering her defiance with gentler shades. He waited for her to speak, but all she offered was stillness—a careful, unyielding line in the hush.

Kaelen's disappointment felt cold as north wind. The others seemed a world removed, their faces shuttered as though a pane of glass had slid between them and him. Lysandra's suspicion did not waver, and Rowan turned away, shaking their head. Unspoken, the unity he had felt in this room—born of shared danger, fleeting laughter, the comfort of someone at your back—fractured along a line he could not cross back over.

Guilt gnawed at his veins, sharper than a sword's edge. All those nights lying awake beside crackling embers, reliving the old oaths muttered in haunted dormitories: *Witchcraft is a blight. Compassion is a disease. The realm comes first.* Years trying to unpick those bindings, pretending that one could simply will an old self away. If exposure came, the witch hunters would carve his name among the kingdom's traitors; if he stayed silent, Elara's people suffered for the sins of his secrecy. He'd lived in the margin between those two fires, breathing the smoke, never wholly cleansed.

Compelled by something softer—needing them to see he was not what he had been—Marek dropped to one knee. The floor creaked beneath him; the oak boards pressed chill against his skin. He raised his gaze to Elara and Kaelen, voice steady but raw.

"I am loyal to you," he vowed. "I kept my past hidden out of fear, yes, but also so I could help you without endangering what you've built. If you cast me out now, I'll understand. But I am with you." Yet as he lowered his head, the voices of the old vows whispered poison at the edges of his mind, and he wondered if trust, once fractured, could ever truly be made whole.

The silence that followed was absolute. Only the drip of wax, the faint rumble of distant footsteps from the inn below, intruded. Lysandra shifted by the door, arms crossed, her silhouette cut from the night's quiet. No verdict came—only eyes that measured, weighed, and held him there, suspended between forgiveness and exile, as the hush pressed into every vulnerable crack.

Footsteps pounded down the inn's crooked stairs, so hard the air seemed to ripple. The kitchen's lanternlight danced over the battered tables, casting restless shadows over blanched faces: Kaelen, Lysandra, Rowan, half a dozen others hunched in clumps. Elara hovered at the edge, her nails chipping fresh grooves in the wood beneath her palm. When the door flew open, a breathless ally staggered in, harsh breaths turning to steaming clouds in the chill.

"They're here—witch hunters. Scarlet crests on their doublets." The words tackily stuck to the stone walls, filling every crack. "Locals saw them flanking the wood at dusk. Four, maybe five men—the rest hidden, I think. Watching."

A faint taste of smoke curled at the back of Elara's throat, bitter as old regret. For a heartbeat, fear tried to take root in her chest, gnawing at the careful boundaries she'd set between herself and disaster. She forced her shoulders straight. "Kaelen, storeroom. Now. The rest—quiet."

From the kitchen's warmth, they filed into the windowless back, past barrels of onions and dried salt beef. Elara knotted her hands together on the table's edge, fending off the urge to conjure a twisting ward of wind—magic preferred for storms, not for smothering dread. Instead, her voice sliced through the hush. "We strengthen our perimeter. Post two on every threshold, and triple the patrols by the glade. If they know our sanctuary—"

Kaelen cut her off. "Or if someone told them. We won't move until we know who passed word. We drag our people out in the open, we risk all of us. Treachery inside stings worse than any blade."

Lysandra squeezed into the corner beside the overturned barrel, gaze darting from one uneasy face to the next. Rowan's brow furrowed, and even the minor allies—faces newly familiar, trust still raw—flinched under the weight of Kaelen's suspicion. Elara's lungs cramped, caught between protectiveness and the scraping doubt in her veins.

"We can't leave our backs open on the faith that no one would sell us for coin," Elara insisted, words brittle as torch glass. "Not now." Her thumb pressed harder into the table, searching for an anchor.

"There's no faith left," Kaelen said. His tone carried none of the gentleness he'd shown her in private, only the iron edge that made his men follow him into fire.

The argument thickened, voice against voice in the flicker and glare. Sawdust-laden air pressed close, carrying the secret tang of sweat and rain, muffling every plea and rebuke until Lysandra slipped out, all silent purpose.

Elara let her eyes settle on Kaelen—on the line of his jaw, the brush of copper hair at his temple, the silent command in his bearing. She wondered, not for the first time, what strings might still bind him to that world outside, where honeyed words and threats turned loyalties like a wheatfield in storm. Across the kingdom, the witch hunters' shadow coiled methodically through every crevice—fattening their purses with gold for each betrayal, raising scaffold and noose wherever a whisper of magic lingered. Each month, more faces disappeared from her lists, not with a scream but with a hush, plucked by the promise of safety or the crack of a coin purse. To live was to trust, but trust grew as hazardous as spellcraft in these days.

Heavy boots and the wet scrape of cloaks snapped her from the spiral. Lysandra stormed back, the hem of her skirt snarled with nettles and mud, fist high with a bent, crumpled letter. "Found in the bottom of Brin's satchel," she proclaimed. "He swore he didn't know it was there."

She flung the letter on the table. The group converged, limbs bumping in anxious knots; candlelight gilded the paper's creases, the inked code twisting in sharp, unfamiliar curlicues. Rowan snatched it up, lips moving in a low chant as they pieced out meaning from the cipher. Eyes widened.

"It's the pattern they used in the Fallow Massacre," Rowan whispered, voice sharpening and trembling in the same breath. "Timetables. Names. Codes for rendezvous."

Chaos spooled up like a wire pulled too tight. Accusations spat out in low, venomous hisses. "You vouched for Brin—" "Why would they single us out unless someone gave them reason?" "Anyone here could have—" Elara watched the room fracture, alliances splintering under suspicion. Fingers pointed, old hurts reawakened, and she recognized the cold calculus of the witch hunters at work—corroding trust, weaponizing fear to wash away resistance from within. It was not enough to hunt with fire and blade; suspicion did the bloodletting for them.

Elara's resolve teetered on the knife-edge of reason. She strained to believe the best of her comrades, but the certainty she'd clung to was dissolving. If she erred, if she trusted a traitor, everyone she cherished could be thrown beneath a headsman's axe. And if she turned her wrath on the wrong soul, what would they become, except a mirror of their enemies? Her eyes burned, longing to dissolve into the next rainstorm, to let the soil drink her away.

She caught Rowan's hand, squeezing once, a silent plea for steadiness. But the group's fevered shouts battered her from every side—the world shrinking, spinning, tilting.

"You'll tear us apart, all of you!" Kaelen's fist crashed against the wall, making the lantern gutter and spit. "Enough! Not while I lead."

A sudden blast rattled the window. Candle wax trembled; Elara's heart beat in her throat. As silence shuttered down, the ache of mistrust pressed colder and closer than ever before.

Elara's footsteps whispered through grass still wet with the night's chill. The inn's warmth and quarrels faded behind her, replaced by the hush and shimmer of the Moonlit Glade. Here, silver-birch trunks rose ghostly around her beneath the fractured glow of the moon. Drops clung to her hem as she brushed aside ferns, the air laced with the resinous tang of yew and an undercurrent of something older—magic, soft as sighing water under earth.

In the glade's heart, moss shrouded stones ringed a shallow pool, black and glassy, reflecting a slivered moon and the tangled uncertainty behind Elara's eyes. She dropped to her knees, cool earth dampening her palms, breath knotting in her chest. Her reflection stared back, spectral and uncertain— her hair loose, a single muddy smear on her jaw, and, beneath the surface, a flicker of power she no longer recognized.

The echo of voices haunted her: Rowan's quick wit deflecting, Lysandra's unwavering certainty, Kaelen turned inward and unreadable, Marek's betrayal spilling through the tense room, cracking the shelter she'd so carefully built. It was her oathbroken magic that had drawn them all together—her choice to bind herself to Kaelen, her promise shattered at the altar of necessity. Now even friendship wore the sharp edge of suspicion, and she felt the weight of every careless word, every uncertain glance.

Shame clung tight, a living cord around her ribs, and she pressed her fingers into the moss as if it might root her soul again. She should have been stronger— should have found another way to save him, or turned away. Ancient promises hammered through her memory: a witch's word is as iron—once broken, it cannot be made whole. Yet in the moment between his death and her desperate magic, there had been only an aching clarity, and now it seemed her hands had set fire to everything she loved.

Her magic hurt differently now. It lived inside her bones, restless and wild, flickering beneath her skin on nights like this. Sometimes, she felt it thrumming in her pulse, hungry and changed—no longer a gentle ally, but something on the verge of slipping her grasp.

She traced a trembling line through the pool's cold surface, watching ripples distort her face. What if the bond she'd created chained Kaelen as much as it saved him? What if her defiance unbalanced the old order, drawing the witch hunters ever closer? She imagined flames sweeping the woods, friends divided by her mistake, every comfort burned to ash. Was it always like this, when witches broke their deepest vows? Did their hearts fracture and bleed until nothing but guilt remained?

The grass hissed behind her. Elara stilled, readying a ward, but only Rowan's gentle footfall disturbed the silence. Rowan crouched beside her, the gleam of the moon outlining the stubborn set of her brow.

"You didn't have to come after me," Elara said softly.

Rowan's voice was a whisper, roughened at the edges: "Some silences shouldn't be kept alone. Not tonight."

For a space, neither spoke. Night insects hummed across the pond, reeds stirring with secrets. At last, Elara found the words crawling from her chest. "I thought if I could save him, it would be simple. A life for a life. I didn't expect the magic to... to twist inside me—and between all of us. The oath was sacred, and I broke it. I keep thinking, if I were less selfish, more faithful..."

Rowan's shrug was barely perceptible. "And if you hadn't, would you sleep any easier, knowing you left him to die for a law older than your heart?"

"It isn't just Kaelen," Elara whispered. "It's all of them. The way Lys watches me now—and Marek, afraid his secrets damned us all. I can't help but feel I started the unraveling. Trust comes apart so easily. Even magic feels like a labyrinth suddenly; I can't find where my power ends and the curse begins."

A hush stretched, and Rowan stared out over the water, as if the moon might offer a gentler answer.

"Is this what it means to be a witch?" Elara asked, voice cracking. "To hold love and loyalty in either hand, and break both with a single choice? What if my magic keeps changing—what if the promise I broke is just the beginning of what I can't control?"

Rowan's reply was soft, each word threaded with care. "Being a witch means choosing, always. Sometimes choosing wrong. But your heart is still yours, Elara, oath or no."

A longing grew inside Elara—a wish that she were different, braver, able to hold every promise unbroken. She saw the faces of those she cared for flicker atop the pool's surface, each one distant, and herself impossibly small before the world's vast design. The glade felt poised at the edge of change. Could magic ever heal what it had torn asunder? Was it possible that love was the sharpest blade—and sometimes the salve?

She sat back, brushing muddy grass from her knees. "I can't outrun what I did—or what I feel. If there's punishment to come, I'll face it. For love, and for loyalty both." Her voice wavered, doubt shadowing the resolve. "That's all that's left, isn't it?"

"Sometimes it's enough," Rowan murmured.

The two witches sat together, shoulder to shoulder as the glade deepened into quiet. The night's air tasted of moss and new leaves, and an owl called from the woods. Tears pricked along Elara's jaw, cool and silent, but in their place her resolve gleamed, clandestine and unyielding, as she faced the uncertain dark.

The faint glow before dawn bled across the sky's edge, pressing blackness into velvet blue. Kaelen stepped into the inn's battered training yard, rime-glistened cobbles uneven beneath his boots. Marek waited in the center, hands loose at his sides, eyes shadowed in the hesitant light. Kaelen gripped the practice staff, wood worn smooth as river stone, and motioned for Marek to ready himself.

Neither spoke as the sparring began. The steady rhythm of their footfalls, the thudding clash of wood ringing in the cold air, replaced words that threatened to splinter something already brittle. Kaelen struck, every movement precise, each feint edged with the frustration roiling beneath his calm. He measured Marek's reflexes—the hurried block, the flicker of hesitation. The memory of whispered confessions and betrayed trust tightened Kaelen's chest, sweat stinging his brow as aggression found its path through muscle and bone. The scent of churned earth mingled with the metallic tang of his breath.

Kaelen's mind roamed the faces of those cloistered upstairs—Elara's sleepless eyes, Lysandra's wary silence, Rowan's guarded posture, the others whose allegiance now seemed as fragile as a spider's thread. It uncoiled in him, the axiom learned in corridors and courts since boyhood: trust was a commodity best hoarded, never freely given. He feinted left, then pivoted, driving Marek back until the man faltered, expression wary.

They circled, exhalations fogging in the chill. Kaelen's anger was a pulse beneath his skin, less for Marek's betrayal than for the filigree of fractures that now ran through their alliance. How many would scatter if pressed too hard? What oaths would shatter under the threat of fire and gold, or the promise of mercy from the witch hunters' noose?

"Again," Kaelen said, voice hoarse. They clashed, staffs biting together. With every blow Kaelen pressed harder, each movement a silent question: Will you break? Are you truly one of us now, or merely the knife in the dark?

A final strike sent Marek's staff spinning away, clattering against a stone wall. Both men breathed hard, hearts thundering in their ears.

Kaelen released his grip, jaw taut.

"We move forward only in truth," he said, words hewn as much from bitterness as necessity. "I won't let anything—anyone—jeopardize what we're building. Elara will be protected. So will the others. Whatever mine and your past, our purpose now must be above anything else. Do you understand?"

"I do. And I give you my word," Marek answered, voice low.

"See that you remember it."

Kaelen turned away, letting Marek collect himself. His muscles trembled—not only from exertion, but from the weight of resolve settling around his shoulders.

He crossed the yard, heading toward the lichen-mottled back steps of the inn. Elara sat there, the hem of her cloak trailing in dew and dust, her hair a tangle of moonlight and midnight shadows. Kaelen hesitated, then knelt beside her, feeling the world narrow to the space between them. The wood beneath him was damp and cold; the press of their uncertainty hung close, unsaid.

"You're up early," she murmured, her gaze unmoving.

"I couldn't sleep." The words slipped from him, bare. "Too much to fret over."

She didn't reply, but her hand—pale, scarred, marked with the remnants of last night's sorrow—

rested near his. He reached for it, the warmth of her skin shocking in the ashes of night.

"I haven't been someone you could trust easily," he said, voice higher than he intended. "But I find myself... believing that our bond isn't a mistake. Whatever it is between us, it's stronger than I anticipated. Some days, it frightens me—how much I'd risk for you, what I'd lose."

Her eyes searched his, moon-bright with cautious hope.

Kaelen swallowed. "I have to believe it's not only pain our joining will bring. I want to believe it could be... salvation. For me, for you, for all of us."

Her fingers tightened around his, just long enough to anchor him—or perhaps to hold herself from slipping under again.

"I can't promise it," she whispered. "But I feel it, too."

For a moment, everything except the tentative press of their hands, the rhythmic thrum of their joined heartbeats, faded away. The world stilled; in the hush after ruin, something delicate began to form.

Kaelen rose, reclaiming his sword and slinging it across his back. He climbed up to the roof, the stairs groaning beneath his weight, tiles slick with condensation. He faced east as dawn unfastened its colors over the city. Hearthstone's slate shingles glimmered under the first sun, and the streets below remained hushed, as if holding their breath before the day's chaos descended.

He pressed his palm to the hilt, gaze sweeping those alleys where witch hunters could already be slinking, red crests hidden by cloak and fog. How many would try to undo what they fought for before they tasted freedom? Kaelen wondered how long defiance could weather betrayal and dread—if loyalty would fray until they stood alone, or if something born of Elara's magic might awaken in him, rising vast and unpredictable as a summer storm.

Could anything endure with so much in shadow? With each morning he grasped the hope that their connection would sustain them past suspicion and loss. He braced himself for the day's battle—the sword in his hand less weapon, more ward against the world's hunger—mindfulness, a lifeline as the city stirred and their circle awoke, hope and fear tightly interwoven with the coming light.

Chapter 12

Embers of Desire

Ash and ember played along the rim of Elara's vision, the campfire at her feet a stubborn, sputtering core in the deepening forest shadows. Orange light licked across her wrists and cheekbones, shifting as she moved—slowly, warily—trying not to press too hard on the gash in her arm. The blood had dried to a thin russet thread over skin still tacky with sweat and the bitter essence of crushed willow. Her fingers, marked with tiny crescents from years picking thorns and herbs, trembled as she dabbed the wound with a cloth she'd soaked in healing tincture. Above the muffled snap of branches outside their fire's circle, the wilderness inhaled, damp and loamy, the air thick with dew and woodsmoke.

She took care to keep her eyes down. Even here, hidden amid tangled roots and velvety moss, memory would not leave her alone—memories of refusing to kill, of the oath fractured in her hands, of the moment fire and forbidden incantation spilled out and entwined her fate with Kaelen's. Each heartbeat reminded her of the cost. Each flare beneath her skin —a sudden ripple of blue-white light tracing veins from her shoulder to wrist—testified to instability she could no longer ignore. The lines pulsed faintly, alive beneath the bandage, the way lightning sometimes hid in stormclouds: never fully dormant. Sometimes she imagined the magic itself would thicken and spool out of her, taking the best parts of what she was with it.

There had been a time when solitude, discipline, the certainty of her hands working alone in leaf-shadow and birdsong, had felt as if it could shield her from anything. But magic born of broken promise threaded a new hunger through her marrow. It left her uncertain where her own will ended and the compulsion of the forbidden bond began. She was not supposed to be afraid of power. That was what they had taught her, all those years in the Shadowed Wood, all the lessons whispered over mortars and moonlit runes. But fear shivered through her as she pressed the cloth tighter, the lesson of the witch's sacred oath ringing in her ears: what is mended by forbidden means must bear a heavier cost.

She risked a glance sideways. Kaelen sat across the fire, framed in a slant of light, his posture tense but unreadable. He watched her work—still as a shadow, hands resting between his knees. Beneath his hood, firelight caught in the pale lines across his face and the sharp set of his jaw, rendering him at once otherworldly and desperately human. He had survived the day's violence beside her, had thrown himself between steel and spell, and yet his presence disrupted the shape of her world as thoroughly as the day she saved his life. There was something brittle in the air—a thin, taut expectancy, like the edge of a spell before it lands. Alone, she would not have spoken. But the darkness was thick and close, her resolve softened by exhaustion.

She drew her cloak higher, feeling the tingle of errant power itch up her wrists. With the wind shifting the fire to gold and shadows, she found herself speaking, voice barely above the hush of embers.

"It isn't just the hurt," she said, more to the wound than to him. "Sometimes I feel it building inside me.

The magic. I patch these cuts—I heal, I fend off hunters, I do what I must—yet each time, it slips a little further out of my hold." The words tasted raw. "I think...I'm losing pieces of myself, Kaelen. As if the more I save, the less I remain."

He was silent for a breath. She heard his knuckles crack where he clasped his hands, heard the small catch in his exhale. Above, moths spun and darted in the warm updrafts—drawn to the same flame that illuminated her fears.

"I understand," he said, voice ragged, lower than she recalled. "Since I woke to this—whatever lives between us—I can't shake the emptiness. Like there's a hollow carved in me where trust or memory should exist." The fire flickered, painting uncertain patterns on the moss. "Even now, I keep waiting for some part of me to wake, something I can claim as my own. But all I seem to do is question: how do I trust you, or anyone, when I barely know if I am real? Or if I'm just the sum of what's been stolen and what's been given back."

She dared to look up this time—met his eyes, hesitant, and felt the bleakness there echo something she would never have named aloud. His vulnerability was an invitation she hadn't expected, an echo of her own fractured certainty.

Kaelen moved first—awkward, fingers curling slightly as he reached across the space between them. She saw the tremor there, a tension not born of fear but of hope denied too long. His hand brushed hers as she lowered it from her arm, skin connecting in a way that sent a shimmer through the lines of magic beneath her flesh. She held his gaze, steady as she could, and let her own hand remain over his—cool, battered, scarred, yet alive.

They stayed like that. The campfire crackled and threw shadows up the trees. She felt the charged warmth leap between their palms—wary, not yet surrender, but the promise of something that might one day let her breathe free.

No more words passed. Elara listened to the lonely music of the forest and the hush of his breath, the quiet around them as spare and trembling as a new spell. For now, the bond between them was not something to fear, but a pulse of possibility waiting in the firelight.

Kaelen nudged a brittle twig into the embers, coaxing up a coil of sparks, then let the stick slip from his hand to the fire's edge. Across the ring of light, Elara's face was cast in moving shades—deep amber and gold where the flames licked her cheek, umber shadow along her brow. They had spoken already of wounds and fears, the sort of things one stitched or buried, but now the hush between them was gentler, filled with the hush of dew falling, the slow shuffle of owls among black branches. Kaelen shifted closer, knees pressed to his chest beneath his worn traveling cloak.

He spoke low, uncertain at first, as though his voice were a thread he might lose in the restless night air. "When I try to remember my life before waking up in that tower... certain things come back. Never the beginning or the end. Only the middle, small and bright as a blue banner whipping in the sunlight. There were so many—banners—strung across a marble courtyard so pale it hurt to look at in summer. Someone—I think my mother—laughed. Hers was the sort of laugh you could hear echoing all the way through the pillars, even when the rest of the court wore their silks and silence."

Kaelen rubbed the heel of his palm over one eye, as if the gesture might coax memory into substance. "I keep dreaming of the smell of rosemary. Not the dried sprigs we sometimes burn to mask a campfire —real rosemary, green and thick-leaved, growing in warm stone planters. It's always there, just as I walk down endless halls—her voice, that scent, sunlight flashing on blue. But as soon as I try to hold it, it—" He broke off, shaking his head, a rueful sound escaping his lips. "It slips away. Like the rest of it."

He tried to laugh, but it tangled in his throat. The longing pressed against his ribs, sharp as hunger. All those pieces of memory—bright banners, polished marble, sunlight and something safe; they felt truer than anything he might claim about himself now. The weight of them built in his chest, a mixture of loss and desperate, aching hope for the world he might have called home.

Elara listened in silence, knees drawn up, the tips of her fingers tracing shapes across a patch of moss at her side. She hesitated, then leaned a little nearer, as if letting him close would not cost her. Her tone was measured, brittle with caution at first. "When I was a girl, I used to slip out before first light—quiet enough that even the old spirits didn't hear me go. The Shadowed Wood is loud when you know how to listen. The moss there is softer than any blanket, cool and damp underfoot, and if you dig down, you'll find root-threads that sing a little when rain's coming." Her voice warmed by degrees, uncertainty melting as she spoke. "My mentor—her name was Maelis—she taught me to read the wind. Not just to sense coming storms, but to catch secrets whispered from one tree to the next. The first proper spell she showed me was to coax the night lilies open with nothing more than a word and patience. I woke every season to try it—just to prove I could."

Her gaze flickered up, the firelight glinting off her burn-marked fingers. "Not many know that. Not even Lysandra. I think... it's easier to let people believe the only magic I trust is the sort born from discipline. Sometimes I almost believe it myself."

Kaelen watched her in the silence that stretched between them—grasshoppers creaking softly just beyond the ring of firelight, wind stirring the loose strands of her hair. He felt the urge to fill the stillness with more memories, but the well was dry, and the things he most wanted to understand about himself wavered at the edge of knowing.

The fire shuddered as a breeze moved through, reshaping the shadows at their feet. Kaelen reached for possibility, letting the future drift out on his words. "If we ever outrun these witch hunters, do you think your Shadowed Wood could be more than a hiding place? Could it be... a home people come to for sanctuary? For celebration? Sometimes I lie awake and I wonder what it'd feel like to walk through a city where people didn't flinch from magic, where a fire like this would draw laughter, not suspicion."

He did not say how the question cut through him— uncertainty coiling beneath his skin. The fragments of past grandeur did not belong to the fugitive he had become. In the face of that lost world, he imagined a different one, built not on bloodlines but on purpose—where he could shape his own belonging, even if the name on his tongue remained an echo. Some part of him feared he would never be untethered from the heavy shroud of the past, yet Elara's presence hinted at a way forward—if only he could let go of what no longer fit.

She smiled, slow and small, and nodded. "I'd like that. Magic unhidden. A place where none of us run."

She closed her eyes a moment. "Maybe that's what we're making now, little by little."

Their words dwindled as they leaned toward each other, joined by a hush thicker than any charm. Kaelen's pulse steadied in the kindling glow, the bitterness of longing softened by her nearness. He did not draw away as embers faded to bronze, or when the scent of moss and woodsmoke grew heavy.

Though the woods beyond remained dark and wild, here in the glow of the dying fire, Kaelen listened to the settling sighs of night. Peace felt possible—distant as the dawn, but no longer unreachable.

The quiet hush of midday was shattered by Rowan's breathless arrival, her boots scattering damp leaves as she hurtled through the undergrowth. The hazy sun reached only in slender shafts through the tangled canopy, lighting her profile in brief flashes—a silhouette charged with warning. "Scouts," Rowan said, voice rough from running. "Three, in the fern grove. Southbound. They'll find us if we stay another minute."

Fear tasted sharp on Elara's tongue, metallic and cold. She rose, every fiber braced. The world snapped into focus—the musk of wet earth, the sharp tang of bracken, the pulse of magic throbbing under her skin in sync with her quickening heartbeat. Rowan knelt, catching her breath, hand already on the hilt of her knife. Elara nodded once, trusting; it was a wordless language, built in crisis.

Kaelen was already moving, fingers deftly slipping talismans from a leather pouch. They shared a look—brief, weighted; the awkwardness of the previous night replaced with an unspoken understanding. Elara's own hands pressed to the mossy ground, cold soaking through her skin. She shaped the breath in her chest, whispering the old syllables. Power curled from her lips, unseen but real, weaving itself into the wind—an invisible veil encircling their makeshift camp.

Kaelen rose, marking points around the clearing with mute precision. Ferns shuddered where he knelt, a faint scent of scorched resin left in his wake as he pressed each talisman into the earth. The magic hummed between them—a net, delicate but resilient, born of their fragile trust. Elara tasted his anxious focus in the air, as if her own nerves had a second echo. Rowan moved lightly at the perimeter, senses alive, her storm-grey gaze never still.

The first hunter broke the screen of undergrowth with little sound—a shadow swathed in boiled leather and iron, helm glinting, blade held tight. Behind him, two more followed, eyes sharp and predatory. Elara pressed her back to a slender trunk, fingers swirling ribbons of fresh magic. Every lesson—every whispered warning around midnight fires—crystallized into this moment. She was not alone.

The witch hunters hesitated as they met the edge of her ward. The lead man stepped forward, suspicion writ plain in the angle of his shoulders. He thrust a gloved hand through empty air—and recoiled as sparks crackled invisibly around his wrist. Elara exhaled, steady. Kaelen, nearby, whispered a guttural word inherited from a lost language; from his palm, fire bloomed, swift and feral.

Elara reached inward, drawing from the restless energy of the wood. Earth and air answered. A barrier rippled skyward—translucent, humming. Kaelen's flames leaped through the spaces between, wild but contained by her guiding hand. The world shrank to this—two bodies moving in rhythm, a dance of trust forged in calamity.

Steel rang out as the hunters pressed harder, one swinging his sword at the air where the barrier shimmered. Sparks trickled off the invisible wall, acrid smoke curling toward the treetops. Kaelen's next flame burst forced the attackers back. Their boots churned the loam, faces twisted in confusion and fear. For an instant, Elara glimpsed herself reflected in the metal of a shield—sweat streaked, eyes bright with something more than terror.

She felt the presence of Rowan behind her, steady and watching, every sense attuned to danger. It struck Elara—the bone-deep certainty of interdependence. Foolish to have believed she could face this life alone; it took Rowan's warning, Kaelen's fire, her own resolve now burning fierce as any torch. Together, they bent danger to their will.

"Now," Rowan hissed from the shadows, gesturing toward a dense tangle of brambles. Elara sucked in a breath and moved, Kaelen close behind, Rowan darting ahead like a fox through dew-damp undergrowth. The magic shield flickered in their wake; behind, the hunters scrambled, blinded by smoke and shimmering light.

They ran, branches whipping, thorns snagging at sleeves. Elara's heart hammered—fear, yes, but threaded through with a heady exhilaration. Kaelen's hand at her shoulder was a silent promise. The ward snapped, a current discharged, and they burst from the cover of brambles onto a rise dappled with cool shadows and soft moss. Rowan circled back, face tense but unmarked.

They crouched in silence atop the knoll, watching as the hunters circled below, stymied by Rowan's misdirection and the lingering shimmer of Elara's fading magic. For a moment, no one spoke. The world was all sharp pine and breathless quiet. Elara's skin still stung with the imprint of magic spent too quickly; adrenaline ebbed, leaving her hollow but unwavering.

The sun slid toward the horizon, flooding the woods with slanting amber. Elara glanced at Kaelen, who met her gaze without flinching. Sweat soaked his brow, but his eyes were clear—trust radiated between them in the hush. Rowan crouched nearby, knife at the ready, a reminder that loyalty was not assumed, but earned in moments such as these.

Twilight thickened. The memory of their escape hung with the mist—a bond newly forged, fragile as the first thread of dawn. Elara straightened, shoulders squared by exhaustion and something more resilient. Here, where the woods began to fill with shadows and the threat had retreated (for now), she let herself imagine a day when fear would not be her only companion. For now, she stood at Kaelen's side, Rowan a steady force nearby—together, a line that would not break, not yet.

Dusk clung to the glade in watery ribbons, the sun's last breath caught among twisting willow limbs and delicate banks of fern that glowed faintly in the half-light. The scents of scorched leaves and trampled moss hung in the air, reminders of violence still too near; beneath it, the tang of cooling earth, as if the land itself exhaled—equal parts pain and quiet hope. Kaelen moved beside Elara, matching the rhythm of her bruised breath in the hush. The silence pressed around them, broken only by soft, uneven inhalations and the hush of their footsteps in the loam.

Kaelen's skin tingled where adrenaline had left its ghost. His body was marked with the day—scrapes along his forearms, a streak of dried blood near his thumb—and though exhaustion weighed in his bones, something urgent thrummed beneath it all.

He watched as Elara reached for her shoulder, her palm splayed over the crescent mark etched into her flesh. A faint, luminous shimmer pulsed under her fingers, its light trembling like a living heartbeat. She drew a ragged breath. In that moment Kaelen saw her as both wounded and magnificent—strength and uncertainty knotted together.

A current flickered between them, sharper than anything he had felt since awakening in the Tower. Suddenly, energy snapped up his spine, fire and cold at once. The trembling in Elara's hand leaped into his chest. He gasped. The world contracted to a single, blinding rush—magic humming through the glade, spilling out from her mark. Kaelen staggered, clutching his side, and as the force poured through him he was flooded by an awareness so vast it stole the last of his words. Elara's emotions pulsed through the tether unbidden: fear, coiled and brittle, hope darting between the cracks, a pain so deep it shuttered in his own ribcage until he could hardly breathe. He saw the shadow of her worry, felt the fragile longing she carried, as if her heart had opened just enough for him to glimpse the storm inside.

It was terrifying, baring—yet the terror melted, replaced slowly, inexorably, by wonder. Was this how magic was meant to move—through two bodies, two hearts, no longer alone in their burdens?

He heard himself whisper her name.

Without a word, Elara reached for his hand, her palm hot where it pressed to his trembling fingers. Kaelen's lips parted but no sound came. Instead, the energy beckoned; he closed his eyes and let himself lean into her, the soles of his boots rooted in damp moss. Between them, the magic coiled, thickening, then blossomed outward—a living thing, neither wholly his nor hers but something new, exquisitely balanced. The pulse of their bond quickened, urgent and alive. Light flared at their joined hands, gold and violet curling in delicate veins across Elara's skin, looping through his. Healing warmth surged in his blood, mending bruises, soothing aches. He felt his fatigue dissolve; lightness bloomed in his chest. A gentle heat radiated from their clasped hands, spilling into the dusk, seeping beyond the shelter of willow and fern.

A soft gasp came from the shadows—Rowan, hidden among the ferns, exhaling as her own pain eased, the light rippling across her limbs. The air shimmered, motes of gold falling on leaf and skin alike. Kaelen sensed none of Rowan's private thoughts, only the reverberation of their shared magic, a perfect resonance that healed without needing speech.

The afterglow receded slowly, an ebbing tide. Kaelen opened his eyes. Elara's cheeks shone with sweat and wonder; between their hands bloomed a thin ribbon of brilliant energy, floating just above the pulse in their wrists. Its edges flickered, always on the verge of dissipating, yet endurable, as if a promise made not just by flesh but by something older and wilder woven into the marrow of the world.

Kaelen's chest filled with possibility and dread in equal measure. Before, magic had meant power—fire hurled and wind called—but this was different: a fusing of intentions and wounds, a channel that made them stronger together and frighteningly susceptible. What would it mean if their bond grew? There was power, yes—it might shift the tides, disrupt the equations that kept witches hidden and their enemies emboldened. He imagined confronting Lord Dalen, this bond burning between them, unchecked. Could they, united, unmake the old order? Or would their joining only make them more visible, hunted not only for what they were but for what they could become?

He swallowed, suddenly aware of every heartbeat threading between their bodies. This connection demanded trust, a thing Kaelen had never given freely and hardly understood now; yet it crackled across his nerves, making withdrawal unthinkable. Her emotions wound into him, fragile but fierce, a gift and a test in the same breath. If he faltered, if he protected himself behind old walls, this bond might poison them both, or worse—unlock something neither was ready to wield.

But Elara's hand was steady—a trembling steadiness, true, but strong in its vulnerability. Kaelen looked at her face illuminated by the lingering light and sensed hope rising in her once more. He let himself wonder, for the first time, what it might mean not just to fight for survival but to claim belonging at her side— a promise forged in danger, growing in the hush of a world gone wild.

Together, breathless and awed, they watched as the ribbon of magic hovered between them, glowing and mutable. Night crept through the woods, and neither spoke of tomorrow; the changes in their bodies and hearts whispered enough. Their entwined hands, and the whispering light, were proof that nothing would be the same again.

Chapter 13

Tides of Rebellion

Elara lingered at the edge of the clearing where the Wildlands pressed in, close and secretive. This was not her forest, but the hush of anticipation beneath the boughs tasted familiar on her tongue—wet moss, old bark, and the sharp, acrid memory of smoke still clutching to the leaves from the last skirmish. She pressed one palm against rough bark, channeling a tremor of magic, grounding herself as Kaelen led the procession into the waning light—torchless, as if one careless glow might draw death down upon them all.

Kaelen lifted his hand, and the Ironwood Band stepped from the underbrush first. They bore old scars and newer wounds, studded leathers smeared with the day's dust, eyes as ready as hounds before war. Their leader, a woman with arms crossed and a jaw set like an anvil, moved with the battered caution of those who had survived too many betrayals. Next, the Ashen Sisters—five veiled silhouettes in silver-threaded ash-grey, bare feet silent against the needled earth. Behind, slower and less certain, the Nightglass Outcasts, shrouded all in black linen, hands almost always hidden, voices barely more than a murmur. Hunger rimmed their faces, an absence of sunlight stretching long in the bones.

The fractured kingdom had bred these splits. Each faction was the answer to a wound: the Ironwood

Band honed hard by a massacre in the timber camps, their loyalty soldered by the memory of felled children and crops razed in punishment. The Ashen Sisters, last remnants of a lineage driven underground, shared language, song, and custom older than the stones, swearing never to cede tradition for safety. The Nightglass Outcasts, once townsfolk, now carried the stigma of vanished kin and destroyed villages, persecuted to the edges, living in the hollow between witch and refugee. Where the king's hounds had burned and hunted, resistance budded—petals grimed with ash and blood —each group certain only in their need for survival. This was a rebel patchwork, strength stitched through with the weaknesses of old feuds and the constant risk that the very seams would tear if tugged.

Elara drew a steadying breath, feeling the push of her pulse against her wrists, fire and water underwriting every thought. Her mind flickered with the warnings of her teachers: Do not trust too quickly, do not forget old debts. Still, the clearing seemed to vibrate with possibility. As she stepped forward, the hush was absolute, a hundred wary eyes marking every gesture.

"We are not here because we are unbroken," Elara began, her words a thin silver thread. "We are here because we have no choice left but to stand together, lest none of us remain at day's end. Your wounds are known. Your losses are not forgotten."

Muscle and memory, these old rites, but still her voice left her lips colored new—carrying the edge of hope and the deep ache of longing. She let the air cool around her, coaxed a shimmer of light across her palm, the faintest pulse of river water winding in her veins, a hush of wind that made the Sisters' veils flutter. The Ironwood leader nodded, wary approval in the set of her eyes. Elara met her gaze—and then Kaelen's, further back, offering a small gesture of solidarity.

"We offer intelligence from the court," Kaelen said, voice lower, more measured. "Patrol schedules. Weaknesses in the northern outposts. Anything our cause requires."

"You'd sell your own for us?" The Nightglass spokesman's voice was jagged, almost hollowed from disuse.

"I would see the tyranny end," Kaelen replied. "And what is noble blood if it stands for nothing?"

The factions began to speak, words gathering weight and sharpness in the cool air. The Ironwood Band, brusque and unbending, recounted the razing of Hartsbridge—how the river ran choked with the bodies of their kin, the toll exacted for a whispered rumor of sheltering a witch. The Ashen Sisters, their eldest unearthing language strung like beads, spoke of traditions outlawed, of children chased from sacred bonfires and homes repurposed as gallows. The Outcasts hissed their story in parts— dispossession layered on exile, bribes paid and hounds loosed, how promises made in moonlit glens had been shattered by dawn.

They demanded autonomy. Swore they would not follow another's rules, not after what unquestioned trust had cost them. Elara felt each declaration land heavy in her ribcage—a call, and a warning: power could be found here, or a fracture wide enough to bleed them all dry if unity remained only a word.

She kept her stance open, voice pitched soothing, naming the old gods, referencing the sacred rivers, bending the talk toward what they had in common rather than what had torn them apart. Slowly, resistance bent, not broke. Magic hummed beneath her skin and she let it show—a subtle crown of blue-white fire flickering above her brow as dusk fell, the earth's heartbeat echoing up her legs.

The Ironwood leader reached out, rough hand extended. "We join," she said, "but know this—past wounds run deep as roots here. Betray us again, and we become your enemy."

The Ashen Sisters' matron's reply was a ritual chant, refusal to follow any command that would sever them from their ancient rites. The Nightglass spokesman spit in his palm before the clasp—an oath laced with old dirt and defiance.

Each leader clasped hands beneath the eldritch branches where green lichen shivered, the pact sealed in the shadows. Elara watched the hands linger, saw the calculation and hope flicker in narrowed eyes, the glimmer of trust yet unsteady as a child's first step.

As the sky bruised violet, final signals—birdcalls, stone patterns, fingers crossed in secret signs—were agreed on. Elara held her breath, pulse tripping fast with mingled dread and longing, aware that only love for her people and the fragile tug of fate kept her from breaking herself apart for them.

As the last light vanished and the clearing emptied, Elara's heart ached in its chest, knowing unity tonight rested on the trembling whim of trust and desire—and that this was only the beginning.

The Hearthstone Inn, its timber beams swelling with the scents of spiced ale and baking bread, pulsed with the quiet electricity of imminent conspiracy. Evening shadows gathered in the corners, molasses-thick, as Kaelen slid into his chair beside Elara at the heavy, scar-scored table. The room glowed amber with lantern light, but uneaten food cooled, glistening with condensation, and mugs formed halos of pale ale about stacks of parchment maps smeared with candlewax and coded glyphs. Lysandra and Rowan pressed in from the far side, the two women's heads bowing close as the Nightglass Outcasts, the Ironwood Band, and the Ashen Sisters drifted in, trailing wariness and mud.

Kaelen's fingers trembled ever so slightly as he thumbed through the newest batch of reports. Nightglass scouts, it seemed, left traces as delicate as charcoal on old birchbark: signs of witch hunter posts shifting in the dark, supply carts rattling past ruined wells, unfamiliar banners hauled through storm-pocked fields. Rowan uncapped a battered scrollcase and let a crumpled map spill across the table, its edges torn and corners singed. Lysandra arranged runes—opal and riverstone—along the grain of the wood, her hands deft, face unreadable.

The Ironwood Band's leader, broad-shouldered and breath sharp as winter pine, jabbed a finger at a star-shaped mark. "You talk of strategy, but how long before the hounds sniff out half our number? Ambush and vanish: it's how we survived." His words sank beneath the grumble of shifting chairs, received by nods and a few coarse laughs from his kin.

A voice like flint rapping glass rang out from the Ashen Sisters—grey-clad, eyes hooded and lips pressed flat. "Strategy is for those who have time to lose." She flicked her gaze over Elara first, Kaelen next, her tone clipped. "Redstone Watch should burn tonight. No clever feints, no running. Strike, and let the ashes warn them."

At the far side, a thin Nightglass woman, her braid tied with a crow's feather, lingered over her own map, voice quiet but knife-keen. "Sabotage. Their cart wheels. Their watch clocks. Let them wake to smoke but never see a blade. We don't win by lining up for slaughter."

The arguments caught and tumbled in Kaelen's mind, each proposal bleeding mistrust into the next. The Ironwood Band eyed the Nightglass Outcasts with history etched deep in their frowns—there were old betrayals in those glances and in the pauses before anyone spoke. The Ashen Sisters, faces painted with ash and blue woad, recoiled at any compromise that threatened their customs. Their unity felt brittle, strung to breaking by the bending light above their storm of plans.

Lysandra, ever a soft flame where there should be frost, lifted both palms as if weighing water. "You risk old grudges in a new war," she intoned, runes glinting as she turned them. "An overt assault—noble, perhaps, but it could fracture the lines we so lately wove. And sabotage, though clever, leaves captives to die in silence. We must be bold, but not blind."

Rowan's mouth quirked, a smirk cracking the gloom. "If you two quarrel any louder, the witch hunters will join us here and ask for stew." The Outcasts stifled a snicker. "Listen. If I have to pick one of you to watch my back and not stick a knife in it, well, I'd rather take my chances with the marsh serpents. But we don't have that luxury. We need everyone—or we'll get slaughtered piece-meal, like last autumn by the valley."

Kaelen's gaze lingered on Elara, seeking her pulse beneath her calm. She leaned forward, letting her words pour gentle but sure. "Redstone Watch is weak now but won't remain so. We can strike as one, when the night's at its deepest. The Ironwood Band can cut patrols at first bell—Nightglass, you'll cripple the wagons, free their horses. Ashen Sisters, your flames will mask our true numbers. If we fall to infighting, we give them their victory without a single spell cast. We claim it together, or we do not claim it at all."

In the shivering lantern-light, Kaelen sorted through the fragmentary plans and bristling egos. He read in every twitch a history: old grief stacked atop new, honor forced to bloom among weeds of suspicion. He felt the fragile possibility of alliance—a blade pressed to its own hilt. Responsibility pulsed in his chest, a painful anchor. He worried over his body's weakness, hated the dizzy intervals when words swam and breath caught, but he clasped his reports with purpose, offering what clarity he could from his former world. Elara's patience, her unfurling voice, became the constellations by which he steered his trembling resolve.

As consensus wove itself—tentative, frayed, but holding—the group turned to mark roles and signals. Secret hand gestures mimicked spells: a twist of thumb, a flick of wrist. Each faction, each leader, marked their place with palpable reluctance and a few muttered curses, but the current of commitment ran beneath the posturing. Rowan uncorked a gourd of sand, pouring a grainy cascade over the battered map. The lantern's light sputtered and died, and in the deep hush that followed, Kaelen heard their united destiny gathering like a spell at the tip of a tongue—not yet spoken, but waiting.

The room held its breath as the rebellion's first operation set itself into the marrow of everyone present.

Rowan's boots tracked in a spatter of mud as she entered the back hall, the hush of midnight hanging thick—so silent Elara could almost hear the strain of every single heartbeat. In her hand, Rowan held a folded scrap, inked with the careful angular script that only spies or desperate outlaws used. She pushed it across the heavy oak table where Lysandra sat, the only light a single trembling candle that painted the walls with restless shadows. Lysandra's fingers moved deftly, peeling back the code and tracing the cryptic glyphs with an anxious intensity. Around them, the air vibrated, thick with unspoken dread, as the cipher revealed a network of troop movements—details no one outside their circle could possibly have known.

Whispers built in the cracks between the stones. The scent of damp wool, woodsmoke, and fear pressed at Elara from all sides. Every footstep beyond the door felt like it could herald ruin. She pressed her hands together, feeling the subtle burn of her own magic restive at her fingertips, as Rowan's voice cut through:

"Someone's selling us out. This... they couldn't know about Redstone, not unless one of ours handed it to them."

A cold ache draped itself around Elara's shoulders, each word from Rowan pinching inward, sharper than needles. They could not afford this fracture—too many eyes, too many watching for weakness. She let anticipation build inside her, the fire and river churn of elemental promise, as the circle's trust began to dissolve, invisible, in the shifting candlelight.

Elara waited in the storage room, surrounded by bundles of dried heather, crates of bitter apples, the air close and windowless—a refuge that felt more like a snare. She drew the bolt as Seraphine's footsteps sounded on the stone, determined and almost lyrical, face illuminated by the uncertain glow of the fire. The door thudded shut, steel sliding home. For a moment, only the hush of burning logs filled the little space, the shadows fluttering between the two women.

"Sit," Elara said quietly. She gestured to a battered stool opposite her. The silence sharpened, coiling in the gap between them, neither accusation nor plea. Elara's spine was iron; her voice a hush that dared not waver.

Seraphine lowered herself into the circle of firelight, eyes glinting with reflections—blue, like distant mountain storms. Her fingers wrapped tightly around her own wrist, the shifting tattoos at her skin's edge glowing and receding with her breath.

"You know why you're here," Elara began. She kept her tone measured, a careful balance between inquiry and restraint. "There's been a breach. Coded messages, troop movements leaking from behind our walls. The witch hunters know what no outsider should." Her mouth tasted of ashes.

Seraphine's lips trembled, just barely, before she drew herself rigid. "You think it's me who brought them here?"

Elara nodded, her pulse loud, surfacing through the quiet, the forbidden magic inside her churning with every word. "Not think. I know. The cipher Lysandra broke matched your pattern—root phrases pulled from Sutri old tongue, ones only you've ever used with me. Why, Seraphine?"

For a long, trembling instant, Seraphine stared into the tangle of shadows behind Elara's head. Then: "I passed them messages. Only small things. Nothing with names, never with intent for harm." A shallow, ragged breath passed between her words. "They found me. A hunter. He knows my past—my family, the massacre at Raven's Cut they covered up. I saw what hatred can do. I—Elara, I couldn't see it again, not after my parents burned for someone else's rebellion. He threatened to bring the same fate to others, to all of you if I didn't—"

"You should have come to me," Elara said softly, voice rough around the corners. She pressed her palm to the rough wood, feeling the grain, anchoring herself. "Anything was better than this." The betrayal was a sapling's rot, quiet and spreading.

The door rattled, then flew open. Rowan burst in, breath quick and straight-backed indignation formed in her posture. Lysandra stepped in behind, calmer but eyes sharp and unwavering, her cloak trailing the fresh scent of rain. Rowan's gaze darted between Seraphine and Elara.

"You let her talk?" she demanded. "We should cast her out—tonight. No mercy for traitors."

"She's scared. That hunter is real, and she's not the only one with ghosts behind her," Lysandra said.

"She jeopardized everything. Someone could die," Rowan shot back.

Dialogue rose and overlapped, tense as drawn wires. Lysandra tried to reason, Rowan's rage fanned the flames, Kaelen's deeper voice cut through from the hall as he entered, proposing, "We confine her. I'll take first watch. Until we know more, we can't risk the plan." They all spoke—fear, grief, anger plaited together like old scar tissue.

Elara stood unmoving as the debate fractured further, the cacophony swirling around her until Lysandra's calm, Rowan's thunder, and Kaelen's iron all faded into white-noise.

Her chest ached with unspoken regret. Every word Seraphine had spoken was a mirror held to Elara's own vulnerabilities—a leader who dared trust, and for what? Courage in this place meant carrying others' failures, absorbing every drop of fear and disappointment as her own. She felt the exile of responsibility in her marrow: if this shatters, it was her hand that drew the line in the sand. If they failed, if the witch hunters closed in and another massacre followed, history would reach back, black-fingered, and it would be Elara's name carved in the ruins.

In the world beyond this cramped and flickering room, alliances were not forged in glory but in desperate bargains, cautious silence, and relentless scrutiny. Every secret risked lives. Every fracture signaled opportunity for the kingdom's hunters—who thrived on discord, on hint and rumor. Witches fought for every hour of safety, united only by the threats that sought to unmake them. Trust was a spell as fragile and rare as spring frost on September grass.

Rowan outlined steps for restricting the flow of information, speaking in clipped, decisive tones. Seraphine's head bowed as Lysandra guided her from the room, Rowan following close behind. Kaelen lingered only a second by the threshold, gaze solemn, before disappearing into the shadows. Elara was left beneath the slanting light, hands pressed to the battered wood, the circle of trust splintered. She could hear the indistinct sounds of locks and new guards; she could feel the fault line opening beneath their cause as though she was the one who had cast the spell.

Weapons and words passed from hand to hand beneath the thin, colorless light of an expectant morning. Swords lay sheathed in bundles across woven grass mats, their hilts polished to a weary shine. Bows—some curved and elegant, others hacked roughly from storm-felled trees—were pressed into calloused palms, binding stranger to stranger for the chance of survival. Marek's steady voice counted out blades, his fingers running over the bindings to check for flaws. Rowan ducked through the knot of rebels, cracking dry jokes as she taught trembling hands the anchor stance for a stave. The Ironwood Band, their cloaks forest-dark and muddy at the hem, parceled out quivers and shield-charms marked by the scars of older wars. Over all this, the air vibrated, not from noise, but from a layered listening: hope searching for reassurance, dread searching for weakness.

Kaelen moved with brisk efficiency among crates stacked with stones veined in sigils, pausing to check each rune's glow against the hush of the dawn. The magic they had borrowed—spells from books left buried in hearth ashes, symbols crafted from stolen gold—formed a lattice beneath their feet, and he frowned at each flicker, each uncertain blink from the protective wards etched into bone and clay. Occasionally, someone leaned close and asked for another talisman, and his answer was gentle but assured: the runes would hold, the signals would not betray.

Elara waited for Kaelen where bramble met shadow, the sky overhead a bruised gradient from silver to blue-black. Her hand found his—a wordless press, a transfer of silent fears and stubborn faith. For an instant, the world narrowed to the pulse she felt under his skin and the roughness of his thumb as it traced the edge of her palm. She let her gaze rest on him, noting each freckle, the subtle tremor at the corner of his mouth. No one could see beyond the outer shell—the gentle burden he carried, the history he wore like a second spine—but she read something in his eyes that was real, unvarnished. Betrayals pressed heavy as river stones, but his next words came low, for her alone.

"Whatever tomorrow brings—whatever tonight breaks—I trust you, Elara. All of it. Not because you have to protect us, or because you're strong enough for everyone. I trust your judgment, and I choose it. I choose you."

A tightness in Elara's chest unfurled, both hope and ache wrapped in the warmth of his breath against her cheek. She squeezed his hand once more before drifting back toward the firelit heart of the encampment.

In a ring of churned earth and crushed wildflowers, Lysandra led a ragged procession through drill after drill. Her voice, composed as the frost's bite, sent runners skittering down mapped escape trails and guided younger witches in the complicated flick of fingers required to send a shield spell arcing over friends. Rowan stalked the periphery, sleeves pushed up to show her tattooed runes, barking reminders over the hush, "No heroics! Stay with your partner, shield left, blade right!" The Ashen Sisters, resplendent in their bark-patched armor, charged and retreated in a flurry of practiced formation: centuries of tradition pressed into each measured stride. The Nightglass Outcasts watched through narrowed eyes, their own signals sharp and private, their faces unreadable as the moon behind the dawn mist.

Smoke gathered uneasily above their fires. Elara moved among her fighters—Ashen, Ironwood, Nightglass—her mind cataloguing each scar, every quiver of resolve, each borrowed spell. She saw suspicion spark between Nightglass and Ironwood, the grim resolution of women who had lost kin to soldiers and storm; the flicker of fear in eyes still green with youth. The circle clustered close as she called them to order, her voice sounding both within her own body and across the breathless morning.

She hesitated on the threshold of speech, burdened by the galewind of outcomes. She imagined the forest blackened by fire, wagons heavy with new prisoners, the crackle of captured magic torn from trembling hands. What would it mean, if she failed here? If the trust that linked these rebels—already threadbare and patched with desperation—tore under the strain of another betrayal? The memory of Seraphine lingered, raw and bitter: one secret become a chasm, one weakness a poison in their shared hope. Would the world remember them as villains or martyrs? Would the kingdom's children inherit only bones and warnings, magic winnowed to myth and ashes?

Yet Elara could see, just barely, a future gilded with possibility—a world where witches strode sunlit streets, bright-eyed and unafraid, where the stories told around village fires ended in renewal, not slaughter. The forbidden bond twisting inside her—power and longing braided tight—threatened to burn her alive, but it also made her believe that revolt could remake more than law, more than memory. If conviction could cross the roots of these ancient trees, perhaps mercy would sprout in unlikely soil, breaking the cycle. It would cost everything she had. It already had.

The rebels watched her, sun shadows tangled around their feet, the hush vibrating with what-ifs. She spoke, and her words laced the air like a promise, like spellwork.

"We move together. We fight for those lost, for those still left, for what might come after. Watch for the signs, trust only your teams. Guard the old and the young, and remember—this dawn is ours only if we claim it together."

Weapons and talismans vanished into folds of cloak. The forest swallowed them, one after another, their boots muffled on moss, their hearts joined by frail but burning threads. As the first birds began to sing, Elara lingered at the edge, letting the weight of many fates rest—just for a heartbeat—against her ribs, before stepping into the mist.

Chapter 14

The Witch Hunter's Fortress

Under the vault of the moonless sky, the forest pressed close—trunks rising in solemn parade, branches weaving a shroud that smothered every glimmer of starlight. Night's chill seeped through Elara's cloak, carrying the scent of iron, damp leaf rot, and the distant tang of torch smoke. With each cautious footfall, frost-dusted leaves whispered secrets beneath her boots. Elara's senses stretched beyond sound and shadow, searching for threads of warding and malice in the air. Ahead, the Witch Hunter's Fortress cleaved the horizon: a monolith of cruelty, its sheer black stone hunched, bristling with iron spikes that gleamed faintly, catching and swallowing what little light the world offered. Arrow slits yawned like the empty eyes of skulls. The fortress loomed not only over the land but over memory itself.

Moving silent, her allies in a crouching line behind, Elara pressed her palm to an ancient root and let her focus narrow. Every child born to witches in the kingdom grew up beneath stories of this place—its halls stinking of fear, its windows alive to the cries of executions in ages past. Each slab of stone bled history; each echo in the cold halls a reminder of mothers and brothers dragged from bed by night, promises broken under interrogation, secrets snuffed beneath boots or brands. She drew a trembling breath, knowing that within these walls, oaths had shattered—even as new vows might be forged tonight.

Kaelen halted at her side, his hand a mere shade in the dark, two fingers splayed briefly at his temple before sweeping toward the outer wall—a silent signal: stillness, caution. Elara nodded and pressed forward, eyes catching the faintest shimmer rippling across bramble and stone—wards, woven with artistry and violence, wards built not to warn but to maim and expose. Her fingers curled, drawing warmth from her core, shaping lines of elemental magic so fine they could only be seen by those initiated in the old ways. Glowing just under her skin, the light was a secret caress, burning where she concentrated. Words, honed and precise, spilled from her lips—murmurous, threading through the dark like a lover's whisper, breaking, changing, soothing the shrieking edges of each magical barrier.

The walls responded reluctantly. Magic shifted with reluctant groans inside the mortar, yielding in flashes of dull blue before fading to silence. In the charged stillness, Elara's heart raced, not with fear but with a quicksilver pulse of something perilous and precious: love harnessed to purpose, hope fastened to rebellion. She thought of each life caged behind those stones, of the way Rowan moved with feline stealth at her back, of Lysandra's quiet courage, of Kaelen—his presence a steadying weight at her side, his watchfulness a wordless promise.

A distant crunch of gravel—the soft hiss of armor, too close. Elara stilled, closing her fist on magic until the power ached in her veins. Kaelen melted into shadow, poised like a hound before the hunt. She risked one glance as he glided ahead, daggers flashing briefly in the meager glow from high-set torches. Two witch hunter patrols, bored or careless, never saw him coming. The violence was swift and silent. Bodies slumped, the thud muffled by moss. Kaelen's silhouette lingered a moment, then vanished into the deeper dark, leaving only the hush of fatal resolution behind.

Elara's thoughts flickered: Would tonight bring freedom—or simply another entry upon the fortress's long ledger of suffering? She tasted resentment alongside resolve, anger pressed hard against old grief. Each stride toward the wall was rebellion. Each minute act of subversion was a love song for her people.

Lysandra slipped ahead, agile in the half-light, her form flattening against cold stone. Elara watched her friend's boldness with mingled pride and anxiety; she saw Lysandra's braid catch where rusty wire winked, saw the small shake of her head—another trap, razor-fine and thirsty. With deft precision, Lysandra sparkled her palm against the wire. Magic surged— crisp, blue-white—and the tremor of violence faded. From beneath her cloak, a slender pin gleamed. Lysandra coaxed it into the ridged guts of the old gate and, within a heartbeat, iron surrendered. The lock gave a soft sigh. The way was open.

A rush: the team pressed in close, hearts loud in the hush, blades gleaming, magic alive between knuckles and teeth. Arrow slits overhead promised sudden death, but Rowan made a careless gesture with two fingers, and the courtyard bloomed with phantom mist—cool, swirling vapor that clung to boots, hair, skin, hiding all but the pressing sense of danger, masking breath and sound.

They darted—first one, then three, five shadows across naked moonstone, slipping between columns and past torches burning bitter. The edges of reality seemed to thin; Elara felt every heartbeat not just in her own chest but as an echo in the rhythm of those beside her. She reached the archway, palms tingling with magic, and signaled an "all clear"—two taps against stone.

Inside, the fortress bared its belly: vast, echoing halls, walls heavy with memory and malice. Their bodies pressed together behind a broken column, breaths shallow, shoulders brushing. As the sound of footsteps retreated into the gloom, Elara's gaze met Kaelen's across the shadowed span, bold promise kindling between them, nerves strung tight as bowstrings. They pressed deeper, every sense alight.

Down the stairwell, torchlight flickered in trembling pools. Lysandra pressed her fingers against the damp, grooved stone, the cool grit grounding her as she listened for danger—boots slid in the passage above, metal brushing stone, the steady thump of adversaries that knew only discipline and cruelty. She willed her breath quieter and fixed the trembling in her hands, weaving a barrier with the faintest brush of power: a thin lattice threaded from her own pulse and the warmth of the torch. The ward shimmered, heartrates merging with the pulse of ancient stone, masking the echo of her descent. She ducked beneath a splintered beam at the passage's mouth, wishing for the comfort of morning sun and the lullaby of cicadas in the glades she'd abandoned.

Her thoughts kept circling back, unbidden, to that terrible memory—her siblings' cries when she failed to hold a barrier strong enough, careless for an instant, and a shimmer of wild fire had leapt the line. In the smoky midnight after, guilt had grown like a bramble within her, twisting roots through every line of spellcraft she'd learned since. Even now, she felt the memory's chill settle along her collarbones, a warning and a promise: She would not fail the ones she loved again.

Rounding the corner, Lysandra nearly stumbled into the path of four witch hunters, their silhouettes made monstrous in the wavering torchlight. She checked her momentum, heart pounding—a controlled exhale, the taste of old fear on her tongue. She raised her hand, murmuring a word that bent shadow and flame, and with a thrust shut the iron grate behind, the clang ringing in the close air. Let them think she was frightened, fleeing. She fixed her gaze on the meanest of the four, eyes that glinted like daggers, and let her stance quiver, coaxing pursuit.

"Got you cornered, witch," one spat, voice thick with relish.

She replied, fingers brushing the crumbled mortar. "Not today." And then she ran, boots silent, flicking the next torched sconce loose so it crashed in a riot of sparks, leading them deeper, away from her friends threading below.

She had trained for this—night after night, discipline hammered into nerves and sinew, practicing containment, misdirection, escape. Protection was an art. To shelter demanded more precision than force. Here, under ancient stone, she felt each lesson in her marrow: stay focused, trust the world's secret leylines, never let panic take the first step.

As the hunters followed, their armor scraping, Lysandra forced her trembling hand to steady and touched her palm to a loose stone jutting from the wall. She drew from it—not too deep, just enough to feel the shudder of elemental potential. She shaped it, guiding energy and memory together. Memories of the fire that nearly claimed her siblings, of how she'd rebuilt herself spell by spell, wound by wound. The charge built until her skin tingled, that blend of fear and purpose intoxicating, and with a single word—

breathed rather than spoken—she unleashed the light.

A searing flash detonated in the corridor, bursts of white and pale violet flinging jagged shrapnel and stinging pebbles. Yelps and curses echoed. Two hunters staggered, eyes streaming, and a third crashed hard against the wall. The fourth, blade drawn, surged through the haze—her nerves caught fire, muscles anticipating pain. She ducked right, but not fast enough. The sword grazed her shoulder, searing a thin gash that burned hot and then cold. Lysandra pressed her hand to the wound, stifling a cry, and let the pain anchor her focus.

She would not yield. Pain, she'd learned, was a message—keep moving, be careful, survive for those who need you. Every sense sharpened. She darted back, drawing the last two into a half-collapsed storage chamber thick with the scent of mildew and the bite of old iron. The air trembled with her power. With careful, deliberate gestures, she wove an arcane snare just past the threshold—a spiderweb of cinching force. She kicked a stacked shelf, sending crates and dust clattering down, the sound a ruse for helplessness.

"Stay back! This shelf won't—" she shouted. Footsteps thundered after her. As the two hunters stepped inside, the snare snapped tight, tangling their boots and dragging them to their knees with a metallic shriek. Shelves toppled, barrels spilled, barricading the doorway behind their shouts.

Lysandra allowed herself one shaking breath, feeling the rough reality of her aching shoulder, the tremor in her bones from borrowed magic. She gathered a strip of fabric snagged from splintered wood, binding her wound as blood oozed beneath her fingers. The stone corridor rattled with the echoes of the brawl—cries, footfalls, shouts unanswered. She closed her eyes, steadied her heart, and listened for the sounds of pursuit.

She pressed the makeshift bandage tighter, kneeling between shadow and shattered wood, and exhaled through clenched teeth. The cost was sharp, but her path was clear: she would buy them time, no matter what. The memory of her siblings' terrified faces, of how failure once cut deepest where love lay, hovered close—a reminder and a vow. This time, she would not falter.

Shadows pooled thick against the stone as Elara pressed herself to the dank wall, the cold of the Witch Hunter's Fortress seeping into her skin. The low chamber ahead flickered with smoky torchlight, bars running in hard black lines across what had once been cells for the long dead, but now imprisoned the living. She moved between islands of wavering gold, each light illuminating things her eyes would rather not see—faces warped with pain, bodies curled on filthy straw, wrists ringed with iron, young and old alike bound by chains warded with red and black sigils.

She caught the sweet-metal tang of blood, rank with the cloy of old sweat and fear. Moans drifted through the bars, broken and unsure, trailing through the air like ghosts clinging to the stones. Elara's heart stumbled; her breath came shallow as she registered the burns marring pale skin, the raw welts that magic could neither heal nor disguise. One prisoner's eyes pleaded, their irises dull as river stones. Another, hair tangled and matted across her jaw, made no sound at all. The world narrowed— torchlight, iron, the pulse thrumming in Elara's fingers, the ghosts of agony that would not let her turn away.

Uneasy memories flooded up, sharp as knife-blades: the execution square in her childhood village, the crowd pressed in tight, the sound of a girl not much older than herself screaming as the flames took her. Elara remembered her own frozen terror, the hopelessness in her mother's steady hand, the brute indifference of the men who called themselves righteous. That day, all she could do was watch and weep; her voice was too small, her magic too forbidden, the law too absolute. Now, years and scars later, she tasted that same ash in her mouth—a frozen helplessness that left her knees weak but her jaw clenched in a vow harder than steel.

The fortress was a wound in the world—its walls layered thick with horror, each stone older than any of the imprisoned. Magic had failed here a thousand times, hope smothered beneath the boots of men who believed pain could drive the wild out of a witch. Elara drew a breath, but the air was thick with despair and the faint stench of burning hair. She pressed her palm to the cold of the bars, feeling a sick tremor rattle through her bones.

She forced herself onward, past a half-conscious boy who flinched from her shadow, past an ancient woman whose fingers twitched with the memory of spellwork, the skin raw where they had scraped at iron bands. She could not look away—not now, not ever again. Guilt gnawed at her. Foolish to imagine she had protected anyone with oaths. Her loyalty, she saw plainly now, meant nothing to men who relished suffering as a weapon. What were ancient laws worth, if they only kept her shackled to inaction?

A table stood to her right, stained red and bristling with the bone-white glare of surgical tools—hooks, razors, clamps twisted open wide. A scattering of shattered crystals glimmered weakly in the faint light, leaking dregs of what had once been power. Spell inhibitors carved with runes lay beside silk cords darkened by dried blood; beside them, enchanted gag-chains still hummed with residual silence. The threads of magic that wound through Elara seemed to snap tight, pain lancing up her arms as she clenched her hands. For a heartbeat, her resolve wavered. But the trembling of her hands steeled as she turned, signaling Rowan with a tight flick of two fingers.

Rowan met her gaze and moved to the first cell, lips working in quiet rhythm as pale blue sparks flickered between his knuckles. The tumblers of the lock clicked, ancient iron surrendering to stolen magic. Elara flinched as the groan of hinges scraped the hush, but forced herself to kneel beside a girl half slumped against the bars, eyes unfocused and bleeding magic from a wound at her neck. She pressed one hand gently to the girl's cheek, feeling the tremor, the fever afterwards, the uncoordinated reach for sanctuary.

"They'll come if we don't hurry," Rowan whispered, words dampened by the dread that filled the chamber.

"We free as many as we can. I'll get them out," Elara answered.

Across the opposite corridor, Kaelen's shadow slipped ahead, the glint of his daggers just visible as he crept toward the sound of boots. Elara strained to listen, catching the chill bite of Lord Dalen's voice cut through the corridor—a voice colder than splintered iron.

"Show no mercy. Use the prisoners as leverage. The rebellion will fail when they see their kin broken."

The words seared through her. If she had doubted before, she knew it now—there could be no peace, no safety, as long as men like Dalen commanded suffering.

Rowan hissed an incantation—sound and light merged, a cell swung open. The girl collapsed into Elara's arms, whimpering as she cradled the limp form, smoothing blood-matted hair from a battered brow. Elara whispered, "You're safe. I promise. We're leaving." But inside, the old shame gnawed; no promise felt strong enough.

A guttural cry erupted farther down the corridor—a sentry, discovering the breach. Bells peeled, metallic and furious, shivering through stone and flesh. Chaos blossomed as boots pounded on flagstones, steel screaming against scabbard.

Rowan shouted, "Guards!" as he tore open another cell. Elara's magic flared—earth answering her frantic pulse. A guard lunged, mace raised, and the torch flames twisted, lunging up in a shield that sent him reeling. She hauled the trembling girl upright, arm wrapped secure. The clamor grew, rough voices shouting as more doors banged open, footsteps closing with jarring finality.

"Go! To the archives!" she barked, pushing forward, Rowan at her side, Kaelen appearing out of shadow as the din mounted behind them. They surged toward a narrow stair. Elara's heart hammered against her ribs, breath sharp and wild, every sense straining. Rebellion was no longer an idea, nor duty— it was the only answer left.

At the locked door, Rowan's magic snapped. Elara spun to face the guards bearing down on them. With another desperate knot of power, she drove a gust of shuddering wind down the passage, scattering the armored men. Kaelen flung the door wide, Rowan reinforcing the frame with a shimmering barrier as they tumbled inside, slamming wood and iron behind them.

Bells tolled a wild litany and the fortress roared alive. In the sudden hush of the archive antechamber, pressed between fear and hope, Elara's trembling resolve crystallized into something unbroken at last.

Kaelen's palms pressed into a fine pelt of dust layered on ancient oak, the scent—dry, almost perfumed with the memory of old ink—thick in his throat. The archive's meager lanterns shed muted circles of light redolent of scorched brass and tallow, smoky shadows pooling between rows of ledgers. Somewhere overhead, iron hinges groaned. Kaelen's heartbeat hammered a pace beneath the thumps of distant boots. His fingers closed around the cracked hide of a tome, half-swallowed by cobwebs; the family sigil pressed in faded gold—a rampant hart entwined with delicate runes—sent a silent current through his skin, as if the ink itself remembered his touch.

He dragged the book into the lantern's circle. Dust flaked away in little stars. The others—Elara, Rowan, Lysandra—moved in the periphery, their breaths a rough, shared rhythm. Kaelen's world tunneled into the brittle crackle and the labyrinthine script that wound across vellum soft and graying with time. Light trembled on his knife-scarred knuckles as he turned pages, seeking a shape amid the maze of family names and court decrees, some etched in a hand so steady it seemed inhuman.

Beneath a cluster of pressed wildflowers, a thin document was sealed with the broken wax of his house. The words—To Aleron, Firstborn of House Aelthyr, by will of the Witch Council—caught his eye and would not let go. He tore the envelope, every movement rustling centuries into the present. The ink within had bronzed, the hand formal but smudged by haste. A pact, line after line, its power coiled like a sleeping serpent: that one heir, always, would bear the charge of guardianship and enforcer, their fate fused by law and blood to the oaths of the witches themselves.

The text burned through Kaelen's mind like acid. He saw in that curling script the weight given, generation by generation, as if his veins ran not only with human blood but old magic, sacred and perilous. His ancestors had stood in moonlit chambers with the Witch Council, trading freedom for a peace none could trust. Their line, marked to act as both shield and sledgehammer—enemies, sometimes, of those they longed to protect.

He passed the document to Elara. Her eyes devoured it in silence, the air between them fragile, pulsing. Her mouth parted in realization, her gaze steady and searching as if she saw, for the first time, not Kaelen the healer or rebel, but the inheritor of an unbreakable chain.

Something inside Kaelen twisted. The fortress was a living thing—the stone thick with the cries and secrets of centuries—but here, in this suspended moment, the world narrowed to the fragile parchment between their hands and the truth it unveiled. What was he if not a living instrument of this old, merciless bargain? He wanted to recoil from it, to refute the cruelty of binding one family's soul to another's survival, but beneath the grief was the flicker of a deeper meaning, the heady terror and possibility that his purpose was bound to hers, and to the fate of witches everywhere.

His thoughts pulled back through the tangled corridors of memory, past the shrouded faces at royal banquets, the way nobles turned their eyes away during witch trials, never thinking that the protector's burden meant infection—guilt, fear, and secret hope—passed down alongside privilege. The luxurious halls where he learned court etiquette were haunted, he now understood, by sacrifices unrecorded in any history book, the quiet magic that sometimes must have flickered at the edge of his vision, disguised as tradition and duty.

A crash echoed beyond the door. Boots approached, sharp and growing closer. Rowan's hands blazed with sigils, sweat on his brow as he layered spells across the wood. Lysandra, pale and panting, slid into the chamber—shoulder slicked with blood, garments torn, her eyes warning of disaster. Kaelen's grip on the document tightened, the fine parchment trembling between his fingers. Panic and clarity formed a razor edge; he slipped the document into his tunic, waving Rowan to release the barricade as Elara gathered the dazed, shuffling prisoners.

Elara's voice rose, low and swift. She sent a pulse into the foundations, each word weaving with ancient resonance. The wall behind them groaned and cracked, stones shivering apart to reveal a tunnel choked with rot and the stench of centuries-old water. Kaelen plunged after Elara, Lysandra at his heels, Rowan shoving weakened witches ahead as the cacophony behind them swelled—shouts and steel, cries that splintered the stone.

Cold, foul water clung to Kaelen's skin as he crawled, every scrape alive with the scent of mildew and iron. He tasted fear and hope at the same time—sour and sweet on his tongue—knowing each inch forward was a defiance etched across generations.

At last, the tunnel sloped upward, spitting them into a thicket of willows weeping into the pale dawn. The group slumped in the silvered grass, shivering, lungs sucking at mist that glimmered faintly with lingering enchantment. Kaelen met Elara's gaze, breathless, the broken dawn painting her face in shivering gold and shadow. Though past and present warred within him, though the burden of his lineage ached like an old wound, something unwavering filled his chest—a knowledge that whatever future waited, it would be shaped by the fragile, indelible bond they had forged and the pain and wonder of promise fulfilled and broken alike.

Chapter 15

The Cost of Magic

Mud sucked at Elara's knees as she toppled forward, her hands pressed against her chest. Pain prickled beneath her ribs—not a simple ache, but shards of fire threading through flesh and bone. She dragged in a ragged breath. The world warped: earth tilting, treetops spinning, color smearing into chaos. Swarming through her were fragments—Kaelen's voice whispering her name, a caress of terror, a memory of clanging metal, the lingering echo of that night when she had broken everything sacred. The oath's words spun around her mind, each syllable a blade across her skin. She shut her eyes, gritting her teeth. Her body hardly belonged to her now. Every pulse reminded her of the forbidden promise—its barbs anchoring themselves into her marrow, feeding on hope.

Somewhere ahead, Kaelen reeled against a lichen-scabbed beech. Blue fire coiled and burst out along his arms. His jaw clenched in a silent scream as magic convulsed in his veins, crackling violently before sputtering into mist. He heaved for air, slick with sweat. For a moment he was only a shadow shivering against the pale bark, terribly distant. Elara stared as the joining thread between them thrummed with his agony. She could taste the burn of it—something metallic on her tongue—and it made her stomach twist with cold dread.

She crawled through nettled leaves and sodden earth, her shaking fingers digging furrows in the muck. Reaching Kaelen, she slid her palm over the tremor of his hand. Relief traveled up her arm—a faint cool balm to the fever that raged within her. She bent her head closer and tried to steady the racing of her breath, willing some small comfort into the strange, flickering current that now bound them. Her own nerves sparked in sympathy, as if she were wound tight around the same invisible coil. When Kaelen's grip closed around her fingers, he was trembling, eyelids fluttering in half-conscious relief.

"Stay with me," she whispered. Voice or thought, she couldn't say. The tendril of her magic threaded softly beneath his skin, seeking the smallest foothold of calm.

His lips moved. "I'm here. I won't—" The word faded. He exhaled against her, his body straining for stillness.

They slumped together at the foot of the tree, finding what stability they could in its ancient roots. Elara leaned her head back against the mossy trunk. Breath mingled with the lingering chill of coming night. The hush of the forest pressed in, heavy as a secret. Kaelen reached to sweep sweat-damp hair from her brow. His hand lingered, a trembling brush, a fragile act meant to root them in the world. She managed a ghost of a smile, though her lips threatened to split into sobs instead.

"We'll figure it out," he said, too gentle. The words rose between them, weightless and unsure.

"We have to," she answered, but already the next burst of magic sizzled somewhere deep within Kaelen. He shuddered, his back arched, hands curled into the dead leaves. The wild light flickered orange

—then vanished—leaving the forest smelling faintly of burnt pine resin and damp earth.

Elara's chest hitched. She felt herself hollowing out, a gaping chasm where guilt and fear pooled. The power that had once obeyed her now moved with its own hunger, leeching out from both of them, never sated. Each time she used it—each desperate spell, each wild flare—she could feel it demanding payment in flesh and spirit. The truth trembled in her, bitter and crystalline: every healing came with a cost, every effort to keep Kaelen safe carved another fragment from her own life, or his.

Such a bond should have been a blessing. She had never imagined it might become a gnawing parasite, devouring both their futures. Sometimes she caught herself praying for oblivion, for their magic to simply wink out, releasing its grip. Other times, she saw only the horror—Kaelen convulsing in the dirt, burning away piece by piece until nothing living remained but the trace of her failure. Could she sever it? Or would their undoing unspool until they both were dust, their hearts extinguished in the same breath?

She squeezed Kaelen's hand tight, grounding herself in the press of wet bark and the heat of his palm. His skin was too warm, pulsing with feverish energy. The silence around them thickened, broken only by wind rattling through dead leaves. All the ordinary music of the woods—tree frogs, distant birds—had evaporated, as if the world itself held its breath.

She swallowed hard. "We don't have much time," she murmured. The words curled up and faded between them.

Kaelen's hand turned over in hers; his gaze flicked toward the sky and then back down to their interlaced fingers. Both of them knew—felt it in shudders and in the haunted rhythms of their magic —that every moment now ran thin, brittle as spun glass. She pressed her forehead to his shoulder, desperate to remember skin and breath and closeness.

For a heartbeat the world narrowed to the quiet ache of two bodies entwined by promise and peril, and the creeping certainty that if neither found a way to master what bound them, even this thin amber twilight would soon gutter and die.

Twilight spilled pale blue and gold across the glade, its hush broken only by the faint whisper of water against stones. Elara walked the bank with careful steps, her boots sinking into moss thick with the memory of rain. Bordering the stream, half-buried roots tangled in the earth, their gnarled fingers mirrored in the wavering surface below. She paused, staring at her reflection, drawn and uncertain, her amber eyes fractured by the current's gentle movement. A shiver wound up her spine. She heard her own voice—ghostly, ragged—echoing the words of the vow she had sworn when moonlight and desperation had bound her fate.

The water caught her features in a dozen shifting forms: witch, oath-breaker, savior, exile. She could not decide which mask belonged most to her. Kneeling, Elara pressed her knees into the dew-damp grass, feeling blades bend and cling. Her hands covered her face, blocking out the world, the scent of moss and loam rising up to cradle her grief. She let the tears slip hot across her cheeks, not even trying to silence the tremors in her breath. The chilling press of forbidden magic was with her always now, coiled behind her heart—a living brand. Each sob was a memory of what she had lost, what she could never return to: the quiet pride of lineage, the trust of the coven, the certainty in her own place among witches.

She mourned for the self that might have been— obedient, careful, untouched by the sting of rebellion. Yet all she could feel was the ache of having chosen otherwise, a fracture down the center of her soul. Memories pressed in: her mentor's voice, low and stern, repeating the lessons that once seemed unbreakable law. "The sacred oath is the marrow of our magic, Elara. To sunder it is to invite the unmaking of the self." She remembered the chill of those nights, the scrape of bark beneath her fingers as she traced runes into trunks, practicing the rituals that should have shielded her from the world's cruelty. But what shield could keep out the needs of a dying stranger? Was compassion itself a curse, or only the way she had wielded it?

Eyes closed, she heard again the crack of the spell shattering between her palms, the desperate plea in Kaelen's gaze as she defied every warning. Her chest tightened; she had become the cautionary tale elders whispered around midnight fires. The rules she had once clung to felt brittle and distant now. Part of her raged to turn back, to unmake the moment she offered mercy, to reclaim her name as something unstained. But behind her anger quivered doubt, shame, and a deep fear—fear that she was sliding toward something monstrous, her powers corroding from within.

She pressed a hand over her heart. Beneath skin and bone, the forbidden magic hummed—a restless thing, as much wound as lifeline. Her fingers curled into the wool of her cloak. Thoughts of Kaelen surfaced in her mind unbidden, vivid and sharp as the gold at dusk. His fear had burned through the bond only moments ago, mingling with her own. They were linked in pain and hope alike, and the strangest thing was how his gratitude, gentle and unfamiliar, still managed to reach her amid the storm.

A warmth flickered through her vision, a pulse of gold that glimmered in the spaces between her ribs, melting some small part of the gloom. Not forgiveness, perhaps, but the first hint that she was not wholly lost to herself. He needed her—not just as healer or protector, but as something more. If her life must be forever marked by exile, torn from all she had known, let it mean something beyond regret. Moving forward hurt, but the alternative—remaining mired in guilt and fear—felt worse.

She found herself wondering, if she survived this storm, what shape her life might take. Could the world bear a witch who broke her oaths and yet refused to be swallowed by ruin? Would she become legend or warning, the pioneer of a new kind of witchcraft, bonded not by blood rules but by the alchemy of mercy? She saw the stream wander on, carving new paths through old land—always changing, yet part of the same whole. She longed to believe that she, too, could adapt, forging a place somewhere between salvation and sacrifice.

Yet for every hope, shadows pressed in. If her power unraveled further, if Kaelen's life slipped through her grasp, nothing would remain but the ashes of her defiance. She pictured herself exiled, feared even by those she had long called sister. And still, the pulse of their bond was a lantern in the dark—a testament to what could grow from shattered vows. Was it possible that love, or something like it, could transform what tradition deemed unforgivable?

Raindrops began to peck at the stream, sending fresh distortions over her reflection. She wiped her face with trembling fingers and drew in a long, unsteady breath. The ache remained, but so too did

the impulse to rise, to move. Slowly, Elara sat
upright, the last light of dusk flickering in her eyes.
The glade felt changed, thinner and more honest, as
if her silent confessions had been accepted by the
ancient woods themselves. She did not know if she
belonged here, or anywhere, anymore—but she
would walk forward all the same.

Marek crouched beside the embers in the half-dark,
sharpening his dagger with a careful rasp-rasp of
metal on stone. Smoke curled into the rafters of the
Hearthstone Inn's safe room, the fire's heart
throwing an orange glow over the battered shelves
and stacked barrels. Shadows pooled in the corners
where the lamplight dared not reach; here, the air
carried the secrets of lost travelers and whispered
plans. The familiar metallic scrape steadied his
hands, the repetitive motion anchoring his mind even
as his gaze drifted to the far edge of the room.

Elara hunched over her bedroll, her elbows braced
against drawn knees, strands of dark hair glinting
with sweat. Across from her, Kaelen's breath came
too quick, his face gaunt beneath the flickering
firelight. Magic seemed to writhe just beneath his
skin, flickers of blue threatening to leap free. In their
shared silence, pain pressed down, heavy as sodden
wool, and Marek's jaw set with a sour ache. He
weighed the blade in his palm—useless for this kind
of wound. His mother's words looped through
memory: hurt, even when you can't heal, because
standing by and watching means you've chosen their
pain.

He set the dagger aside. "Let me see your hands."
His voice sounded softer than he'd intended, filtered
through exhaustion, cutting past the regret that had
carved lines into his face. Elara blinked up, glassy-
eyed; Kaelen only nodded, shoulders tense. Quietly,
Marek knelt beside Elara and unclasped the pouch at

his belt. The bitter root within smelled of earth and biting wind—it was the kind his mother had gathered long ago, when magic surged wild in border winters and nothing else could blunt the headaches that followed. "Chew this," he said, pressing the folded leather into her trembling palm. "Slowly. It dulls the backlash, helps the body remember itself when the magic pulls too hard. My mother used it for burns. And for heart troubles."

He watched Elara hesitate—who could blame her?—then raise it to her lips without a word. Marek crouched until he met Kaelen's hooded gaze. "There's an old trick from my village," he said, wrapping a damp strip of cloth around Kaelen's wrist with surgeon's hands, "when you can't stop the shake in your bones. You breathe with the wind—long in, slow out—let your mind ride it while the cloth pulls the wildness down to your skin and out." The gesture was awkward, comforting and clinical all at once, but Kaelen let himself be guided. The scent of wet linen and root mingled with the acrid ghost of burned magic, thick as a storm coming in off the marsh.

In Marek's mind, old doubts jostled for air. He'd carried the prejudices of his childhood for years—border fears of witches whose spells could raze crops or sour milk, whose anger smoldered like peat underground. But there was nothing monstrous in the way Elara looked at Kaelen, nothing in Kaelen's steadying hand as he braced Elara's shoulder. What he saw was a different kind of danger: that those who loved too fiercely might burn together rather than let go.

He cleared his throat, forcing a wry note into his voice. "You two have a knack for trouble," Marek said, managing what might pass for a smile in better weather. "Back home they'd have called it a curse—but my mother always said curses were just problems you refused to work at." The fire snapped, sending sparks spiraling toward the ceiling. Marek used the lull to prod another log into place, watching Elara's eyes soften and Kaelen's lips curve faintly upward.

"You think a root can save us from ourselves?" Elara asked, a tremble giving way to a thread of humor.

Marek shrugged. "If it makes you spit and curse and forget the ache for a minute, that's something."

Kaelen's voice was low, threaded with weariness: "And if the magic refuses to be tamed by tricks and bitter roots?"

"Then we do what we can," Marek replied. "Survive the night and try again at dawn."

The walls between them, built by suspicion and necessity, felt thinner now—a hair's breadth between certainty and chance. Marek shifted to sit cross-legged, laying his battered boots against the cold flagstone. He told a story of the year frost took his brother's hand—a fire gone wild, the healer's desperation—and how they'd learned to cover wounds with laughter even when the skin stung raw. His memories tasted of smoke and loss, but in sharing them, Marek sensed a thread of connection knitting itself through the battered trio.

Elara laughed, a startled, fleeting sound, and Kaelen's reply was a smile hidden at the corner of his mouth. For a heartbeat in the hush, Marek allowed himself to hope this strange alliance might become more than pain held in common. He gathered broth from the hearth, pouring the steaming, spiced liquid into battered cups, the warmth promising something gentle. "Drink. I'll keep watch," he said, voice half a vow.

They huddled together, shoulders close, their eyes growing heavy beneath the crackle of the fire, and

Marek resolved—as sleep claimed them—that he would not let the night have them, not while breath and bone endured.

Elara leaned back, her shoulder blades settling against the cracked timber wall, and the frail bones of the Hearthstone Inn embraced her with their familiar creak. The hidden quarters smelled of old wood, lavender sachets tucked in dark corners, and the thick, earthy comfort of burning peat. Candlelight spilled across her face, flickering each time the wind rattled the distant shutters. She drew her knees up, warm under the coarse woolen shawl, the magic in her chest humming steady as a heartbeat—faint, but insistently alive.

Marek pushed through the narrow gap—heavier tonight with his arms full of rough-woven blankets. The door whispered shut behind him, muting the muffled raucousness from the world outside these walls. He set the pile on the cot and spared Elara a crooked smile, the shadows softening the lines of exhaustion wearing at the corners of his eyes. "You two planning to freeze before the witch hunters even have a chance?" His voice, gruff beneath its care, tugged a hesitant smile from her. He tossed the top blanket toward Kaelen, who caught it, a half-smile curving his lips.

Kaelen sat by the makeshift window, one foot braced on the rickety stool, city lights winking through aged glass smudged with rain. "I shouldn't complain about the cold after the haunted library of Alderborn," he said, as he wrapped the blanket around his shoulders. "The place was rumored to devour any child who mispronounced a spell. I... may have said 'luminae' instead of 'luminare,' and the shelves rained forty dust-drenched tomes on my head. The librarian was not amused."

Marek let out a low chuckle. "Serves you right. That's why I never picked up magic—stick to metal and muscle. Fewer mishaps." He slid down to the floor, stretching his weary legs, then tossed a glance at Elara. "Go on, Elara. You must have one story that trumps slippery books?"

Her cheeks warmed in the candlelight. "Only one?" She cleared her throat, found herself smiling at the memory drawn from some safer, more innocent past. "There was a lesson in water-shaping when I was twelve. My mentor warned—never blend emotions with a calling spell. I ignored her. The pond erupted. Except the fish came up bound in tiny ice spheres... for nearly an hour. We spent the morning thawing out frogs and apologizing to the sprites." Kaelen's laughter loosened the stitch beneath her ribs.

The tension curled between them all, slowly unwinding as the laughter faded. Kaelen's hand found hers—just the faintest touch, fingers brushing, calloused skin warm against her chilled knuckles. She wrapped the woolen shawl wider around them both, letting Kaelen's pulse and the quiet thrum of their linked magic form a fragile cocoon. The bond's glow, ever restless, had slipped into a tranquil hush, humming where their hands met. The fear lodged behind her eyes softened, if only for a breath.

They let the evening stretch thin, small comforts weaving themselves into the silence. Marek divided the cooled broth, passing it over with a mumbled warning about the bitterness—Elara found herself savoring the earthy taste despite it, the heat spreading down her arms. Outside, rain tapped at the glass, tracing latticed rivers down the panes; the sound was hypnotic, a lullaby against the trembling world beyond the false wall. The magical wards—serpentine and unseen—tingled faintly, holding danger at bay. For this hour, at least, the world's claws seemed blunted.

Elara's gaze drifted between Marek and Kaelen—the swordsman's rough hands cradling his cup, Kaelen's quiet smile, shuttered but sincere. A thought surfaced unbidden: That the world could be made new by moments such as these—not by thunderous victories or ancient magics, but by the knotted blanket between friends, laughter shared in the dark, the simple act of safeguarding one another. She dared, as she listened to Kaelen describe the crackling fire-warded corridors of his boyhood home, to imagine a time when the Hearthstone Inn's hidden chamber would not be a cell—when such warmth might blaze openly, and not as fugitive embers smothered by fear.

She pictured—though the notion felt as fragile as dandelion fluff—a future where witches might gather at any table they chose, where the sharp edges of distrust dulled to understanding. In this vision, the inn's walls became not barriers but pillars for rebuilding trust, for laughter ringing loud and free, for bonds blessed by the open air. The pain in her chest, old guilt and new longing entwined, twisted sharply then softened: a wish so dangerous she could only cradle it in the secret corners of her spirit.

Yet in the same motion, anxiety sharpened her senses, tensing the cords in her arms. It would be folly to forget—peace here was only the hush before storm; even now, Marek's eyes flicked to the door every so often, Kaelen's grip unconsciously tightening when distant thunder rolled. Elara grappled with the swell and pull within—relief braided with fear, desire for belonging clashing with instinct to flee. Was it wrong, she wondered, to wish for this night to stretch longer? Was daring to hope an act of defiance unto itself?

She pressed closer to Kaelen's side, silent vow shimmering beneath her skin: She would protect this haven, however fleeting, as fiercely as she could, and guard the peace found in simple togetherness, even while bracing for the next shadow.

She blew out the candle. Darkness drew close, soft and near as breath. The three of them settled back, listening to the quiet drip of rain, the far-off thunder rumbling—a lull that, for now, was nearly enough.

Chapter 16

The King's Decree

Gilt-edged light slid through stained windows and carved banners of red and gold over the gleaming council chamber. The air here always seemed thick with anticipation—silk shoes on lacquered floor, the rustle of embroidered linen, the brittle clash of expectation set against dread. Courtiers gathered in grave clusters beneath woven banners emblazoned with the rearing stag, a symbol that once promised plenty, now shadowed by the rumors curling through every alley and hovel of the Capital. Each advisor's brow was drawn; their glances gathered and scattered, congealing into knots of old rivalries and new fears. From the far end, Lord Dalen's voice rang out—sonorous, cold, beloved by those who feared the shadows more than the loss of freedom—while Lady Miren's silver rings caught the morning as she gestured sharply, her argument braided with warning and empathy.

At the heart of this storm, King Varric took his place on the throne. His fingers curled over the dark mahogany arms, the wood sunken and smooth where generations of monarchs had strained under decisions that altered fates. He let his gaze drift over the room, past Lord Dalen's pale, angular profile—marked by the wolf tattoo curling along one thick forearm—to Lady Miren's ageless steadiness. Around them, layered in whispers and sideward glances, the structure of the kingdom's court unfurled: a lattice of obligation and ambition. Conservative nobles, their fortunes tied to the memory of old wars and ancient pacts, pressed ever tighter behind Dalen, insistent that iron and flame were all that stood between civilization and chaos. Across the open parquet, reformists like Miren moved quietly, intent on mending the torn seams between palace halls and city streets, the world outside hungering for certainty.

How fragile it all was, Varric knew. At the city's core, he saw the council not as a tree but a bramble—each thorn a vote won through dinners, debts, or veiled threats, each branch leaning with the wind but refusing to snap. Below the council chamber's windows, unrest flowed like a fever, fevered by rumors of forbidden fires and faces glimpsed in moonlight. The forbidden magic radiating from Elara and Kaelen's bond—whispered among bakers, muttered in soldiers' barracks, suspected in every shifting shadow—was not just an aberration but a pebble flung into a lake whose surface had already trembled. The capital thrived only so long as the court hid its cracks behind the gleam of well-tended armor and the scent of rosewater.

Lord Dalen's voice cut through the din. "Your Majesty, panic clutches the guard. Shopkeepers lock their doors by midday. Mothers speak of their children's blood running black with witchcraft. You must be decisive. Patrols must double. The law must be sharpened. Fear spreads faster than any pox—let us fetch fire before it consumes every household."

He stood framed by the sigils, eyes pale as slate. "If we do nothing, every peasant in the countryside will learn to shelter witches beneath their floorboards. The oath was broken—once that wall is breached, what will hold back the flood?"

Across from him, Lady Miren's fingertips glittered with rings and urgency. "My lord, you court rebellion. The city teeters not merely due to magic, but the rumor of magic. The last time such decrees were signed we saw three winters' worth of riots and market squares drowned in blood. I beg caution. We cannot hang suspicion in every doorway and expect peace by morning."

Varric watched the play of fear and calculation across each face. Dalen sought order, but his was the order of locked doors and silent nights. Miren reached for peace, but hers leaned on brittle trust. Varric's own father—whose scar he carried, whose principles he inherited—had taught him: the capital is a tapestry woven from a thousand brittle threads. Strain too hard and it tears; too soft, and rot spreads unseen.

He raised his hand. Conversation shattered with the grace of fine porcelain. His voice, burnished by hours of silent considerations, filled the hush. "I have seen what comes when fire is met with fire. I have buried too many sons of this kingdom beneath banners meant to shield them. And yet, to do nothing is to open the gate to chaos." He pressed his palm over the sealed document at his knee—its crimson wax still marred by the signet's weight. What price, to preserve the heart of a kingdom already wounded by suspicion and loss?

Memories pulsed behind his words—winters illuminated by torches held not in welcome, but warning; the loss of his father in a silent corridor, the taste of regret as bitter now as it was then. In the eyes of these counselors, he saw his own haunted hope: a longing not merely for power, but the delicate chance to love and be loved by a nation that could, perhaps, one day learn gentleness over cruelty.

"The consequences of either extreme—violence or inaction—will be felt not only in these halls, but in every cradle and every grave," he said, voice soft as silk and firm as the stone beneath the city. "We seek a path that preserves order without surrendering our humanity."

His decision, like so many before, would be measured in the silence on the streets and the heaviness in his heart. The divided council murmured as he signaled his steward. Thunder grumbled over the rooftops, hinting just beyond the glass at storms too great for any man to hold back. Varric paused at the threshold, his silhouette caught between velvet and rain, searching the city lights for some sign that compassion might yet outlast fear.

A hollow hush clung to the crypt beneath the market square, pierced only by the scrape of boots on stone as the witch envoy led her measured descent. Candlelight trembled on ancient walls lined by soot, glinting off specks of mica and the faded sigils of some long-forgotten burial. Cloaks whispered—a blue-edged merchant's mantle, a noble's gold-threaded cape, and her own emerald-green hood veiling her face. All gestures here were deliberate: the merchant tapped fingers thrice on the table in silent greeting, while the noble let a silver ring flash, signaling recognition. She nodded to each with just enough deference, masking the tension corroding dry air.

Wax-sealed notes and hand-inked maps cluttered the battered wood table. The merchant, voice cool as a stream, opened the dance. "Our guild keeps the spice routes clear and the granaries full. Prosperity rests on stability. If leniency in taxes and tariffs can be assured, we see no reason to hinder your interests—provided riots do not close the streets."

The envoy listened, letting the pause hang. Words in crypt meetings tasted of old fruit: sweet, ripe with promise, rotted with threat. She caught the noble's sidelong glance, his thumb idly tracing the stitched crest of a rose on his doublet.

"My family maintains loyalty in the western wards," he murmured as if reciting a lover's secret. "Councillor votes don't come free. I want stewardship over the northern forges, should this decree pass. Favor bought once can be bought anew."

At last her chance to bargain. She pushed a note across the table, wax stamp gleaming with the subtle emblem of witchkind—a feather and flame entwined. "All territory and profit are windblown if a witch's blood stains half the city," she said softly. "I propose the council offer safe passage for our siblings—no trials, no lists. Keep our kin from the fire, and your routes and forges will not burn in turn."

The merchant's eyes narrowed above his veil. The noble's lips twitched, hungry as a moth by candle. Everything in this crypt was a transaction dressed as devotion. The envoy kept her voice honey-smooth, despite the memory of watching a friend's hands shake as city guards dragged him from a cellar stair.

Their bargains were rehearsal for the greater theater unfurling above. She sensed both allies' patience and hidden knives: the merchant's smile a folded threat, the noble's promises spun tight as a snare. Allies for an hour, perhaps a day. Some had signed away kin before, for fewer coins than what glinted now on the table. She weighed her own tongue, refusing urgency. Her price must seem fair, but not desperate. Tonight, necessity had its own seduction.

"My informants say Elara's name falls on every whispered tongue," the envoy continued, feeling the words as pebbles dropped into a still pool. "To some, she is hope—a lantern in the dusk. To others, she is the lightning inviting the ash. If King Varric's hand wavers, the city will not wait for morning to choose sides."

A silence, scented with tallow and stone-damp earth, pressed by the thrum of unspoken longing for safety, for a future wrested from fate's closed fist. She watched their faces, searching for cracks in calculated façades.

"Her—sacrifice, her defiance—has made her a living promise. That's a dangerous thing. If she falls, so do our chances to bargain. If she rises, the blade swings sharper for us all. You—" Her gaze flicked between merchant and noble, "must decide if your futures are tied to hers, or if you'll help sharpen the axe raised for her."

The rebel leader rustled parchment pamphlets, edges still tacky with blue paint. "We'll fan the flames where we can," he said, eyes skipping from face to face. "In the Guildhall hallways. In the night markets. I'll plant word of secret amnesty, or riots if it's false. Divisions grow fertile when watered with rumor."

"You'll follow our instructions?" The noble's brow arched.

"You'll see them in the morning," the rebel said. His fingers drummed against candlelight. "But be wary, both of you. A mob turns on its shepherd, and royal coin spends as well as gold for anyone who lives in shadow."

The envoy folded her hands atop a note bearing a single name in careful script—Elara, again and again, curling through her mind like a lover's whispered endearment or a curse. The city's fate, the rebellion's hope, pressed into those letters, fragile beneath stone and oath. She found herself wondering—if Elara survived, would witches have more to fear from their rescuers, or their would-be saviors? If Varric handed compromise in the square above, would it bring dawn or another night's reprieve doomed to shatter?

Candles guttered as coded instructions flickered between hands. The envoy pressed a signet to a sheet marked with owl feathers—orders to sanctuaries, links in a fragile chain. She wished briefly for the comfort of trust, of a cause undivided, but alliances were currency here. Only longing and calculation, entwined in fleeting accord, held them together.

One by one, shadows rose. The merchant snuffed his candle, gliding away with the promise of anonymous coin. The noble draped his cloak, vanishing into a tunnel of wet stone. The envoy gathered the remaining notes, heart thumping. Her faction's cause moved tonight not on faith, but on careful bargains, weighed between hope for freedom and fear of betrayal.

She slipped into the labyrinth, footsteps echoing with all she dared risk, all she longed to save, all she feared would be lost if Elara's hope caught flame or drowned in the deep, silent dark.

Elara drifted through the bright, bruised veins of the Capital City, the crowds so thick and loud she could feel the weight of bodies pushing against her magic. Sunlight slanted between gabled roofs and painted banners, but in her shaking hands the chill of autumn clung, insistent and sour. Every sense sharpened. The market sang with ripeness and risk— vendors hawked scarlet apples in piled heaps, their waxy skins reflecting crimson onto the cobbles; raw honey glistened in glass jars, their golden viscosity tempting and cloying all at once. Behind every offer, every smile, she glimpsed the jaws of a city that would devour her without even the courtesy of bitterness.

She pressed her hood lower until the rough wool scratched her brow. With each step, a current of unease tugged at her. The pulse of the broken oath thudded in her wrist, a private drumbeat beneath the lamb's bleat and the click of the money-changer's tokens. A man with a pale, narrow face—was he a baker's assistant or a city informer?—kept reappearing behind barrels and between a pair of bickering fishwives. The second time their eyes caught, the world seemed to narrow on the silver flash of his signet. Her heart ratcheted; elbows tight, she eased toward the gatehouse, careful not to trip on a cabbage leaf or let her urgency betray her.

There was no safety in movement, only the illusion. The city had become a snare of eyes and whispered names: witch, oathbreaker, traitor. Sometimes she imagined hands closing around her shoulder, or heard the scrape of armored boots just beyond a cluster of costermongers, and every nerve in her body threatened to burn through her disguise. She paused near a barrel of salt, inhaling the briny tang, fighting to calm her breath. In the aftermath of breaking the oath, every shadow grew teeth.

The pressure of expectation pressed through her cloak far heavier than any autumn chill. She saw herself reflected in the metal rim of a lantern— features distorted, eyes ringed dark with the weight of her own decisions. Was she paranoid, or could someone truly read her crimes in the way she gathered her skirts, or how she declined an apple with a murmured, "Not today"? Did the world sense how badly she wished to disappear, to be just another woman trading coins and once-distant dreams for bread?

Kaelen skirted peril with less disguise. The streets pressed close to the palace library, all cold facades and hawk-eyed guards with swords polished bright as moonlit bone. Elara kept the library façade in her periphery as she slipped closer, watching from behind a cart of dried herbs. Kaelen waited with too much stillness outside its columned entrance, a charcoal travel cloak disguising his fine bearing, the hood casting his features in unreliable shade. She watched as a palace guard in black armor moved in. The steel at his hip glinted. There was an exchange— quick words lost to the city's clamor, a display of a folded pass, the guard's suspicion as taut as a drawn bowstring. The moment Kaelen's accent caught on a syllable, she saw the guard's hand drift to the sword hilt. Kaelen kept his chin steady, a slight tilt of arrogance Elara recognized. The guard did not yield.

Elara turned away, blood roaring in her ears. She had her own watchers to evade. The market's aromas— roasted walnuts, yeast, a faint ribbon of lavender from a perfumer's cart—were no kindness now, just further proof that every sense could betray her. In a city smelling of hot stone, sweat, and cinnamon, it was easy to believe she was being hunted by scent alone.

She ducked through an arch into a quiet lane, letting the city's frenzy narrow to the muffled thrum of her own pulse. There, behind a shuttered spice shop, Kaelen appeared—his cloak drawn close, face slack with tension. They met as if guided by hunger more than planning, eyes darting for threats even now.

"You saw him too? The pale one by the orchard sellers," she whispered, glancing toward the alley's mouth. Her voice scratched, half wind, half invocation. "He's been circling me since dawn."

"I know. The city's crawling with new 'watchers' today. I barely talked my way past one outside the library. Your name comes up now, even in rumors no one dares voice," Kaelen replied, voice pitched low, back pressed to the damp stone.

"I feel like every time I breathe, someone marks it down for the next patrol," she said, hands flexing as though something wild threatened to break through skin. "Lysandra needs to send word. We don't know how safe our people are—or if anyone's still listening."

"We can't stop searching for leverage," he countered. "If we lose one more ally in council, this city becomes a noose. We split. You take the scribe by the aqueduct. I'll try for the cobbler's contact near the wall."

She hesitated. "Keep sharp. They're more ruthless than before. If you sense anything—"

"I'll vanish. You do the same," he said, the briefest smile flickering—an old promise, renewed. They touched hands for a moment, fingers careful not to linger, as if affection itself were culpable.

" We'll meet at dusk. If not, you run," she murmured.

Their hands slid apart, leaving a warmth that trailed up Elara's arm even as the city pressed colder around her. Her heart stuttered with longing and reluctance. She moved first, melting into the alley's dusk; Kaelen vanished in the other direction, their parting shadowed in caution and unvoiced pleas.

Doubt tailed her every stride. Could all this dread be trusted—a sign of real danger, or merely the inevitable corrosion of hope under so much fear? Even with Kaelen's whispered vow, the city felt stacked against her, every stone set by someone who would see witches driven into dust. She moved with her head down, heart armored in brittle resolve, but the ache in her chest reminded her that trust, even now, was a dangerous form of faith.

As lanterns flickered on and the streets shifted toward curfew's hush, Elara pressed herself into the shadow outside a scribe's house. Night fell slow and absolute, blurring the chasing outlines of spies and guards alike. In her part of the city, every footprint was an accusation, every muted cry a summons. She waited, nerves set on a blade's edge, straining for the smallest reassurance—a glint of Kaelen's cloak, or the silence that meant, this hour at least, they remained unbroken.

King Varric stepped from the shadowed colonnade and out onto the stone balcony, the wet gold of dusk pinning the city's breathless anticipation to the flagstones below. The main square teemed with bodies pressed shoulder-to-shoulder: merchants in their russet and blue, noblewomen clutching silver-threaded shawls, the ragged and the righteous encircled by a ring of torch-bearing royal guards. The columns of light from above flickered against faces upturned in hope, suspicion, and dread. In their midst, King Varric tasted the city's fear—the thin tang of sweat and something older, more animal, that shuddered at the edge of order. The wind teased the silks at his throat, curling in with the smell of coming storm and iron.

He stood at the rail, his back as rigid as the carved mahogany of his throne, and drew the parchment from its black silk tube. The wax seal caught the last daylight, crimson and intact. Far below, a young girl hoisted onto her father's shoulders squinted with a stubborn faith he did not deserve. He inhaled, the air as heavy as an unspoken vow. Every word about to leave his lips would be carved into the bones of the kingdom.

His voice rang, steady and sonorous, through the hush. "By decree of the Crown, for the peace and endurance of this realm—" As he continued, a tension settled, the crowd held in thrall by the shape of fate. Each phrase—registration of magic-wielders, oaths taken anew, conditional mercy for those who submit—fell into their midst like stones into a troubled pond. Not even the banners stirred. Somewhere in the crowd, Lord Dalen's presence cast a shadow colder than the stone beneath Varric's boots.

He read on, forcing his tongue not to trip, refusing to allow even the finest tremor to betray him. Conditional amnesty. Oversight. A path for witches both chained and freed, if they surrendered to his authority. The murmurs rippled—a sharp, rising sound this time—and he caught, even at this height, the flick of restraint in the guards' knuckles curling on shield brims.

Beyond the sea of faces, the city pulsed with memories of last winter's riots—merchants with their stalls overturned, little fires gnawing their way up alley walls. The magic, newly ungoverned, had sent nightmares through every corridor of power. He remembered Lady Miren's quiet voice over council tea: "Bend too far, Your Majesty, and you will not shield anyone from the wind." But crack down, as Dalen once whispered, and the wind must break or rend.

Watching the faces—so many more lives than one mind could ever hold—Varric imagined futures unfolding in bright, bloodstained banners. Would the witches see this as a door or a trap? Voices split the hush. Some cheered the promise of law, of hard borders that might restore sleep. Others sobbed or struck out, violence blooming as a young witch and a merchant's son collided near the old fountain, their struggle swallowed by armed guards and the thunderous leaps of fear.

Varric could not let his hands betray him. But beneath the ceremonial rings his skin was cold, blood rushing against the dam of old sorrow. He wondered —could there ever be a middle path where no one's child vanished at dusk, unaccounted for? Yet the city demanded decisions cut clear as glass; every compromise an invitation for fracture. Was this decree mercy, weakness, or simply a pause before the next blade descended?

He remembered his father's council: mercy is the most dangerous gamble, for those spared will never forget the hand at their throat. But sometimes, mercy was all that stood between a ruler and the ashes of his own making. If Dalen pressed harder, if the rebels wove truth and lies into proof of betrayal— the streets could run wild. The stones would remember whose blood stained them.

Inside, he ached for council, for a friend—a love, even, to share the weight pressing his heart into quiet desperation. But the throne, carved with all the promises of his forebears, permitted no such frailty. He must wear the iron mask, even as the world shifted beneath him.

Somewhere in the city's winding maze, he knew his decree was already shifting destinies. In a cramped attic, lamplight trembled on Elara's face as she bent to read Marek's message, Kaelen's shadow straining to interpret what the parchment did not say: that amnesty bought at the price of an oath could yet become a fresh chain, soft and cold. Varric imagined them—witch and stranger—bound together beneath the storm he had summoned, both their lives balanced on the blade of a word.

Thunder boomed, rolling down from the palace roof to the awnings in the square. As Varric receded from the balcony, rain fell in thick, metallic sheets, scattering crowds whose hope and anger left strange music behind. For one brief moment, he looked out over the torchlit city—wishing, with a sorrow that tasted almost sweet, that any decree could assure peace. But tomorrow would dawn on a kingdom divided, and he, the one who had chosen this path, would walk alone beneath its storm.

Chapter 17

Under the Shadowed Wood

Elara slipped from the faint, mossy path, her palm trailing along velvety bark. The forest pressed close with predawn quiet, each step into its depths loosening her shoulders, grounding her in the old hushes of the Shadowed Wood. She moved around tangled roots and low boulders dressed in lichen-webs, careful not to snap a twig or stir a startled thrush. Cool bracken brushed her calves, damp in the blue-gray gloom. The world beyond—the mutter of Rowan's sharp laughter, the dry cough of Lysandra's fire—fell away, replaced by the pulse of hidden rivers, the gradual brightening east, the way the air itself vibrated with magic's invisible promise.

Here, sanctuary felt ancient and secretive—a cradle for every anxious breath and lingering doubt that clung to her since their escape from the marsh. She let herself slow, attention falling inward. Beneath her ribs, an ache laced with longing: for solace, for clarity, for a sense of belonging wrenched apart by broken oaths and forbidden bonds. She pressed her fingers against the rough trunk of a birch and listened, as she had years ago, before exile had a name. Only the forest's pulse welcomed her fully, unjudging, unafraid.

The memory of childhood ritual—a coil of thyme, the smell of new rain—rose there in her mind. Elara recalled the reckless delight of power uncorked, before grief and duty carved their silent rules. Her teachers had spoken of risk and purity, that elemental magic demanded everything and returned nothing except, if one was lucky, a fleeting sense of peace. Despite all she had lost—parents, kin, and even the right to her own name in the wider realm— the old words hummed behind her teeth, promising anchorage now as the world threatened war.

She found her clearing—a hollow cove beneath a lattice of arching cedar and towering elms. Damp, fragrant earth pressed against her knees as she knelt in the spill of uncertain sunlight, the sky above paling to honey and grey. From beneath her hands, grit and moss and rooted secrets answered her call. She spoke in whispers, syllables seldom uttered since the night she broke her oath for Kaelen.

In the hush, she felt the soil flex and power roil beneath her skin. The spirits came gently at first: earth's fecund hush rising to greet her palms; wind tumbling soft ribbons through the glade, spinning her cropped hair about her cheeks; a sleeping glitter beneath roots—fire held like breath in coals waiting for her trust; the distant gurgle of water slipping from a spring, veiled in ferns, threading cool promise through her spine.

Colors unspooled across her vision. The forest pulse quickened with each flicker of her will. A soft blue shimmer circled her wrists—water's laughter. Emerald and umber swirled from fallen leaves— earth's old patience. Gold flared—fire's warmth gathering under flesh, and silver danced in spinning motes—wind playing with her heartbeat's tempo. The aura built around her, prickle and comfort layered, until she was properly herself—more than exile, more than oathbreaker, more than what the kingdom saw.

Beneath the glowing hush, memories darted: her first lesson grasping the difference between asking and commanding elemental spirits; the hot flush of shame after a failed incantation singed her brow; the cool, damp hand of her mother guiding her away from fear. Yet those moments were always followed by another—a council elder's disappointment, the hush following her father's death, friends who disappeared into cages or the earth itself. Still, ritual offered what nothing else could—an unbroken circle, some ancient thread she could always follow back through doubt and loss.

The forest shivered. Birds ceased their song, a warning hidden in the sudden silence. Wind chased through the highest limbs, lashing cool air against Elara's cheeks. Beneath her, the ground thrummed. Danger, the old warning sang, quickening her pulse with anxious certainty that even here, somewhere sacred, the world pressed in with greedy fingers.

She held steady, calling the energies closer, letting go of the urge to flinch away. The magic roared through her now—a wild tide blazing from earth to sky, each element braided into strength. Warmth radiated from her chest to fist, a brightening so intense she nearly wept with relief. The hush filled her limbs, her senses alive to every shift in the wind, every subtle crackle beneath the surface. She had come into the forest as a woman uncertain, battered by guilt and the pressure of betrayal; she rose now, suffused with purpose.

Elara breathed in slowly and opened her eyes. Every color in the dawn seemed turned toward her—muted sapphire, deepest emerald, rose-gold veins slicing the sky between the leaves. Her aura burned just visible, soft embers flickering about her head and shoulders. She found her thoughts steadier: strength was not without fear, but it was hers, rebuilt day by day from these rituals, these old soft invocations.

"Spirit of ash—do you feel how the air listens for us now?"

"If I told you I did, I'd be lying. The forest's on edge. But it remembers you, Elara."

She offered a small, wry smile, her palm still pressed to the sun-dappled loam. "I suppose we're both learning how to remember. Just let me linger a moment longer."

"Stay as long as you need. The others will wait."

The breeze shifted, sweeter now, and she let herself cradle the warmth and certainty forged from gathering the old magics—knowing dawn's hush would wane, and the hunger of the world lay just beyond the roots and thorns. For now, she stood taller and turned her gaze toward the paling sky, ready.

The late afternoon sun caught between the tangled branches above, breaking into pale golds and cool blues that swept the Hearthstone clearing. Elara watched its play across the mossy ground as Lysandra slipped into view, parting a willow's veiled curtain. Drops of dew glistened on Lysandra's weathered cloak, catching faint glimmers of what little warmth the day still promised. The hush of the sanctuary pressed in, the kind of hush that came after hard news—she didn't need Lysandra's urgent step to know the world beyond the wards had shifted once again.

Lysandra's voice was quiet, precise, as she stepped closer. "Dalen's sent more patrols beyond the eastern hills—double what it was last moon. The king's new decree has the nobles in disarray. No one trusts their shadow." She brushed damp hair from her brow with fingers that didn't quite conceal a tremor. The air between them—normally filled with old, easy camaraderie—held the careful distance of people who had seen too many friends betrayed. Elara searched Lysandra's eyes, finding only measured concern, never the old assurance that everything could be fixed if they just worked together.

Before Elara could muster response, Rowan burst into the clearing in a tumble of energy. Twigs crowned her wild black hair, and streaks of mud cut up the leather of her boots. In Rowan's hands was a bulging, battered satchel, which she let fall at their feet with theatrical flourish.

"Brought a gift," Rowan announced, lips split in a grin edged with both mischief and exhaustion. "King's men are getting sloppy—picked these up from an 'expendable asset' who really ought to find quieter meeting spots."

A few stolen leaves drifted down as she shook herself free of the woods, plopping beside the smoldering campfire. The satchel gaped open, revealing intelligence papers stamped with the same seal that had haunted Elara's dreams for weeks: the wolf's head emblem of Lord Dalen's private guard.

The familiar fire crackle and Rowan's brash humor could not entirely banish the ache tightening through Elara's shoulders. She met Rowan's bright gaze with a tension she tried to mask, managing, "Let's hope you weren't followed. If these aren't useless decoys, they'll try harder next time." She tried for levity, but weariness sapped her edge.

"Please," Rowan scoffed. "If they knew half as much as they pretended, we wouldn't have made it through the marsh last week."

Lysandra sat with folded knees, staring into the faintly blue-tinged coals, her hand resting atop the birch bark she often used for sketching field notes.

The Witch's Forbidden Promise

The old rhythm of their council might have been comforting once. Now every gesture felt measured, every word weighed. Their circle had been tested too many times: allies turned informants, defenders gone missing. Now, even trust was given in rationed, careful offers.

Rowan ran fingers through her tangled hair as she looked at Lysandra. "Heard the eastern post has been compromised?" Her tone was teasing, but Elara saw the searching glint beneath the words, the way Rowan's shoulders stayed half-tensed, uncertain of welcome.

Lysandra's reply was mild but sharp at the edges. "I heard. We lost the old contact routes. And if Dalen's doubled his men, we'll lose more if we're not cautious—especially now, with the king's politics turning colder."

Elara's head throbbed. The magic she'd gathered that morning simmered deep in her blood still— warm, yet restless. The temptation to trust in her newfound strength warred with the exhaustion heavy in her joints. The bond with Kaelen was a constant presence, invisible and strangely tender, yet she feared what would happen if her resolve faltered for even a moment. Nothing in the old teachings had prepared her for this kind of vulnerability.

She gathered her knees in, arms tight to her chest. "None of this would be enough," she said, voice low, "if we can't hold the wards. The magic from this morning feels... sharper than before, but also more frayed." She didn't say broken, though it trembled at the back of her throat. "Tell me I'm not the only one who questions if we're ready."

The fire's heat pulsed across her hands, half-warming, half-mocking. Rowan tossed a pebble into the coals, the ember flare catching briefly in her eyes. "Ready or not, they won't wait. I say we take the fight to their scouts. Had an idea—moves through the old badger trails, flare up a false ward and lead them off course. If Dalen chokes on his own traps, it'll be thanks to me."

Lysandra smoothed the birch bark on her lap, drawing rough lines with the edge of a charcoal stub. "We need fallback routes. If the sanctuary's breached, we guide the younger witches out southwest—here, along the river bend."

Elara watched the pair—the familiar push-pull of Rowan's reckless bravado and Lysandra's structured caution. In their faces she could read the residue of old wounds, the new lines of suspicion and fatigue. Yet beneath it, there lingered the old faith too: the kind that had seen them through narrow woods dusted with fear.

A hush settled in with dusk. Elara pressed her hands over Rowan's and Lysandra's, drawing them close, seeking the silent pledge that lived between old friends and cautious new ones alike. The world beyond their fragile sanctuary pressed tight with danger, but in that moment, their circle held firm— bound not only by magic, but by chosen, persistent loyalty.

Evening pressed silver and shadow through the latticework of boughs, dappling Elara's path between cottage and sanctuary. The air was thick with anticipation—the kind that stretched taut and silent, just before a storm will break. She moved steadily, small items cradled in her arms: milky quartz, bundles of feverfew and witchhazel, slip-thin strips of birch seeded with runes, and vials sealed with beeswax. The table where she always watched the seasons change—scratched, warped, and lovingly carved—waited in the hollow heart of the clearing like an altar. One by one, she arranged her arsenal atop its surface: each crystal aligned with the compass rose, every rune oriented to soak in the last light clinging to the west.

The old lessons pulsed in her: sanctuary built on ritual, love made armor only by will. But her hands shook faintly when a memory surfaced—one of another sanctuary razed, the only child of her line dragging broken wards with her as a shield. Those nights—fires painting the sky, desperation scraping bare her throat—seemed close enough to touch. Even now the Shadowed Wood felt impermanent, a miracle carved from the kingdom's rot, precious only for how close danger pressed against its borders. The cruelty of Lord Dalen, the suspicion that festered in the capital, the king's cold, gnawing decrees—they all beat against this stillness.

Rowan's boots crunched behind her, carrying a careless confidence that made Elara ache with a strange affection. Rowan's battered staff caught the last threads of dusk as she spun it in tight arcs, calling currents of air to whirl, then split. Silt and loose stones churned up from the earth's skin, molded by practice into coiling shapes before settling again. Farther along the perimeter, Lysandra moved with quiet diligence—Elara tracked her, pale robes vanishing between the aspen trunks. Each mark Lysandra inspected bore the fleeting warmth of her touch, the fine silver of her magic binding cracks, correcting imperfection with quiet devotion.

Across the years, witches like them had learned: defiance could be measured in the time spent mending, in the willingness to meet each shadow with more light. Yet nowhere in the kingdom—its dark stone cities, its fields, its sundered coast—was there safety not bought dearly. Every patrol that prowled the hills wore the teeth of old fear, every decree from the palace was another blow meant to drive them into extinction. Their sanctuary was a wedge of hope against centuries of persecution—a hope each night threatened to tear open.

Elara signaled, and Lysandra knelt within a thicketed alcove, shell charm pressed to her lips. The melody was soft, a language lost to the villages where Elara's grandmother once gathered moonlight in jars. The charm pulsed in Lysandra's hand, and for a moment Elara's world narrowed to hush and waiting. After a heartbeat, signals returned—distant outposts still standing, a lull but for now. Elara took in the news without relief, only the steadying clarity that came with purpose.

She pressed a crystal talisman into Rowan's palm. "If the wards fail, throw this against the trees. It'll buy us time to regroup."

Rowan studied her closely, the firelight carving hollows beneath bold cheekbones. "And if the line gives before dawn?"

She allowed her lips the smallest curve—half gratitude, half warning. "Then we improvise. I'll hold until the last tree burns."

"Should've known you'd say that." Rowan's tone was dry as snapped twigs, but she squeezed Elara's hand quick and fierce before striding to her watch.

Elara and Lysandra exchanged a look—years of shared worry etching paths in the air between them.

"Signal if you need me to reset the perimeter," Lysandra said quietly.

"You're the map, Lys," Elara breathed. "I'm... only the hands."

"Don't ever say you're only anything. Without you—" The rest vanished into the gathering dark.

They circled the inner boundary until only the hush of night, a chorus of crickets, and the pulse of something ancient rose around them. Standing together at the sanctuary's edge, they joined hands. A cool breeze lifted the strands of Elara's cropped hair as she called the words to gather her power—old syllables, older than the kingdom's crowns. Rowan's grip grew fierce; Lysandra's pulse thrummed in harmony with the weave of their spell. Their joined strengths streamed outward, feeding into the sapphire wards stretched between the trunks.

Blue fire arced in fine threads along the sanctuary's edge. The shield hummed—alive, hopeful, fragile as spun glass—casting spectral light over the three. For that instant Elara felt the sum of their survival: bruised hands holding against annihilation, the taste of ash clinging to hope and fear in equal measure. All her doubts, the secret longing that one act of broken trust would destroy them, braided into the spell's luminous curve.

The wards shone bright, then faded to pale embers. The three women stepped back, faces lit by the last flickers—so much of what they loved pressed into this place, this night. They caught one another's gaze: tired, loyal, and unyielding as roots that refused to be torn free. As the sanctuary fell quiet, Elara folded her arms across her chest, head bowed. There would be no more time for grief—only this breathless pause before battle, fraught with possibility, wrapped in what fragile courage she could kindle.

Moonlight laced through the high branches, etching pale ribbons across Elara's palms as she traced the edge of her lantern's small circle of light. The glade breathed around her: leaf-litter muffling every sound, silver dew strung across roots and fern fronds, the sharp, chill scent of earth rising as the hour pressed toward midnight. Down the slope, a flicker—a cloak brushed against bramble, a shadow detached itself from the trunks and then Kaelen's form resolved, figure limned in blue-white sheen. She watched him approach, tension in the set of his shoulders and the way his hand worried at the hem of his sleeve. Elara's heart rose to her throat. She had summoned fire and wind, had tangled with death and forbidden magic in recent days, but the hush before this moment felt like the most precarious magic of all.

Kaelen stopped just within the lantern's glow. For a beat, neither moved or spoke, two souls suspended in the hush of sleeping beasts and wind in the leaves. Elara's own words came softer than she intended: "You found me."

His answering smile was fleeting—a quirk, quickly dulled by the shadow in his eyes. "You always seem to know where to disappear, Elara." He crouched near her but not quite close, his gaze catching on the trembling light. "I had to see you—before..." He let the silence finish shaping the fear neither had named.

The glade around them seemed to drink in their voices. The lantern's flame hissed, throwing their faces into relief: Kaelen's angled cheekbones gaunt with exhaustion, eyes hollowed by sleeplessness, but a restless determination flickering in their depths. Elara wanted to reach out and brush the dirt from the cuff of his coat, to tether him here in flesh and blood when every dream reminded her of loss—of bodies swinging from oaks, voices silenced, the cost of breaking the oath thrumming in her veins like some old wound. She found her fingers curling around her knees, grounding herself in damp soil. This is what forbidden power felt like—always a knife's edge between hope and ruin.

"I keep thinking," Kaelen began, "that if I fail now, every sacrifice will have been for nothing. Marek, all those we lost... You. The whole kingdom is bent on hunting what we are. Nights like this, I can't help but wonder if we're only feeding the pyre."

Elara felt the tremor in his voice ripple through her own chest. The first time she'd seen Kaelen, dying in the dark, she'd believed him a threat—another tool of the hunters, perhaps a spy to root out the last witches. But then she'd seen the pain bleeding from beneath his ribs, the flicker of desperate hope in his eyes when her hands pressed fire into his chest. Now, months and betrayals and near-deaths later, he sat before her—still carrying that fear, but unguarded, the rawness in his words unwinding something tight inside her.

"You're not alone in that." Her own words slipped out —ragged, unpracticed. "Every day I ask if I did right. I broke everything sacred to save you, and it's— unbearable, sometimes, carrying that bond." The confession tore through her, bitter and sweet as the memory of the burning stake that haunted her sleep. "I'm terrified of losing anyone else, terrified I've ruined what hope the rest of our kind had left. The magic between us, all that it's cost... I don't know if I'm strong enough to carry it to the end."

She squeezed her eyes shut. The glade pressed in: frost in the grass, the sharp tang of lingering smoke from the defensive wards, every shadow alive with the memory of pain and duty. Elara remembered the faces of witches lost—her fingers entwined with Rowan's in a circle, Lysandra's steady hand at her back, the wild rush of reckless hope when she'd first drawn forbidden magic and knotted herself to Kaelen. Ritual by ritual, wound by wound, she'd learned that leadership was the loneliest fire.

Kaelen's hand found hers, gentle, callused. His thumb brushed slow circles along her knuckles.

"I fear the same things. But whatever fate's made of us—oathbreakers, exiles, worse—I choose you. Tonight. Tomorrow, if we live. I've never believed in destiny, Elara, not until I looked at you and saw something left worth fighting for. We can't promise easy days. Only that we walk the next one together."

Elara met his eyes. For an instant she saw herself reflected—not as a leader or a witch cursed, but simply as Elara, tired and hopeful and flesh-and-bone real. The moon, high and whole, silvered Kaelen's lashes as he leaned in. Her stern composure crumbled; she let her fingers clutch his tighter, unable to guard the ache or the yearning anymore.

"You changed everything about my world. It isn't just magic that binds us. It's every moment we've bled for each other." Her voice broke. "If we fall tomorrow, I want you to know—I would never take any of it back."

Kaelen nodded, silent, pressing his forehead gently to hers. Warmth radiated through Elara—something like flame, something older and deeper, twining through her ribs and settling the tremor in her heart. All the words that might have been left unsaid felt irrelevant as breath mingled in the chill air.

Under the tangled branches, the hush between them became its own kind of sorcery, a shield against the terror of approaching dawn. When finally Kaelen rose, Elara watched him slip away among the silver-lit trunks, her chest swelling with new resolve. For the first time in weeks, her magic sang steady instead of fragile, hope coiling at the heart of her fear as she let the shadows close around her.

Chapter 18

The Breaking Storm

At first light, the Shadowed Wood came alive with sound: a warning bell hammering through the low morning mist, the frantic scurrying of woodland creatures sensing upheaval, and—almost beneath those—another rhythm, as hundreds of armored feet crushed the mossy ground. Lord Dalen led the witch hunters into the forest's heart. His silhouette loomed above the iron-helmed columns, sword drawn. With every step, the hunters pressed the weight of their resolve deeper into the soil, their blades catching the first pale rays of sun that couldn't penetrate the thick branches. Frosted ferns crackled underfoot. Crows flapped through the canopy, scattering midnight and dread.

Elara had barely slipped on her boots before she was out the cottage door, cloak trailing like a dark flame, heart drumming in her chest. The warning rang again—someone had made it to the bell. The air was thick with jasmine and fresh fear, and her breath clouded as she sprinted through the tangled roots and whispering leaves. Smoke from a dying fire wreathed her fingers, and she pressed her palm to the old oak outside her window, drawing a sliver of its energy to ground herself. Every alarm, every footfall outside her safe walls, summoned memories of friends who'd vanished in the night, villages emptied but for ash and scattered keepsakes. The purge had grown relentless.

This wood—once a place where lanterns hung from every sunbeam and laughter blended with birdsong—was now barricade and burden. Neighboring towns betrayed them for coins and royal favor. Children trained in spells before they learned to walk. Families divided by one whispered accusation: mageblood or not. Elara carried their names in her mind, imprinted like the marks on her hands—her life's debts and griefs, her every impulse for rebellion tempered by the fragile balance keeping this last haven from ruin.

She stumbled into a clearing slick with dew, Rowan already crouched by the outer ward circle, chalk in one hand and dagger in the other. Seraphine flickered at the edge of vision, drifting through fog, every movement measured, eyes alight with wind-called power. The world felt tenuous as spun glass.

"They're coming faster than last time," Elara snapped, breathless. "Rowan—reinforce the southern bramble, double lines. Seraphine, mask our movements—bring mist and hush their shouts."

"Understood. East flank's thin," Rowan called, already bounding over deadfall, the rune-ink on her arms gleaming, ready to bite back at trespassers.

Seraphine's reply was the hush of wind through tangled boughs; the mist thickened, obscuring the approaching hunters in flowing curtains. For a heartbeat, the air itself swirled with secrets and defiance.

Elara's mind flickered with images: kitchens emptied hastily at midnight, witches forced to trade names for survival, neighbors' eyes shuttered by suspicion and old stories turned weapon. This forest was rebellion's last heartbeat. All around her, magic trembled—not uncertain, but braced: a garden wild, pushed to fight root and claw.

Kaelen—somewhere west, where the young witches gathered—would be there. Elara's pulse thudded; she trusted him now as she might trust her own heartbeat. She ran, limbs pumping, the brambles tearing at her hem.

Smoke curled high on the far ridge, and she reached Kaelen as he conjured a wall of shimmering force—a barrier woven of leaf-green light and memory. On the other side, a tide of armor surged forward. Crossbow bolts shivered the air, steel heads bursting against Kaelen's shield in sparks and shrieks. The younger witches behind him huddled, their fear cold and raw. He stood, jaw set, sweat beading his brow. Elara reached out, quickly tracing sigils in the loam, lending him the touch of earth's strength as she pressed a hand to his shoulder.

"Hold, Kaelen! If they breach, fall back to the birches —don't let them herd the children," she ordered.

A crash echoed as the witch hunters reached the outer wards. Their shields locked, glinting with ward-breaker runes. They threw nets laced with iron filings and surged forward, swords raised. Rowan let fly a blade of fire, carving through the haze; Elara flicked her hand and sent a river of vines snaking over the ground, wrapping ankles, tripping legs. The air stank of scorched moss and burning silk.

Seraphine's winds swept loose leaves into whirling barriers—one moment's refuge, the next, shrapnel. Rowan, a streak of defiance, darted among fallen logs, pulling wounded back, yelling over the carnage, "South path! Breach! I need two more here!"

Elara forced control. For every step the hunters gained, she pushed back with flame. Villages were gone, but the stories folded into her, bone and nerve —she would not let another name join the lost.

The lines were breaking, smoke thick about her face as she drew her strength for one last surge. Elara hurled a burst of fire into the fray, light exploding in the tangled melee. Nettles singed and iron clashed. She saw, with a clarity that tasted of iron and longing, that their sanctuary was not hidden anymore—it was the last, battered heart of their world, and the world had found it at last.

Rowan's shout for backup split the chaos. Elara braced herself, eyes bright with flame. The siege had begun.

The walls of the inner sanctuary breathed with a tension that tasted of sweat, fear, and wood smoke. Morning light—pale and bruised—filtered through high slits and splintered latticework, trickling across battered tables and canvases hung with crude maps. Every noise echoed in the chaos outside: the clash of steel, the snap of a burning branch, the animal howl of wounded magic. Elara strode quickly through the corridor, boots slipping once in a puddle of spent potion, the copper tang of spilled blood just under the heavy scent of smoldering moss. Her knuckles were raw where she'd gripped her staff too tight.

Lysandra moved through the gloom ahead—she was a shadow, quietly slipping toward a knot of witches hunched near a concealed exit draped in charms and dying elder leaves. Elara's heart lurched as Lysandra stilled, gaze intent: the huddle glanced back, a flick of hands, a touch at a rune-marked wrist, then soft glimmers through the cracks. The witches were signaling, not to fellow sentries, but outward—toward the indistinct line where the sanctuary met the unknown. Betrayal lived here, subtle as fungus on a root. For a span of heartbeats, all that training, all the enforced unity of their magical order, flickered like a candle in a gale.

A flood of memory swept through her—old lessons by firelight, her mother's strict voice, the sacred oath spoken with hands in cold river water and moon on bare shoulders: "When the trust breaks, the wood will splinter. When the wood splinters, all will burn." This place had always been their last promise, but promises meant nothing if fear could worm through even her closest circle.

A slap of hurried boots and Marek appeared from the passage's mouth, his face creased and eyes bright with something that wasn't just battle worry. He blocked her path at a battered alcove spattered with drying herbs and abandoned sigils.

"Elara, I need you to listen." Marek's voice rasped, low so the others wouldn't hear—jaw worked as if he chewed through thorns. "Dalen... Dalen found me. He promised me news of my brother. If I just—if I delayed the warning. I told myself I could control it. That I could protect you all, in my own way. I was wrong. They're here sooner because of my silence."

A swirl of shame, cold and molten, crashed through her. The ache that came with realizing trust was not an impervious shield, but a brittle husk. She clenched her staff tight, pulse drumming behind her eyes.

She wanted to scream, to unleash every searing ember in her veins, but instead her tongue formed only a shaky, near-whisper. "Why would you—how could you let him twist your blood like that?" The urge to loathe him warred with her memory of how every heart fractured differently under loss. She swallowed the taste of bile, steadying herself.

Kaelen stepped forward, jaw set, eyes flicking from Marek to her. Nothing about this battle—outside or in —felt simple.

A fresh commotion burst through the hush: Rowan, windblown, splattered with soot and clutching a crumpled, blood-specked note in one trembling fist.

"They've been signaling. Someone was feeding spells through the roots before dawn. Found this on Lira, the lookout." Rowan slammed the paper on a splintered crate. "It's the healer—look!" She strode to a corner where the healer stiffened, eyes darting. "Show them. Now."

The healer hesitated. Rowan seized the sleeve, twisting it up: code-ink, a lattice of shifting symbols staining the skin from wrist to elbow. Spare strands of failed ward spells, barely visible, still curled in the air—unraveled protections, woven thin on purpose.

A chorus of voices rose—in anger, in disbelief, in horrified silence. Elara stared at the healer, feeling the old fire and the old fear battling beneath her ribs.

A dialogue block:

"What do you say to that? What could possibly be worth selling us to them?" Rowan's words cracked like kindling. "We trusted you. I trusted you."

The healer's voice shook. "You don't understand. They promised to spare my sister if I—if I just weakened the roots, loosened the wards. I... I had no choice."

"You had every choice. We all do, even when it burns."

Elara felt herself sway, breath short. The wounds of the outer world seared less than these invisible cuts —good faith mangled by desperation, hope swapped for survival. She looked into their faces—Marek's, haunted; the healer's, smeared with fresh regret; Rowan and Lysandra, alight with fury and sorrow.

This sanctuary had been built on centuries of whispered vows—oaths etched into bark and bone, rules meant to shelter against the day when the world outside remembered its hatred. Her parents had taught her to prize unity above all else, to believe that a circle unbroken could stand against anything, even the storms of kings and hunters. Now, splinters of betrayal shuddered along every edge.

She dug her heels in, refusing to unravel beneath doubt's bite. If suspicion took hold, it would rot them from within faster than any outside blade. Forgiveness felt impossible, but leadership required more than personal wounds.

Her voice cut through the tension. "Rowan, Lysandra —separate those who answered the wrong call. Reinforce the inner sanctum. Don't let this fear spread further. Not today."

A dialogue block:

"What about the ones who falter?" Lysandra asked softly.

"Isolate them, but don't punish them yet. We don't have the luxury of purges or trust games, not when the wood is burning. We survive together, or not at all."

The room moved—Rowan herding the accused, Lysandra securing new wards. Marek slid down against a beam, head bowed in silent misery. Elara clamped her teeth together, holding the center of herself as the sanctuary shook, refusing to bow to the fractures. She motioned for the defenders to follow, not waiting to see if hope would obey— outside, the roar of battle begged for her resolve.

Smoke curled, thick and stinging, twisting above the north barricade as Kaelen drove through shattered branches, boots sliding across churned earth. Splinters hung in the air, mingling with ash and the sound of pained cries and metal clashing with tooth and bark and shield. The acrid tang clawed at his throat. Ahead, Elara's silhouette materialized from the haze, her hair dark and wild with sweat, staff raised. At her shout, he ducked beside her as a line of armored witch hunters heaved forward.

Elara swung her staff with precision and a muttered word; brambles surged in a green wave from the soil, curling around greaves and ankles, spined with thorns. The nearest hunter screamed, his sword caught by vines that bled sap when hacked. Kaelen, reading her intention as if it were his own thought, slashed burning glyphs through the smoke—long, arcing shapes that blazed red and gold, their heat born in the marrow of his bond to Elara.

He didn't need her words; the tug at the edge of his senses guided him, urging his magic into the gaps she cleaved. Searing fire jetted from his hands, weaving through the defensive breaches like eager hounds unleashed. Torches dropped as fire licked at the line of attackers. Behind them, Rowan leapt atop a fallen log, casting spindly willow roots to ensnare another vanguard, while Seraphine spun ribbons of wind between the trees, funneling confusion and turning arrows off their mark.

Each movement belonged to a dance, ancient and fierce. Kaelen's chest ached with the effort, power running thin, but the pulse tethering him to Elara steadied his hand when nerves threatened to betray him. She shifted, eyes finding his in an instant— amber sparking beneath the chaos—her mouth forming a silent plea. He felt it before she finished: cover left. He veered to the left, channeling a wall of flame over the battered barricade even before she drove her staff down, opening a gap for one escaping youth to scramble through.

The din washed together—metal against bone, bark torn free, magical energy roaring in his veins. A crossbow quarrel sang out, slicing past his ear; another thunked into his shoulder, searing agony ripping through muscle. Kaelen gasped, his legs faltering, the world narrowing to red and the taste of iron. The dead leaves felt like water as he sagged.

A hand under his arm—firm, trembling, steady. Elara's breath was hot against his cheek as she crouched, murmuring a string of words laced with effort. Light pulsed between her fingers, feeding warmth through his ribs. Power ripped from her, threading down his spine, and at the flicker of their bond he almost sobbed with relief and guilt. The shared magic ached inside him, as if her courage flamed through old scars he thought long-buried.

He wanted to apologize. To tell her not to risk herself for his weakness. But she pressed her forehead to his, just for a moment, and through that feverish contact, intent and wordless comfort—*not alone*—vaulted between them.

He let the feeling anchor him, forcing himself upright. Together, breath ragged, they faced the next surge—witch hunters, howling, shields up, boots tramping in unison. Elara's arm swept wide, flaming tendrils crackling from her palm, as Kaelen instinctively shaped glyphs that laced his fire to hers. Sparks danced along the twined magic, mesmerizing as a starfall, devouring nets and dampening the hurled oil meant to mute their spells.

The bond between them, that invisible, aching tether, flared bright enough to paint the fronds blue and silver. Kaelen sensed Elara move before she did, felt her impulse as a shiver in his bones—when to shield, when to strike, when to pause so Seraphine's shock of wind would clear a line. Their unity lent a terrible beauty to the slaughter; for those instants, no enemy could breach their perimeter.

Exhaustion stalked his limbs, threatening collapse. Every muscle screamed, lungs scrabbling for breath that tasted of embers and blood. His vision pulsed at the edges, distant thunder rolling over distant battle. Through the haze, Elara's gaze snapped to him again, and though words failed, Kaelen's heart pounded with a ferocity reserved only for her. She was not an enigma now but necessity—his every hope, his anchor.

He remembered being alone—those endless seasons of cold halls, suspicion, pain stitched beneath fine clothes. He remembered mistrust, how it gnawed at him, the way no oath or title had ever truly shielded him. And now, even mired in agony, he moved as more than himself. Vulnerability became the lifeline. Each brush of Elara's magic offered pain, yes, but also the presence he had thought forever beyond reach.

A shockwave roared from them—blue-white, blinding, hot as the birth of a star. It swept the attacking rank back, splitting shields, scattering bodies like dry leaves. For one miraculous heartbeat, every witch and rebel along the barricade felt the rush, the unity. Just as suddenly, silence—distant, foreign—settled in the wake. Kaelen collapsed against a mossy boulder, limbs shaking, Elara's hand finding his. Overhead, embers drifted, goldmotes vanishing into twilight. Across the line, Rowan's shout carried: another assault to the east. Kaelen squeezed Elara's hand, reluctant to let go of her warmth, even as battle beckoned anew.

Lord Dalen's stride sent a hush crawling over the carnage. Elara saw the man through tangled branches, his gray eyes like slits of ice, the jagged scar along his cheek catching what little sun still filtered through the shattered canopy. He raised his ebony staff—rune-carved wood that drank up the light—and the air itself seemed to recoil. Shadows coiled about his hand, a writhing blade of hatred that heaved and shimmered. With a guttural word, Dalen sent a shaft of black energy cracking toward the heart of the sanctuary. The spell raced, splitting fog and air, drawing a line of oblivion meant to unmake.

Elara raced, breath sharp, feet stumbling across roots and sodden moss, her cloak trailing sparks of desperate magic. Kaelen was at her side, hair wild, blood streaking his temple. She fell to one knee at the foot of the oldest tree in the wood and plunged her hands into the earth, fingers curling into cold, living soil. The tree groaned above her, canopy shuddering. Kaelen's arms lifted, summoning the storm pressing at the forest's edge—his face a pale mask tilted skyward. Lightning crackled, eager to answer.

She felt him by her side, an exhale, their bond thrumming in her marrow. Together, they opened themselves to the wildness whispering underroot and cloud. Her pulse quaked as heat flared from her palms. Earth surged upward, cool and old, while Kaelen's outstretched hands drew roaring wind and electric sky. The chill and warmth met, twisting—a luminous column, water and fire, sky and root. Elara's senses blurred; the world sharpened into leaf, bark, storm, and his hand over hers. Dalen's dark bolt smacked into their conjured barrier and vanished, snuffed in a thunderclap.

The forest trembled. Beneath her, roots writhed. Branches knitted together, forming walls alive and pulsing. Vines snapped like whips, bramble arcs rising to shield their wounded. Tree trunks twisted, impossible and splintering, throwing back the armored men clawing for purchase. The air thickened with the taste of sap and iron, the sharp scent of ozone left by Kaelen's magic. Wounded men thudded to the forest floor, groaning, as others pressed blindly on, their swords little match for limbs that bent and blocked and sometimes seemed to whisper in a tongue older than human memory.

Elara's exhaustion ran through her veins like cold water. She bit her lip, feeling the burn of cost behind her eyes. Every spell came at a price—her hands blistering, teeth chattering, but the forest's magic answered, pressing up through her bones.

All around were the sounds of a world colliding: cries of wounded witches, bellows of furious hunters, the deep, breathless groans of giant trees twisting under the onslaught. The sky bleached itself of color. Elara saw Kaelen, eyes burning streak-blue, sweat beading steel along his jaw. They stood at the center of the hurricane, barely upright, two souls lashed to the ancient tree while magic and bone shivered all around.

Yet for all the tumult, neither side broke. The witch hunters rallied, their discipline holding. They slashed and battered at the animate barricades, some casting their own crude magic, colored sparks fizzling useless against the old woods' will. Witches sagged behind roots-turned-walls, tending comrades, flinging charms and desperate shields. The day's war had ground the air into dust.

When the sun disappeared behind knotted limbs, all that remained was the aftertaste of violence—spilled blood, torn moss, the reek of sweat-fear and smoke. Lord Dalen sounded a whistle that cut through everything. His soldiers limped, retreated, shields raised, edging just beyond the zone where trees and magic would strike. The deadly cadence of battle faded, replaced by a silence that tasted of embers.

Elara pressed herself under the massive tree, sliding down the furrowed bark until her knees buckled. Kaelen slumped beside her, their shoulders touching. All that was left was the ache—muscles stretched to breaking, powers near spent. Their hands, traced by veins of pulsing blue light, found each other. Elara's vision swam. Overhead, the branches tangled with the stars, hiding the moon in a net of leaves and sapphire glow.

She let her breath out in a trembling sigh, head resting on the tree's root. Relief, hollow as an old drumbeat, mingled with unease. The sanctuary had held—barely—and she wondered at the balance they had struck by midnight's arrival. The cost had bled through every moment, bodies left collapsed on the forest's edge, the ground heavy with loss.

Elara felt the forest's pulse running beneath her, deeper than any spell, woven by the roots she'd touched. What if tomorrow broke this last home? What if the world's hatred pressed in so fiercely that even these ancient trees could not bear the weight? She tried to imagine a dawn after true victory—a sanctuary reborn, witches moving unfearing through trees that sang with them, no more hiding, no more splitting herself to be witch and something less. Could magic remake the kingdom as well as shield it?

But if defeat came with first light, she saw only ruin —a hollow temple, her people scattered to wind, her own hands empty. Had wielding such power made her savior or monster? Was this awakening in the wood a sign witches might yet become what the kingdom needed, not its vilified ghosts?

She wished, quietly, that peace born of power need not taste like ashes. She squeezed Kaelen's hand, a silent vow between blood and magic beneath the hush of the sentinel trees, hearts tethered on the threshold of a future unspooled and strange.

Chapter 19

The Last Vow

Gray light seeped through the shattered ribs of the Forbidden Tower. Dawn shaped everything in silver ghosts: the fractured altar, frost-layered flagstones, the splinters of stained glass underfoot. Elara stepped with care among the debris, her boots crunching through centuries of dust, Kaelen's steps silent behind her. Shadows fled before them as she knelt beside the altar's collapsed face. Fingers traced spiraling runes frosted by cold—some she had carved as a child in clay, lessons in caution, in promise. She pressed against the stone and felt its reluctant shift; grit rasped against her palms as a hidden coffer emerged—ancient, heavy, its lid choked by vines. Elara glanced over her shoulder. Kaelen nodded once, moist earth smudging his jaw. Together, they pried open the lid.

Blue light bled between their hands, throwing trembling patterns over Elara's sleeves. Nestled within the coffer rested the artifact—a sphere wrapped in incised gold filigree, emanating a hush that crowded out sound and breath alike. Energy prickled against her skin, strange and almost tender, as if the object recognized her. Elara's vision trembled. She remembered the council's histories: the chosen few who forged balance from fear, laws cut into blood and memory, elemental magic shrouded in iron purpose. This artifact was the beating heart of those oaths—the pact that had bound the first witches, that had remade the violence of the founding wars into structure and secrecy, that had shaped a duty she could not unmake. How many dreamers before her had trembled at this burden? The script burned beneath her thumb.

They carried the artifact from the tower, the morning air crisp with dew and distant birdcall, breath condensing as they crossed the overgrown threshold. The world outside was wild and brimming with old sorrow: ancient stones encircled the clearing like sentries left behind, trees ragged and gnarled by storms. Elara set the artifact atop a dais of roots slick with lichen and thick with history. The old magic pulsed under her skin. She unfurled the scroll she'd stolen from the enclave's darkest archives, the parchment sharp with bitter oils and the faintest whiff of rose, and spoke words so old the syllables made her tongue ache.

Beside her, Kaelen lifted the chalice. The water had the faint taste of snowmelt and the tang of copper, harvested at midnight by another witch's trembling hands, hoping this might tip fate's scale. He poured it over the grooves carved into the stone. Water chased the runes in faint rivulets, each stream finding its mark as if pulled by memory itself.

Elara closed her eyes and let her magic crawl upward from the soles of her feet—through dirt and root, the warmth of the earth calling her courage forth. Her palms burned as she pressed them to the artifact's shell, time bunching around her. Fear tugged at her—the memory of the oath she'd broken, the faces of those who'd warned her: strength, yes, but also peril. She had wanted freedom, but freedom had always been a story withheld. Now, she was bound to Kaelen and to a secret power neither wholly understood. Her heart battered at its ribcage as she whispered the final word.

Wind snaked into the clearing, cold and furious, snapping at her cropped hair. Incantation thrummed in her teeth and bones. She felt Kaelen's hand brush against hers, two streams of intent mixing. Above the artifact, the air shimmered, then twisted; thunder grumbled overhead, quickening her pulse. Magic shivered along her arms—a ring of fire leapt from the ground, encompassing them, devouring dew and shadow, its heat perfumed with petrichor and burnt cedar. The roots underfoot trembled; Kaelen staggered as the earth undulated, his grip steadying both of them.

Light curled around their bodies in silvery arcs, raw and wild. Tiny globes spun upward—blue, gold, a thousand colors she could not name—crackling as they rose, bathing them in an unearthly glow. Elara's thoughts fractured and rebuilt themselves in rhythm with the growing hum: she could see herself mirrored in Kaelen's gaze, could hear unspoken words flicker across the air, his consciousness brushing hers—soft, uncertain, undeniable. The elemental forces, once separate, reached across boundaries, golden threads of her power weaving with his until her skin glowed with it, until she could not tell where her magic ended and his began.

She gasped as the storm crescendoed: fire roared at the circle's edge, wind howled, earth lurched. For a heartbeat, it seemed the world split—anger and longing, fear for a future they could hardly imagine. Yet in that space, Elara felt an old grief flood upward —the sorrow of ancestors who forged peace in the ruins of war, who sewed these laws into themselves so no witch would ever face death alone. She understood, almost gently, the way sacrifice and love could become indistinguishable.

Across the dais, Kaelen's aura flared with her own, the artifact between them stuttering with blinding light. A sound like singing bolts across the clearing— then everything fell silent.

Air rushed from Elara's lungs. She sank to her knees in blackened grass, the taste of smoke and wildflowers thick in her mouth. Kaelen knelt beside her, shoulders heaving. Between them, the artifact sang in low, trembling tones, new-made and ancient, as first light bled across the broken stones.

Mist hung among the ancient stones, weaving through the roots and shattered branches of the path. Kaelen pressed forward into the hush of the sacred grove, one arm supporting Elara as her steps faltered, her breath raspy in the close, moss-scented air. Underfoot, old leaves yielded with a gentle squelch that threatened to unmask their fragile presence to anything listening just beyond the circle of old oaks. Sunlight, pale and shy, had barely begun to touch the stones with gold. Elara's weight dragged against him unexpectedly; her hand trembled so violently he thought she might slip away into the bracken if he loosened his grip.

He caught her before she fell, fingers clenching her wrist. Her pulse thrummed erratically beneath his thumb. Sweat glimmered at her temple, mingling with a smudge of ash—residue from power kindled too far, too much. Kaelen guided her to a moss-padded boulder, careful not to let his own knees buckle. Every fragment of his body screamed from the recent awakening—the coiled magic from the artifact had left spiderweb scars along his forearm, traced in bruised blue and angry crimson. Still, he forced a steadiness he did not feel, lowering himself beside her as though his bones had not been hollowed by the storm.

He dabbed at a cut on his lip, tasting the tang of copper and grit. The skin there was split, blood drying tacky at the edges; he wiped it away and, keeping his arm as casual as the tremor would allow, pressed a cloth to Elara's brow. The compress, conjured cold from his last reserves of water, felt like ice against his palm and radiated a coolness into the heated air between them.

"Rest a moment," he said, voice roughened by exhaustion. "Just breathe with me. I won't let anything find us." The words cost him dearly. He slipped his free hand beneath the hem of his sleeve, exposing the fresh marks—the streaks of magic carved straight through skin, burned there by the artifact's awakening. Soft blue light shimmered and faded along the lines, the memory of the surge pulsing in his sinew still. Every movement felt as if it threatened to break him apart, but he hid his limp by tensing his thigh and set his shoulders in a show of unwavering calm. Elara's lashes fluttered, but she obeyed, anchoring herself against him.

Cool green shadows wrapped the grove, muffling the distant world to a hush. The air was thick with petrichor and the musk of living earth, scents that always seemed to signal change—Kaelen imagined them swirling together, entwining as tightly as the fate that pressed him and Elara together, tighter even now. His chest ached with the fullness of sensation: pain from the ritual, the heat of her body close, the siphoning fatigue that threatened to send everything into oblivion. Fear dogged every thought, fear of what they had done and what it meant for everything yet to come.

He found her hand where it gripped his sleeve, knuckles whitening with strain, and pressed his own fingers over hers. Where their skin met, he felt the thread of energy still humming—a faint echo of the power that had nearly torn them apart minutes before. Elara's amber eyes met his. A dozen things boiled in their silence. The magics they'd awakened were old, older than memory, and he carried that weight inside him along with the sharp blade of dread: If her body failed, it would be his fault. He had drawn her into this. If she died—if she traded her life for his, as he had seen noble guards do on bloodied fields from his childhood into exile—he would trade anything to stop it. The wind through the stones carried the scent of burnt wood, and something like longing.

He squeezed her hand. The unspoken oaths curled between them, thicker than breath. For a moment, he almost felt his heart shudder under the pressure of everything he could not say. In that quiet, he reached back through years of false victories and pyrrhic survival, seeing again the faces of the dead, the haunting eyes of family lost to ambition or hubris or war's careless hand. He remembered standing beside dying men on muddy embankments—how the best of them had clung to purpose not for glory, but for the comrades who leaned against them in the night, hands clasped in pain and quiet courage.

"Elara," he murmured at last, "if there's any mercy in what we've unleashed, I want you to have it. I want a world after all this—after them—for us." His voice barely cleared the lump in his throat. He felt her lean into his shoulder, warmth seeping through cloth and battle-scorched leather, the press of her side a salve to his worry. He feared she would hear how close he was to breaking, yet her need for him—the trust she placed in that need—made him dig deeper. He had thought himself weak, frail beneath his noble blood and the strange magic thrumming now in every limb, but for her, for the hope that shimmered between their joined hands, he could find a way to be strong.

The hush lingered, painted with the promise of what might be lost and what could be forged anew. Her head rested against him, both of them silent now, clinging to the heartbeat between them as if it might somehow drive away the darkness lingering at the edges of the grove. In that closeness, Kaelen whispered a vow to the future, breath hot against her hair: "We survive this. Together. Whatever it costs."

Their hands remained locked as sunlight broke over the stones, spilling gold across blood and lichen. Somewhere in the deeper woods beyond, horns blared—a low, distant call that carried with it the promise of steel and death—but for a moment, the world held only them, and the weight of the choices that bound their souls.

The world trembled before Elara as she pressed through the edge of the forest, the air heavy with the taste of coming rain and ash. Her boots left prints in the churned mud, each step echoing the thrum of her heart as Kaelen moved beside her, allies stretching wide in a band of color and resolve. The battered towers of the Capital City loomed beyond the battlefield—a theatre for all that had been broken and all that might be remade.

Lightning stitched silver through the clouds. Elara lifted her hand, fingers blackened with dried blood, and summoned fire. It leapt from her palm, not as a gentle flame, but as a roaring column, twisting gold and orange through the sodden wind. Witch hunters scattered before its heat, shields raised in futility as the blaze struck earth. Smoke curled against her cheeks, stinging her eyes. Behind her, Kaelen's chant thrummed low, and the ground rose—earth reshaping beneath his will into rippling walls that glimmered, sand flecked with veins of quartz, shielding their numbers as they advanced.

Centuries of suspicion and fear had brought them to this: witches forced into hiding, bearing centuries-old scars in silent glades, rulers promising peace while sharpening the blade. Elara knew those stories—they shaped every spell etched into her bones, every lesson murmured in shadowed woods. Now, the lies marshaled by thrones and whispered by priests threatened all she loved. The fabric of the kingdom, stretched by generations of hatred, had finally split. Every footfall pressed her deeper into the blood-stained memory of witches bound to secrecy or pyre, hearts pressed into silence beneath banners flapping in the wind.

She reached for Kaelen, their fingers briefly brushing. As his shield slid into place, she heard the harmony within their bond, a music quieter than thunder. The air tasted charged, saturated with the fear of her people—fear that for all her power, she would prove too weak, or worse, too willing to trade the lives of others for hope. Her chest ached with the weight of the oath she had shattered: the promise she was never meant to break, now stitched into every heartbeat, every ragged breath.

A wall of steel advanced, sunlight glancing from unyielding helms. Then Lord Dalen strode to the fore, cloak snapping around him like shadow made flesh. His eyes sought Elara, cold with conviction older than compassion. He raised his sword and began to recite, the words harsh as jagged stone. Shadow churned around him, coiling up the blade, and with a sweep, he unleashed a wave of blackness that crashed through the field. The elven shields nearest her crumbled, defenders thrown into the mud with cries swallowed by the storm.

Kaelen's hand shot up and Elara felt the bond flare— pain lancing from his palm to her shoulder. The earth buckled in answer, pillars erupting to block a second tide of darkness.

"Elara—left flank! They're breaking through—" Kaelen's shout was nearly lost in the chaos.

She pivoted, flames coiling through her arms as she hurled them into the breach. Shadows shrieked and sizzled as the fire struck armored hunters, the air thick with scorched metal and sweat. All around, the battle pulsed and unfurled: Rowan swept in with a defiant cry, slashing down banners and scattering enemy formations. Lysandra chanted softly, beseeching fragile shields of light around the fallen, her green eyes burning with persistence. Marek's blade moved like an extension of the storm, steady where others faltered. Seraphine stood atop a ruined cart, arms lifted—lightning split the sky, bursting a siege engine into smoldering fragments as soldiers dove for cover.

From the city walls and narrow windows, pale faces pressed against glass. Children hunched behind barricades; elders gripped rosaries or trinkets, knuckles white. Their hopes hung tenuous as spider silk—this war was not only for witches or kings, but for what the world might become. Could fire and earth and thunder, wielded without shame, find a place amid the city's marble and stone?

The storm above broke, snarling wind and rain across the battlefield. Magic surged wild, drawn to the fear and rage, the decades-old dream of vengeance or acceptance. Elara's cloak whipped around her, soaked to the bone. She felt the ache of every spell, the raw burn of overexerted veins, but pressed forward, refusing the trembling in her legs, refusing everything but necessity and the bond pulsing strong beside her.

In the heart of the fray, Dalen's blade met her fire—darkness coiling, fire hissing. Sparks sprayed between them. Kaelen dropped to one knee, pounding his fist to the earth, summoning a shimmering dome that flickered, shuddered, barely held. Their enemies closed in, relentless. The smell of ozone and blood filled Elara's lungs.

She found Kaelen's gaze, saw in him the echo of her own fear and hope. Despite the chaos, the roar, the pain, the world contracted to a single point: his presence, their tangled fates. As the sky tore open above them, as the storm screamed and the city watched, Elara threw her power into Kaelen's, surrendering caution, trusting their bond—a force neither old law nor crown could sever.

For one luminous moment, they became a fulcrum on which the world would tip, entwined by oath, defiance, and the need to keep something beautiful alive—whatever ruin the night brought.

The hush after victory arrived unevenly, as if the earth itself held its breath. Elara stood on the rain-soaked crest of a grassy hill, mud streaked across her boots and cheek, the last ache of battle throbbing low in her limbs. Beside her lingered Kaelen—disheveled, cloak torn, ashes dusting his dark hair. They gazed together at the battered plain stretched below, where the twisted hulks of siege engines slumped like wounded animals in the gathering dusk and broken banners fluttered, tattered and defeated, among sullen mounds of earth. Smoke curled upward in gray ribbons, sharp on the breeze, the air tinged with spent magic and the acrid tang of smoldering wood.

Peering across the shattered field, Elara saw figures moving: survivors stooping to tend the fallen, others searching for something—hope, perhaps—amid the chaos. Lights flickered in the battered windows of the city, and for a moment, it seemed the entire kingdom teetered between despair and something fragile, barely born.

A silence settled between her and Kaelen, as dense and intimate as midnight cloth. He shifted his weight and turned, face etched with fatigue, voice carrying the rawness of truth meant only for her. "There were moments I thought I'd let go," he murmured. "All that fury and darkness—I nearly drowned in it. If you hadn't..." His hand trembled as he brushed a smear of blood from his jaw, knuckles tight as if clinging to the very words.

She let out a thin, trembling laugh, more exhale than sound. "If I hadn't been there, I doubt I would be standing now. I lost myself in the fire. I wanted to give up." Her gaze swept down to the faded burn scars on her palms—reminders, each one, of mistakes and mercy. "We only survived because you didn't let go. Not of me. Not of hope."

He reached for her hand then, fingers tracing the worn crescent of her birthmark where mud stained the skin. For a heartbeat, she remembered every moment they'd stood together—oaths whispered in the dark, magic flaring wild between them, doubt gnawing their edges raw. In that touch, she felt the echo of every vow broken and remade.

Kaelen's thumb brushed over her battered knuckles. "Whatever comes next, I will not yield, Elara. Even if the cost is everything." His eyes found hers, open, afraid, shining with fierce promise.

She pressed her scarred palm atop his where their wounds matched, silent words blooming in the space between them. This bond—the one that brightened every ache, every bruise, every loss—was not curse but the sum of all they had endured. She closed her eyes. If they were to build anything new, it must be with these jagged pieces, bound by the longing she felt whenever he stood at her side.

She let herself lean into him, arms curled around his back, his jaw lowering to her hair. Their embrace lasted the span of three heartbeats—heavy, quiet, complete. Beneath rising stars, Elara felt the shape of her life tilting, every certainty she'd once clung to shifting, redefining itself. It was not the magic or the oaths or even the cause she fought for that had kept her standing on this ruined hill, but something rawer, kindled in long nights of flight and whispered confessions, a force drawing her toward courage no spell could conjure. In the place where pain and pride met, love seeded itself—stubborn and bright as flame.

She drew back, searching his face for the lines hope made as it settled in the aftermath. Her fingers found the ragged edge of his shirt where skin showed, tracing the fresh scar that now mirrored one of hers. The world spun quietly around them while she gathered her words.

Without breaking that gaze, Elara extended her hand, palm open. "Let's see what remains when the smoke clears. Let's build something with it, together."

Kaelen took her hand, strong and sure despite all his wounds, their shadows twining across the grass. Side by side, they descended the hill as battered survivors began to gather—witch, mortal, wounded, hopeful— glancing up as Elara led with Kaelen at her side. In those watching faces, she glimpsed a slow uncurling of faith. Nothing would be easy, but the sharp hunger for vengeance that once fueled the kingdom was giving way to questions, softer voices, the tentative weaving of a new tapestry from torn old threads.

Her heart hammered as she wondered: What would peace taste like, if they could ever claim it? Perhaps streets alive with song, not screams; magic grown wild through gardens and market stalls, children dancing with sparks in their hands, no longer hunted for wonder. She imagined the city opening its gates to witches and humans alike, a place where old laws faded into stories and promises bound people together—not by fear, but by the trust to try again. She let herself picture it—Kaelen laughing in sunlight, Lysandra tending healing in a public square, Rowan teaching the oaths as hope, not shackles, to a new generation.

Guilt stirred beneath the hope—all those lost to fire, to shadow, to silence. But pride grew with it: for holding fast when despair seemed all-consuming, for reaching for love even when it tasted of ash. Pride that she and Kaelen, born enemies, had chosen to bind themselves to a future unwritten, forged not only by sacrifice, but by the courage to imagine what came after.

At the crest of the hill, the hush of dusk pooled around them. Stars trembled awake in a lavender sky. Between their joined hands, a gentle shimmer of magic danced, gold and blue mingling, pulsing not as curse but promise. Together, they faced the horizon —new and unknown, fragile and fierce—a world remaking itself in the echo of wild hope.

Chapter 20

A Future Forged by Promise

In the grand marble hall of the Capital City, Elara's footsteps fell soundless against cold stone that caught and fragmented the colored sunlight, staining her boots with pools of sapphire, amber, and crimson. The stained glass windows climbed from floor to vaulted ceiling, their depictions of kings, battles, and ancient spirits watching with silent judgment as the kingdom's fate gathered here. Representatives from noble houses, faces carved by generations of certainty and suspicion, stood braced in resplendent silks and stolid armor. The city's ruling council murmured amongst themselves, eyes reflecting both hope and dread. Along the periphery, guards—in rigid black, hands resting on hilts—held their breath as if to keep dissent or magic from spilling over the threshold.

Centuries had deepened the rift between the arcane and the mundane. Old laws, inked in panic after burnt villages and vanished boys, had chained witches beneath fear: no spell-woven fire, no territorial sanctuaries, no self-defense. Broken promises lay like bones beneath every foundation—witches vanished in midnight raids or forced to bargain their silence for scraps of safety. Still, in every festivale, in every cottage where a fever broke by wildflower tea, whispers persisted: without magic, the kingdom's fields had once withered and its rivers drawn back into the earth. The council hall crackled with that paradox—the need for witchcraft and the fear of it. In the air, the unsweet tang of apprehension warred with the lingering wax from a hundred candles guttering beneath the stained glass.

Elara walked forward, Kaelen at her side. His posture, upright and deliberate, sent a tremor through the assembly, testimony written into every scar visible at his collar. She drew in a slow breath— each inhale soaked in the petrichor of morning storms, each exhale an unuttered spell for courage. Our future is drawn in this moment, she told herself. Her hands, marred by old burns, did not tremble. The air felt charged, fragile, as if the wrong word could snap the spell of fragile gathering.

She spoke, voice threading brittle resolve through the hush. "Centuries of fear have bred devastation. The cost of broken promises is written not only on witches' skin but in the wasted fields, in the empty beds left by your sons and daughters, in the blood that stains this hall's foundation still." She let her gaze rest, unwavering, on each councilor. "Witchcraft has been hidden, yes, but not absent. How many times have you accepted a healing root or safe birthing charm in darkness, only to cry for our extermination by daylight?"

Kaelen's presence emboldened her. She met his steady glance—a silent exchange where courage kindled in her before flickering outward, visible in the arch of her shoulders. Kaelen's voice followed hers, textured with restraint and haunted conviction. "I carry in my veins a bond forced by desperation—a bond born from your laws. It saved my life, but it cursed us both. There is no safety unless we forge it together. If you persist in hunting magic, you will leave only ruin. Instead, I stand—blatantly, vulnerably—witness to the cost of division, and I plead that we choose another course."

The room erupted. Arguments battered the pillars: venerable barons decried sorcery as a disease, city councilors pointed to firestorms and storms as omens. An elder in gold-threaded robes slammed a gavel, knuckles white—"Witch blood has threatened peace since before my grandfather's time!" But a woman in deep blue—barely more than a shadow hunched toward the light—rose trembling but clear. "How many more children," she demanded, "must be lost before we admit this fear serves only to devour our own?"

Elara scanned the hall—ancient fissures exposed, anger and pain rooting each argument. She found herself unexpectedly steady. Was this hope, she wondered, or the last flicker before annihilation? She felt her heart beat hollow against her ribs, the memory of her own oath-breaking churning within. She remembered burning pain and golden ribbons of forbidden magic. She remembered a vision of the moonlit glade after the first time Kaelen had survived by her hands—a reminder that mercy, even when forbidden, was never a mistake. She owed it to those who suffered in silence—to Lysandra, to Rowan, to the nameless lost—to use her surviving voice for something larger than her fear.

King Varric stood. The room inhaled as one, the king's blue velvet cloak brushing against the pale marble as he surveyed every row, every upturned, anxious face. His beard caught the blasted light, making him older, weighted. "Enough," he said, quiet but unyielding. "I have seen what division has wrought. It has cost this kingdom her sons, her peace, and her future. We must choose differently, or lose ourselves forever to memory and regret."

A slow ripple rocked the assembly as one by one, councilors, nobles, even the most reluctant, bowed their heads. The old guard crumpled first in exhaustion, then in tacit admission. New laws were declared in a single, trembling breath—protection, not persecution; peace, not hunt.

At the hall's heart, Lysandra and the elders stepped forward, their relics glinting softly in the colored shadows. Ancient words, spun from memory and hope, rose and twined above their heads. From their hands, golden light spilled—gathering, swirling, folding into sigils that hovered midair, binding old wounds. The light crept into stone and skin and breath itself. Every person present felt its warmth— soft as a lover's promise, but inexorable.

As the golden haze faded, the crowd sagged in relief. For a moment, the kingdom balanced on the knife-edge of possibility—prejudice and hope interlaced, a fragile peace only just begun.

Elara led Kaelen away from the echoing marble grandeur of the council chambers, her stride quick but silent. The Capital City was restless beyond the labyrinth of stone, but here, deep within the innermost passages, the world was hushed. Lanterns lined the corridor—each globe of glass inscribed with runes, their light golden and trembling, casting slow-moving shadows across limestone worn smooth by generations. A hush blanketed their footsteps. Kaelen could still taste the coppery tang of tension from the council, the scent of sweat and anxious perfume clinging to his skin, but as the stone swallowed up the city's noise, he felt each breath deepen, loosen something tight coiled around his ribs.

Elara paused before an ancient wooden door, fingers hovering for a moment before she pressed it open.

The sanctuary within was small, circular—a secret alcove set beneath an arched ceiling ribbed with roots and curling moss. Lanterns flickered on every ledge, their illumination softening each splintered groove in the table and drawing uncertain light from the clay cups resting near the wall. The air itself hummed faintly with magic, tingling against Kaelen's skin in a way both familiar and entirely foreign: a living, listening silence.

He waited as Elara settled onto a cushioned bench, only then taking the seat beside her. There was no need for words, not yet. For a moment, he let the hush settle inside him. Stillness, after so much argument and spectacle, felt like a balm; he was taut, but not brittle. Aware of every thread that bound him in place.

His fingers, notorious for their restlessness, fidgeted with the embroidery on his sleeve until Elara spoke—her voice fragile and sure, both. "The magic binding us... it's changed me," she said, not meeting his eyes. "Most days my veins ache, as if fire still runs through them. I can feel the mark left by every choice we made." She flexed her hand, as though testing invisible injuries. "Sometimes I feel as though I am only half myself. The rest is... all tangled up with you."

Kaelen's throat closed around old fear—the echoing cold of the oath-breaking, the pain so immense it had felt like falling endlessly through dark water. That night, the darkness had not been empty; it had pressed against him, whispered in the seams of his memory, threatening to split soul from flesh. Even now, with the council's lanterns blazing above, fragments returned: his powerless body cradled by Elara's hands, the taste of earth and blood, the unfathomable rush of a power that was both blessing and curse. The world was quick to judge witches for their spells, but Kaelen now understood the price for breaking oaths, for love's sake. It was a law heavier than any edict a king could issue. Every gain was bartered from bone and heart.

He wanted to say he was strong, that he could bear it all for her. But he remembered the nights shaking, sweat-slick and fevered, wondering whether the magic would one day burn him out from within. Wondering if he would wake to discover he'd lost himself entirely to her, or worse—to the storm that raged in their blood whenever danger struck. The kingdom had always painted witches as threats— creatures to be contained, or destroyed. Now he bore that legacy, stitched into him by forbidden power. The council's new laws hung as delicately as spider silk, easily torn; he understood too well how a single step could unravel fragile peace, how centuries of hatred could ignite again, swift and merciless.

But here, in this quiet alcove, something else stirred —a determination forged in suffering, a hope as persistent as breath.

Kaelen drew a slow breath and turned to her, voice low. "When the oath broke, I thought I would drown in darkness. I couldn't find myself for a long time after—the power felt too vast, too alien. Even now, I'm never sure whether it's truly me shaping the magic, or the magic shaping me. I am not the man I was. I don't know if I can be—" He cut himself off, jaw clenched. He was a noble born to command, and yet he trembled at what he could unleash by accident. He wanted Elara to know that even when he stood steady in public, inside he was barely holding the line.

She touched his shoulder, and the gentle weight drew all his fractured thoughts to rest. She pressed her forehead to his, exhaling shakily, and Kaelen let his armor drop. Her embrace was neither frail nor desperate. Strength lived in the way she refused to let pain make her cruel.

"For all the pain," she whispered, "I would choose this again. I can't imagine surviving this world without you bound beside me. You are the only thing that makes all of this bearable. The wounds, the hope, the risk—I'd shoulder it a thousand times if it means you're here."

He wrapped his arms around her, holding her as though together they might outlast any storm. His own words came out rough, but clear. "You think you are only half yourself, but you are the strongest person I have ever known. I am afraid, but not of the magic. I am afraid of losing you, of what I might become if I do. Whatever shape the pain takes, it's worth it for the chance to stand with you in the light."

They sat side by side, hands intertwined. He could feel the phantom ache where their magic twined, throbbing with a dull, ceaseless promise. Elara lifted her head and met his eyes; in her gaze he glimpsed not only the scars they shared but the future they might build from them.

"Whatever comes next—"

"We face it together," he finished, the vow simple but unbreakable.

A hush lingered in the sanctuary as they stood. The lanterns' glow wrapped them in gold, their clasped hands a small beacon against the dark. Out beyond these walls, the future was uncertain. But here, for a brief time, they were whole. Their unity, quietly forged and fiercely kept, would serve as the foundation for everything that came after.

They stepped into the golden embrace of the Hearthstone Inn, Elara pressed close to Kaelen's side, the memory of the marble council hall's hard, cold surfaces dissolving in the burst of light and familiar scents. Rows of battered wooden tables gleamed beneath lanterns dressed in woven wildflowers, and every chair brimmed with faces— Rowan's eyes sharp with pride, Lysandra's calm smile steady, Seraphine's glinting with secret delight beyond a haze of blue-tipped incense. Laughter shimmered under the hum of voices, and the hearthfire flared with life, drawing in the taste of spice—nutmeg, rosemary, hints of cider—into the warm, breathing air.

As they crossed the threshold, Rowan leapt from the shadows, clasping Kaelen's arm and catching Elara in a swift half-embrace that left the hint of mischief on the air. The crowd pressed nearer, allies and old adversaries layered together, and Elara felt— unexpectedly—a thrum of belonging. Old wounds and rivalries flickered and, for this span of afternoon light, blurred until only hope was left between them.

It unsettled her as much as it steadied—her hands shook as she let Kaelen guide her to the battered dais beside the hearth. Every step was watched, but now their scrutiny felt changed: no longer suspicion, but raw expectancy. Hearts beat in time with her own, with Rowan's restless tap of fingers, Lysandra's measured breaths, Seraphine's unreadable, unwavering stare. The ache of her past choices—the secrets, the betrayals, even the fire that threatened to consume them whole—pressed against her ribs, not in warning, but as reminder of everything it had taken to reach this fleeting pause.

When Kaelen lifted her hand into his, Elara turned toward him, the light shimmering amber across the burn marks on her knuckles and the half-faded sigil beneath his collar. For a moment, they were alone in the inn's glow, the world narrowing to a hush, the audience's breath held. She scanned their faces—

Rowan's scarred hands crossed over her chest; Lysandra, dignified and serene, a pillar in the storm; Seraphine winding her slim fingers around a clay talisman, gaze trained not on the couple but the threads of magic weaving invisibly through the room.

Kaelen's voice, low and steady, broke the hush. "I swore to keep you from harm, Elara. But it's your heart I fear for most. If I am to protect you, let it be as fiercely as I have defended my own life—against the weight of law and the press of darkness both." He paused, thumb tracing the pulse at her wrist, embers catching along the fragile magic tying them.

Sorrow, sharp and necessary, ran through her—so many times she had doubted, almost fled. The bonds of trust did not spring free from shared battles alone. They needed tending: apology, patience, hope blossoming amidst ruin. She drew a shaky breath and offered her vow, eyes unwavering. "This promise —what binds us—is more than my fate. I accept its cost not just for myself or for our magic, but for every witch, every human aching for sanctuary. I will keep this bond, for the future that so many died dreaming of, and for the peace we carve tonight."

For an instant, silence reigned, thick with memory and possibility. Elara's gaze traveled to Lysandra— her anchor during desperate flight, the one who held her together with gentle admonitions when Elara would have shattered. To Rowan, whose laughter and blade had carved open paths where none existed. To Seraphine, enigmatic as always, who had drawn forth truth with as much danger as grace. Each face recalled the fractures—they had nearly broken under suspicion, their alliances brittle as ice. Yet she sensed, tonight, the subtle stickiness of forgiveness beginning to knit.

Rowan pushed forward, a half-smirk curling her lips. "May you both have the luck to never get bored, and the sense to duck when you must. Don't let the bastards make you forget who you are." She winked, tapping a weathered knuckle to Elara's shoulder—a promise, or a warning, never clearly drawn between them.

Lysandra reached for Elara's other hand, her words as gentle as rainfall. "Trust is grown over time. Let yours root deep and weather every storm. And always remember—hope is the only magic that endures after the fires burn low." Her blessing lingered in the air, cool and soothing—Elara pressed it close to the sore, secret places still healing inside.

Seraphine, silent until now, lifted a pendant of woven willow and stone. Silver and blue light spilled from her palm, swirling in air fragrant with rosemary and the after-echo of thunderstorms. She murmured something in the forgotten tongue of old elementals. The charm's glow gathered, then leapt to circle Elara and Kaelen: a quiet benediction, veined with energy drawn from the world's roots.

Hand in hand, Elara and Kaelen stood as those lights rose—a tapestry of gold and amber, spun with the pulse of shared magic. It shimmered outward, wrapping their clasped fingers, crowning them in something new. A hush fell—awe, disbelief, reverence. Elara's own heart thudded against its cage; she dared to hope this unity might last, even as outside dusk bled along the windows, the world waiting beyond these fragile walls.

With the last pulse, a single breath swept the room. Then cheers broke out, mingled with laughter and weeping, and the crowd swept forward. Where suspicion and grief once held tight, something softer took its place—kinship born not of blood, but forged in fire, fleeting and precious as the light slipping through the Hearthstone Inn.

At sunrise, the Shadowed Wood glimmered with a new kind of magic. Mist trailed over moss and root, translucent ribbons that caught gold-pink light between trunks older than any city. Elara walked, her hand woven through Kaelen's, feeling the pulse of life beneath her soles—the hush of dew on leaves, the rich scent of earth and blooming jasmine, a thousand living things quietly bearing witness. Overhead, branches stretched higher and broader than she remembered, every leaf etched sharp against a sky polished clean by storm and struggle. The forest, once a silent witness to hunting and fear, now seemed to stand in careful celebration. Foxes paused mid-prowl, flame-tipped tails flicking, and birds alighted by the path, their black eyes bright with wary hope.

If she closed her eyes, she could almost hear the forest breathing. After so many months braced for flight, this gentle dawn pressed into her chest with impossible lightness. Elara tightened her fingers in Kaelen's—the gesture both promise and proof. Once, she had walked these woodpaths alone, shoulders tensed, every heartbeat a guarded secret. Now: her hand fit alongside his, fingers marked by burn scars and the memory of broken oaths, steadied by warmth and steady stride.

"Look," she said, voice soft as leaf-veil, "the wild primroses should have wilted by now." They rounded a ring of stones veiled in moss; there, flecks of blue and gold petals sparked among the roots, alive and fierce, out-of-season yet radiant. She wondered if old magic had always lain waiting, or if their tangled hearts had coaxed it forth.

Kaelen's expression was intent. He knelt by the primroses, touched a petal as though it might vanish. "The land is answering you," he replied, half wonder, half certainty, "or perhaps it's simply glad for peace."

Elara imagined the sanctuary rebuilt—walls of timber entwined with green vine, laughter spilling from doorways, new apprentices learning not to fear the moonlit hum of power in their veins. "We could teach them. Witches and humans both. Not how to use magic to wound, but how to listen to it—feel the world's breath, the wild language beneath bark and bone."

"We will," Kaelen said. "Sanctuary should be more than hiding. What if we formed schools, not just for your kin or mine, but for any who need guidance? Children who fear their own hands... those who have only known magic as something to be hunted."

She considered the prospect—the work, the unknowns, the faces of the next generation, bright with hope and caution. Even the word hope tasted foreign, strange on her tongue after so many years of necessity. Would the world accept it? Could they, two people once broken by promise, be architects of something gentler? She was not naive—old wounds in the kingdom ran deep, suspicion could rise again on the tide of a single rumor. But perhaps courage was less the absence of fear, and more the act of planting seeds even as winter threatened.

"After we rebuild, we should travel together," she said. "Visit the distant villages. Show them we're more alike than they've been told."

He smiled, just slightly, sunlight catching his gaze. "I'd like that. Our story isn't only for witches. There are others—those with power sleeping inside, those who have never met someone willing to bridge the old divides."

They pressed deeper into the forest, where springs bubbled up in places Elara did not know water once ran. Clear streams traced old scars, their song delicate and new. Sunlight, for so long filtered and cage-bound, spilled through the canopy in glowing columns, igniting glades with gold. Spots once haunted by memories of fire and flight now thrummed with quiet abundance. Salamanders drowsed atop warm rocks, and deer slipped from shadow as if testing the morning's intent. The air was brisk, textured with scents of rain-wet bark and flowering rosemary. Beneath it all, magic flowed—a gentle undercurrent, neither coaxed nor forced.

She climbed beside Kaelen to the crest of a mossy hill—a place untouched by foot in recent memory. From here, the Shadowed Wood unfolded: green and sun-dappled, brilliant veins of wildflowers streaming through clearings, old wounds already healing. For a while, Elara let the silence settle, her gaze tracing the path she'd once fled, the sanctuary lost and now —possibly—reborn. Her fingers slipped from Kaelen's to curl around his wrist; she felt his heartbeat, steady and living, as familiar now as her own.

Could peace last? She imagined a future where her people no longer moved as shadows, where villagers from far fields sought advice and stories, not spells of protection. Where the word witch was spoken without fear, and old songs rose above ground for children with no reason to hide. She did not know if the kingdom would always remember dawn like this, or if darkness would threaten again, but she would stand as shield and guide for as long as she breathed.

He moved closer.

"We did this together, Elara."

"Not just us," she said. "But you, with me, yes. Always."

They held each other, the warmth between them as steady as the first true light cresting the treetops.

Arms entwined, Elara and Kaelen watched the sunrise fracture over the leaves, bathing the changed world in possibility. For the first time, she believed fully in the promise of a peace just begun.